Devils Inc.

LAUREN PALPHREYMAN

Cover Design by: Damonza

Developmental Edit by: Andrea Robinson

Copy Edit by: Bryony Leah

ISBN: 9798691578724

Contact the author:

www.LaurenPalphreyman.com

For Jamie, Debbie, Bryan, and Alex.

PART ONE
EVIE'S GARDEN

"EVIE'S GARDEN BAR" FREE WI-FI TERMS AND CONDITIONS

Section 666

By accepting the terms and conditions of our free Internet service, you hereby sign away your immortal soul to the Devil and agree to be called upon, at any time, to enter into his service.

HAPPY BROWSING!

Chapter One

The past twenty-four hours have been full of bad omens. I broke two mirrors, I had to walk under a ladder to get to class, and I keep seeing crows on campus. I've felt pent-up all day too. Like something is wrong.

I pummel the punching bag. Beating the crap out of an inanimate object usually makes me feel better, but this time, it doesn't work.

My superstitious friend Josie would say something bad is going to happen. Lucas would say I need to get laid. But I'm pretty sure it's because I've been putting off submitting my law internship application. The deadline's midnight tonight.

I right hook the bag one last time, then admit defeat.

What am I going to do? Tell my parents that reading through obnoxious legal jargon is the worst form of torture? Explain to them that even if I get through this pre-law program, I don't think I want to go to law school?

Of course not.

I'm going to review my application one last time, send it, and hope this one doesn't get rejected. If it does, I'm screwed. I've received five rejections already, and I *really* don't want to break the news to them that their one remaining child is not good enough.

I pause in the doorway. I must have been here longer than I thought. The lights have been switched off, and the hallway is deathly quiet. I've been the last one in the gym before, and I know they won't lock up until I've left. Yet still, the hairs on the back of my neck stand on end. Something feels wrong.

I shake my head. What is up with me today?

Unwrapping my hands, I head for the locker room, where I walk to my locker and grab my phone out of my bag. There's a message from Josie.

Rach! Get your ass to Evie's Garden. It's half-price appletinis all night, and they're not asking for ID.

I exhale, leaning against the lockers.

Can't. Got to send that law application.

The dim light bulb hanging above the wooden benches flickers as Josie replies.

Do it here. Free Wi-Fi.

Seconds later, a picture of her and Lucas pops up onscreen. They're holding appletinis and giving me their best pleading eyes. Josie's black Afro takes up most of the shot, her golden-brown eyes bright beneath bold green eyeshadow. Lucas grins, his wide-rimmed hipster glasses slightly askew and his light brown hair swept up from his forehead thanks to his healthy gel addiction.

I suppose I could read through the application one more time at the bar, and maybe a drink would help me chill out. Besides, what's the worst that could happen?

Fine, I write. *But if this all goes to shit, you can explain to my parents why I'm such a disappointment.*

I stuff my phone back into my bag and hit the showers. After, I'm standing by my locker in a towel when the sound of something being knocked over comes from the shower room. Even though I know I'm the only one here.

The light flickers again.

I refrain from calling, "Hello? Who's there?" since this isn't some horror movie. But I also don't dawdle as I pull on my skinny jeans and a white tank top. That "off" feeling builds again.

I grab my phone, then head next door. The stuffy space is empty except for my infinite reflections in the wall mirrors: my long black hair dripping onto the tiles, my tan skin shining because it's still damp. The peacock feather inked on the back of my right shoulder looks darker in the dim light, and my mind goes to Jonathon. He used to let me stay up and watch those old-school slasher movies when our parents weren't home. Why do I feel like I'm in one right now?

That's when I see the source of the noise: an empty shampoo bottle rolling across the gray tiles. As I bend down to grab it, the lights go off completely. I fumble for my phone and turn on the flashlight, standing to clash eyes with my ghostly reflection in the mirror.

And I freeze.

A tall guy with short black hair hovers just a few feet behind me, darkness clinging to him like a cloak. His glinting eyes catch mine.

"Hey!" I yell, spinning around to hurl the empty shampoo bottle in his direction. "What the hell!"

The plastic bottle bounces off the far wall with a clatter. There's no one there.

Something rumbles behind me, and I turn to see a large crack snaking its way through my reflection.

Not again. I know what Josie will say about this. She said it about the black cat sitting outside my dorm room this morning, the ladder I walked under to get to class, and the crow that flew into the food hall at lunch.

A bad omen.

A low chuckle echoes through the locker room, but no matter where I turn, my phone's bright light reveals nothing but shadows—until I catch sight of a pair of dark eyes in another one of the mirrors.

The man leans in the doorway now, arms folded across his chest. He lifts a hand to wave, and the corner of his lip quirks.

The lights flick back on.

The doorway is empty.

I run toward the main locker room, bare feet slapping against the tiles. "Hey! You should know I used to box in high school!" I yell. "You think I won't kick your—?"

I come to a halt. It's empty too.

I rub my face. *Of course* it's empty. Do I really think some mysterious mirror man is watching me? The darkness is just playing tricks. I'm way too on edge today.

Grabbing my bag from my locker, I head back to the broken mirror in the locker room, where I drag the brush through my tangled hair, underline my brown eyes with black eyeliner, put on some mascara, then leave.

Outside, the Californian sky is a burnt orange behind the ugly university dorm buildings that tower over each side of the footpath. A crow caws behind me, the noise sharp against the quiet air. The black bird watches me from atop the peeling Trinity Falls College Gym sign.

No. Not watching me. It's a crow. Doing normal crow things.

I've been watching way too many teen vampire shows.

That's one for sorrow, you know?

Shaking Josie's voice out of my head, I start the ten-minute walk through the palm tree-lined residential roads by cutting through the memorial park on the outskirts of campus. I'll get to Evie's Garden Bar, send off my application, then get rid of all this pent-up energy by partying with friends on the dance floor.

There are no such things as bad omens.

7

Chapter Two

When I reach the town's main street, the warm air is filled with the sound of chattering students getting ready for a night out, the faint pulse of bar music, and the greasy smell of Diablos' chili hot dogs.

Trinity Falls doesn't have much to offer in the way of entertainment—except for a smattering of bars, it's mostly family-run stores, an old church, and a couple of bookshops specializing in textbooks for the students. With LA a mere half hour away, it's as if whoever built this town got bored halfway through the job and went to party there instead.

Just up ahead, dim lights from Evie's Garden Bar spill onto the sidewalk. A black cat darts across my path. Like before, I refuse to think something this cute is a bad omen.

"Hey, buddy," I say, bending down to stroke him.

He hisses at me before hurrying across the road and slipping into the crowd that's already started to build outside Apocalypse. The neon-blue sign flickers above the club's otherwise subtle entrance. The "C" of "APOCALYPSE" is a horseshoe.

"Suit yourself," I mutter as a tapping sound comes from my left. Evie's front is entirely made of glass, giving it the look of a fancy greenhouse. Josie and Lucas sit at one of the high tables in front, rapping on the window at me and pulling faces.

The corner of my lip twitches as I head to join them, but a sharp caw causes me to look up at the entrance. That same crow watches me from atop the white Evie's Garden Bar sign.

The same crow? Crows all look the same, Rach.

It caws again, its beady eyes meeting mine.

"What are you looking at?" I say.

It caws again.

"Jerk."

This time, it just tilts it head.

Inside, the bar is a bubble of noise. The space is small and mostly lit by flickering candles and fairy lights that wind through the gray trellises against the walls. Potted apple trees are dotted across the black-and-white checkered floor, and the air smells like perfume and lime wedges.

I push through a group of sorority girls to get to Josie and Lucas.

"Finally!" says Josie, removing her purse from the white barstool beside her. "It's packed tonight! I've battled the legions of hell to keep this seat free for you!"

A tall blonde in a blue dress shoots us a dirty look. When Lucas throws an evil look right back, she scowls and returns to her conversation.

"She's tried to take your seat three times already," he says.

"We're guy-watching," says Josie.

"Are you two ever not guy-watching?" I ask, sliding onto the stool. From their outfits, I can see they're expecting a big night; Josie's wearing the black dress that emphasizes her curves, and Lucas's white shirt is unbuttoned at the collar, with hipster suspenders cutting over his slender shoulders.

"Hmm . . . guilty," says Lucas. "Though you could do with a bit of guy-watching, Rach, since the crazy cat lady vibe isn't working for you anymore." He slides his gaze to the street outside. "Even cats are crapping themselves at your presence."

"Funny," I say, pulling out my cell. "Right now, I need to send off this application."

"How have you not done that yet, babe?" asks Josie, the silver crucifix around her neck glinting as she leans forward.

"Don't start. I've already had all that from my parents." I mimic my mother's high-pitched voice. "It's almost like you don't want to be a lawyer, Rachel. Such potential. Such disappointment. Why can't you be more like Jonathon? "

I stop when I notice Josie and Lucas's expressions have become serious, their eyes flicking to my tattoo, then back. I'm not sure whether I'm about to get the "sympathy for the dead brother" response or the "stand up to your parents" lecture. Either way, I slide off the stool and force a smile. I don't want to bring down the mood.

"Why don't you tell them you don't want to do law?" says Josie.

"Because then they'll ask me what I *do* want to do."

"And that is?" says Lucas.

"Right now, I want to read through this cover letter one more time," I say, "then I want an appletini."

Lucas picks up his cocktail glass and swirls it pensively before taking a sip of the bright green liquid. "So it's just a coincidence you came to Trinity College?"

"It has a good pre-law program."

His eyebrows raise over his glasses. "*And* it's close to Hollywood."

"Just because you burst into the world waving your jazz hands, Lucas, doesn't mean we all want to be actors."

"Pfft," says Lucas. "You don't have what it takes to be an actor. But after making us sit through all three Godfather movies, you can't convince me you wouldn't rather be in the film program."

"Well, if you can convince my parents it will give me a 'useful' degree, I'm all ears. But otherwise"— I lift up my cell—"I need to send this off."

They don't get it. Jonathon was a genius, and while I don't have his gift for computers, law is an ambitious enough field of study to appease my parents. My announcement about coming to Trinity a few years ago was the first time they seemed invested in me and my future since a reckless driver robbed me of my brother seven years ago. Someone needed to fill that hole.

"I can't find the network though," I add before they can act on their clear skepticism.

Josie nods to the bar. "The router's over there. Signal might be better."

"Plus, you can bring us drinks on your way back," says Lucas, tapping his now-empty glass.

"On it," I say. "Just give me a few minutes."

I push my way across the room, sliding onto a recently vacated stool just as a bartender with her dark hair tied in a ponytail approaches. A name badge is pinned to the black waistcoat she wears over her white top. *Eve.*

"Drinks, honey?"

I order three appletinis, then I go back to my cell. As I find the network—"EVIE'S GARDEN BAR"—a rumble of thunder sounds behind me, and the dim overhead lights flicker. Confused, I look out the window. The sky behind Apocalypse is a dusky blue, no storm in sight. I shake my head and go back to the Wi-Fi.

A long list of terms and conditions flicks onto the screen. I quickly scroll down—I have to read enough of this kind of thing in class. As I do, the "off" feeling that's been plaguing me all day intensifies for no discernible reason.

I click "Accept."

I'm logging in to the Jones and Smith recruitment portal, where all my details are saved, when a low chuckle sounds to my right.

"Something funny?" I ask, turning my head.

Adrenaline washes over me.

The guy sitting beside me is tall and well-built, with black hair shaved close to his head. Although he faces forward, I see the amused tilt to his lips. He looks like he must be in his early twenties or a few years older than me. A swirl of black ink curls up the back of his neck.

And I swear, it's the same guy I saw in the gym mirror.

"You," I say.

He turns his head slowly. "Me," he says, his voice low.

It takes everything I have not to grab the nearby pitcher of water and throw it in his face. His eyes glint. His irises are a cloudy gray, the pupils rimmed by a circle of gold. He looks like he enjoys the reaction he provokes.

"What the hell are—?"

"I'm Crow." He maneuvers his right arm across his body for me to shake. "You must be Rachel."

His accent isn't American. It's Scottish, I think. *Not important, dummy—why was he stalking you through the locker room?*

Realizing I'm not going to take his hand, he withdraws it and shrugs before nodding at the phone in my hand. "You know, you really should read the terms and conditions before you accept those things."

As he leans forward against the bar, my eyes can't help but drop to his body. From the way his black T-shirt clings to his muscles, I'm pretty sure he would look good without it on.

But that's beside the point.

"I saw you," I say loud enough for my voice to cut over the electro swing and the rattle of cocktail shakers. "In the gym."

"Did you now?"

"You were in the girls' locker room."

He chuckles. "Why would I be in there?"

"You tell me."

On the other side of the bar, Eve hits a snag while making my batch of appletinis. She skirts past a male bartender, throws away the empty glass bottle, then heads to the cellar to restock. Crow watches her in the mirror, an odd look on his face.

"How do you know my name?" I demand.

"Lucky guess."

"Right. So you *are* following me."

"Or maybe I saw your phone."

I look down at my cell. The start of a message shows on my lock screen.

Rach—hottie next to you at the bar!

Dammit, Josie.

I shoot a look over my shoulder. Bathed in the neon-blue light of Apocalypse, she laughs at something Lucas says.

"Is this some kind of pickup line?" Crow runs his thumb across his bottom lip. "The old 'you look familiar' come-on?"

I jerk my gaze from his mouth to his eyes. "What?"

"I mean, I've never heard the 'I've seen you in the locker room' variant, but it puts a creative spin on it, I'll give you that."

"I was *not* hitting on you."

He raises a thick eyebrow. "So you weren't mentally undressing me earlier?"

When I don't reply, his smile broadens.

"I'm busy," I say, turning back to my phone. "Go bother someone else."

I bring up the cover letter for my application and start to skim it. As he leans closer, I catch the scent of woodsmoke and outdoors. The air feels charged all of a sudden; the hairs on my arms stand on end.

"Blow it off," he says in a rough whisper.

"Excuse me?"

He looks pointedly at the cover letter. "The internship. Blow it off. There's another one already lined up for you."

I cover my screen. His full lips twitch as he leans back again and takes a swig of his beer.

"What do you know about it?" I ask.

"I know you're about to be recruited by a different agency. Don't know why though."

"Did Josie put you up to this?"

"Josie? Nah, I don't work for Josie. I work for someone much worse."

I shake my head and go back to my phone, where the letter is still open. I've only gotten to the "I am interested in an internship with your company because. . ." paragraph.

"You're wasting your time," he says.

Dislike flares within me. Without even getting to the end, I push send and close it.

"Is there something you want?" I ask.

"Always. But that's not why I'm here."

"So why *are* you here? To annoy me?"

"To warn you."

"What?"

"Things are about to get pretty *Hellish* for you, Rachel."

I swivel on my stool, our knees knocking. "Are you threatening me?"

"I suppose you could call it that. I threaten people all the time." He leans in conspiratorially. "It's kind of my job."

My blood runs cold. I don't understand what's going on. I don't even know this guy. Why would he be threatening me?

Before either of us can say anything else, Eve slides three appletinis in front of me.

"Here you go. Sorry to keep you waiting," she says. "Needed to get some—"

The smile drops from her pink lips as she notices Crow.

"Your kind aren't welcome here," she says.

Crow's smile only broadens. "Eve here's a real xenophobe," he fake whispers. "Hates the Scots."

"Get out," she says, looking down her nose at him.

Crow pushes his stool back and stands to his full height, which must be over six feet. As he does, the candles on the high tables go out, and lights in the ceiling flicker. Ice slithers down my spine, but Eve simply stares at him.

"What are you going to do, Omen?" she asks, flexing her fingers. "Fight me because I won't serve you a drink? You don't have what it takes to kill me."

Kill?

He stares at her for a hard moment. Then he grins, raising his hands. The lights stop flickering.

"That breakup with hubby's done you well, Evie," he says. "Finally grown yourself some lady balls."

"Get. Out," she says.

When he looks at me, his amusement hasn't dimmed. "I'll be seeing you soon," he says, backing away through the crowd of students. As he does, his eyes flick to my shoulder. "Nice tattoo."

It isn't until he's across the road that I realize my muscles are still tensed. Eve watches him with an equally distasteful look. Then her gaze drops to the three cocktail glasses with wedges of apple on their sugared rims. The darkness vanishes from her face.

"That'll be eighteen dollars, please," she says and smiles.

I stare at her for a moment. She's not even going to try to explain that?

"Who the hell was that?" I ask as I pull my card out of my bag.

"Him?" she says. "A bad omen. You don't want to be getting messed up with the likes of him."

Chapter Three

We spend the remainder of the night laughing and drinking too many appletinis. It becomes easier to push the creepy dude out of my mind after my fourth cocktail. By then, my tongue is green, and the sweet apple-flavored alcohol has pushed away the murderous thoughts. Whatever that was all about at the bar, it's clearly between him and the bartender. They obviously know each other. Which means I must have imagined him in the mirror earlier. This has nothing to do with me.

Probably.

"Another drink?" says Josie. "Or shall we head to Apocalypse to get our"—she jiggles her arms—"dance on?"

"Can't," says Lucas. "Got an early morning *Doctor Faustus* rehearsal."

"Yeah?" asks Josie. "What counts as early morning for a theater student?"

The corner of Lucas's lip quirks up. "Eleven."

Josie laughs. "That's ridiculous. You're coming to Apocalypse. Rach? It'll be fun!"

"I dunno."

"If fun isn't your thing, babe, you can look at it as a 'help Josie not be single' mission." She waggles her eyebrows. "I called about the bartender job they were advertising. The guy on the phone sounded hot."

"How can someone sound hot?" I ask.

"His voice was all low and smooth and"—her eyes glaze over dreamily— "British."

I laugh. "Well, as fun as watching you flirt with your potential future boss sounds . . ."—I rise to my feet, wobbling slightly—"I actually do have an early morning lecture tomorrow. I'll catch you for lunch?"

Josie frowns. "You sure you're okay, babe? You seem a bit tense."

"I'm fine."

Her slightly unfocused eyes follow my hand as I pull my hair off my right shoulder. Then they widen.

"Oh, shit," she says, staring at my tattoo. "It's the anniversary, isn't it? Your brother. I'm so sorry, Rach. I forgot."

"No, not until next month. I just . . ."

I shake my head, wondering suddenly if the bad feelings of today are related to him. Applying to this internship feels like a step toward the future. A future without him. A future that would be different if he were still here.

"Maybe I have been thinking about him a bit lately."

Josie takes my hand. "He's watching over you, you know?"

She wants to make me feel better, but I've never been into the spiritual stuff—or, at least, not like she is.

I force a smile. "I'm fine. Honest."

As I take a step back, I brush arms with the blonde from earlier, who's eager to finally get a hold of my stool. We all scowl at her as I sling my sports bag over my shoulder.

"Don't get into too much trouble without me," I say with a grin, then I skirt around one of the potted apple trees on the way to the exit. But when I reach the glass door, I pause, feeling eyes burning into my back.

Eve the bartender watches me with a dark expression. When she catches me looking, she goes back to uncapping a row of cider bottles for a team of Trinity Falls College football players.

What's her problem?

A crow caws as I head back to campus.

I make my way up the six flights of tired stairs to my room. This whole dorm block is pretty old—peeling plaster, light bulbs that need replacing, and a lingering smell of damp—but I don't mind because I have a private room. Josie says it was a miracle; I think it's more to do with the fact this block is falling apart, and they don't want to put any more students in a place about to be under heavy construction. Hence the ladder propped up outside earlier.

Still, I've always admired how positive Josie is about everything. Although it bugs me a bit when she says things about Jonathon being in a better place or looking down on me from above. Even if that *is* true—and the jury's still out for me—I'd rather he was still alive.

When I reach my floor, I have to wiggle the key before the door finally clicks open.

My room is pitch-black, and I fumble for the switch.

There's a guy sitting on the edge of my twin-size bed, right on top of the checkered red-and-black comforter I'm fairly sure I left crumpled on the floor. My window is open behind him, and the half-open slats of the blind rattle in the breeze.

I make a weird yelping sound and stagger back into the wall. "What the hell?"

A sour look crosses the intruder's face. He looks about twenty, with red hair swept neatly up from his forehead, a pale complexion, and a sharp jaw. He sits perfectly upright as if there's a rod reinforcing his spine, and he wears a white blazer with the

18

word "HALO" on the pocket. It's topped with an embroidered circle of gold.

"Finally," he says. "I've been waiting all evening."

"Are you lost?" I ask.

Frowning, he rises elegantly to his feet. "No. I'm Gabriel," he says. "And we have something of uttermost importance to discuss."

As if this day hasn't been stressful enough with my application due and the weird guy at Evie's, now there's a random dude in my dorm.

I pinch the bridge of my nose. "If you're not lost, then you're trespassing, and you need to get out."

Gabriel folds his arms across his chest, clearly indignant. "Do you think I *want* to be here? No. But we need to talk about the broken mirror," he says. He points to the long one mounted by the door. I figured I must have bumped into it when I got up to go to the bathroom during the night.

I try to piece this together. "You're some kind of . . . mirror repairman? That's why you're here? In my bedroom? In the middle of the night?"

"Please. Take a seat," he says as though I've just entered his office rather than found him lurking in my room. When I don't move, he inclines his head toward the tatty desk chair near the foot of my bed.

I frown. I'm sure it was draped with clothes this morning. In fact . . .

I survey my boxy room. The framed *Fight Club* poster I hung on one peeling white wall is no longer lopsided, the glasses of lukewarm water have been cleared from my nightstand—and have the textbooks stacked beside my old boxing trophy been *alphabetized?* They have. They start with Business Law and end with Sociology.

"You tidied my room?" I say.

Gabriel is suddenly very interested in the murky glass of the light above his head.

"Seriously," I say flatly. "Get out."

When he doesn't move, I grab his slender wrist and make to drag him out into the hallway, but despite the fact I pull—hard—his feet remain firmly planted. His physique is willowy. There's no way this dude is stronger than me.

I wrench him again with no success.

Pulling his wrist from my grasp, he rubs it against his white blazer as though he's just touched something filthy. Now we're inches apart, I note that he smells citrusy, like the bath bombs they sell at the beauty store downtown.

Stop sniffing the creep, Rach. Get him out of here so you can go to bed.

"Look, what do you want?" I say.

"I need to talk to you," he says with a scowl. "I shouldn't even be here."

"No shit. So go away before I get campus security."

"You won't do that," he says.

"Why not?" I cross my arms.

"Because they're a group of bullheaded guys who like to assert the small ounce of power they have in an attempt to make other people feel small," he says. "And they are most certainly going to Hell."

"I would've just gone with 'they're a bunch of assholes,' but that works. You've had a run-in with them too, huh?" I raise an eyebrow, remembering the time Lucas, Josie, and I were yelled at for "loitering" in the campus square after a party. Lucas *was* belting out show tunes, to be fair. But still. "Was it because you were lurking around other people's rooms?"

"No," he says. "I threw a pebble at a bird."

"What? Why?"

"It was following me."

I sigh and fall back on my bed. This is pointless. He's not leaving until he's said whatever he has to say.

"Okay. Fine. Talk. Then leave. I'm tired."

He stares at me for a moment, then brings a large white phone out of his crisp gray pants. "I detected heightened Omen activity on the Trinity Falls College campus this morning," he says, starting to scroll. "I'm guessing from the broken mirror in your room."

"Omen activity?" I laugh but then recall my interaction with the bartender and the hot yet clearly dangerous guy at the bar. *A bad omen*, she said. "Is this some kind of weird college prank? Has Josie put you up to this?"

He looks up from his screen. "No."

"So the fact you and some weird guy who calls himself Crow have both bothered me in the space of a few hours is a coincidence?"

He curses under his breath. *"Crow,"* he says sourly. "The bird was one of his. This is worse than I thought if he's getting involved."

"A friend of yours?" I say. *A weird bird-owning friend?*

His face darkens. "He's no friend of mine."

I rub my face, forgetting that I'm wearing mascara. After wiping the black smudges on my jeans, I sit up and lean forward.

"Can you just tell me what you want to tell me so I can go to bed, and you can get out of my life?"

He inclines his head, face devoid of expression. Then he goes back to his phone screen. "I've been monitoring the Trinity Falls area since I picked up on the Omen activity. I've been watching you, Rachel—"

"Who *are* you?"

"I told you. I'm Gabriel, and I'm an Angel." He looks up from the screen. "And at approximately seven minutes past nine this evening, you signed away your immortal soul to the Devil."

Chapter Four

Is this guy high? Am I high? Maybe I shouldn't have had that fourth appletini. Or—no, my money is still on this being an elaborate prank. All of Josie's bad omen talk was just the setup. So was the black cat, the crow, and the ladder.

"I'm not sure which part of that crazy to dissect first," I say. "So let's start with the angel thing. . . You think you're the Angel Gabriel?"

"Why do people always say that?" he snaps. "As if the Angel Gabriel would be sent to visit someone as insignificant as you."

"So they sent someone unimportant?" I ask.

His pale cheeks pinken. "I wasn't sent," he says after a long moment of looking at the blinds. "I shouldn't be here."

"Why are you here then?"

"I told you that. Because you signed away your soul to the Devil." He shakes his head. "You really should read the terms and conditions."

That's what that Crow guy said too. Whatever this is about, they're definitely in on it together.

"What are you talking about?" I say.

"The free Wi-Fi at Evie's," he replies, frustrated. "You didn't read the terms and conditions. Devils Inc. must have hacked it and added in a clause. Either that or they've struck up a deal with Eve. It wouldn't be the first time she's entered into a legal agreement with a third party."

I arch an eyebrow. "Are you telling me I just exchanged my immortal undying soul for free Wi-Fi?"

"Yes!" he says as if I'm finally getting it.

I laugh. "And Lucifer, King of Hell, sent you, the Angel Gabriel, to tell me about this?"

"I told you, I'm not the Angel Ga—" He stops himself, jaw clenching. "No, that's not important. What is important is that Devils Inc. will be in contact shortly. Likely in the next twenty-four hours. So I am here of my own accord to offer you another deal. I think Devils Inc. are up to something, and I want someone on the inside to be my eyes and ears. It will be dangerous, but you will meet with me in secret and relay information, and in exchange, I will put together a legal case to save your soul."

I get up and walk toward him. This time, he lets me usher him to the door.

"Okay, buddy. Thanks for the info. I'll let you know about the 'saving my soul' thing."

In the doorway, he stares at me as if he's trying to determine whether I'm taking him seriously. After a few seconds, he nods, satisfied.

"Good. Here." He hands me a small white card.

"How did you get into my room anyway?" I ask.

"The window," he replies simply.

I don't have time to mention my room is on the sixth floor because he's already striding down the hallway.

"What a strange guy," I mutter, peering into the keyhole to see if it's been tampered with, then rattling the handle a couple of times. Afterward, I put my desk chair against it just to be safe.

Then I look at the white card between my fingers. "HALO CORP.," it says in gold lettering. The same oval-shaped emblem on Gabriel's jacket hovers above the "H." *"For all your Angelic needs,"* it says, followed by Gabriel's name and contact number.

I stare at it incredulously before slipping it into my pocket.

I'm going to bed.

Angels, Omens, and a deal with the Devil . . .

At least it's more interesting than my business law class will be tomorrow.

But this has to be some big prank. Right?

Chapter Five

My seven o'clock alarm sounds like a death toll.

I groan, face in my pillow, then I push myself into a vaguely upright position and turn it off. I feel like crap. My mouth is dry as a bone, and my head throbs. I didn't think I drank *that* much last night, but the threat of a hangover lingers behind my blurred vision.

To make things worse, there's a message from Mom on my screen. She wants to know if I managed to get the application for my internship sent off on time, and if I've thought any more about heading back to New York next month. They like to visit Jonathon's grave on the anniversary of his death, then have a memorial back at their place for friends and family. They want me to come. I know I should, but I like to remember him in my own way, lighting a candle and watching some of his favorite movies rather than being so public with my emotions.

I quickly reply that I did, and I'll think about it. Then I stumble out of bed to the shared bathrooms, toothbrush in hand. The stuffy air smells like shampoo, and I can hear someone peeing in one of the four stalls behind me. It's only when I see the crack in the mirror above the sink that the weird events of yesterday come back to me.

Omens, Demons, Angels. . . What?

"That's seven years' bad luck, you know?" says Lisa over the sound of the toilet flush. She bounds over to wash her hands before smoothing her long black hair.

"Huh?" I say, although it comes out garbled because of the toothpaste.

"Breaking a mirror's a bad omen," she replies.

"Oh, right. Yeah. So I've heard."

"Speaking of, you hear the news this morning? Seven-car pileup on the freeway into LA. Six people died, and two more are in critical condition."

She goes on about the wreck as she applies a creamy layer of foundation, but I tune her out, making the odd grunting noise where appropriate. Lisa's nice and all, but she's one of those irritatingly chirpy morning people. Josie's like that too. I need at least a cup of coffee before I can even string a sentence together.

I rub the smudged eyeliner from beneath my eyes, splash my face, then tell Lisa I'll catch her later. A thought occurs to me as I reach the door.

"Hey, did you see a guy hanging around my room last night? Red hair, good-looking in a clean-cut way, kind of socially awkward?"

She grins. "No. Why? Got yourself a new guy?"

"No, nothing like that. Never mind."

There's no way in hell he came in through the window, so someone must have seen him. Shaking my head, I go get changed in my room, pulling on the same jeans as yesterday and a black tank top. I grab my business law textbook and laptop, then head out, checking my emails on my cell as I walk down the stairs. I stop dead on the second-floor landing, my stomach plummeting.

One of the emails is from Jones and Smith. It's about the internship.

And it's a rejection.

Shit.

How can they even have checked my application yet?

Shit. Shit. Shit. Shit.

I lean back against the wall, dread weighing down my chest. I needed this. An internship is a requirement for getting through this program. How the hell am I supposed to pass this year?

My parents are going to kill me.

Heart beating fast, I refresh the page again as if another email is just waiting to pop up and tell me it was a mistake.

It doesn't.

But a different email *does*.

"DEVILS INC.," says the sender line, and when I open it, the logo at the top shows the "D" curled into a Devil's tail.

Dear Rachel,

Thank you for the interest in our organization you expressed at 9:07 p.m. last evening. We are delighted to accept you into our compulsory internship program. Please report to the office at 5:30 p.m. this evening to begin your training.

Yours devilishly,
Adalind Gardiner,
Secretary,
Devils Inc.

It's followed by an address in downtown Los Angeles. I'm still betting on it being a prank, but if it is real, this might actually save my ass.

Still. What kind of law firm names themselves after the Devil?

Stuffing my phone into my pocket, I make my way outside. I'm halfway to class when I realize two things: one, that stupid crow is back; and two, someone is following me.

After heading across the square, past a couple of girls on an early-morning run and the odd student clasping a paper cup from Lazarus's Coffee, I disappear into the narrow alley between the library and the food hall.

The crow is waiting for me at the end of the path.

I stop.

Then I turn and slam the side of my arm into the upper chest of my stalker, pushing him into the wall. He grunts, surprised, his cloudy gray eyes latching onto mine.

It's Crow.

"Why are you following me?" I snarl.

He smiles. "Following you? I'm making sure no harm befalls you, little Demon. Part of my contract. Did you know there was a seven-car pileup on the freeway this morning?"

"What's that got to do with anything?"

"You'll see."

I take a step back, adrenaline surging through my veins, and look him up and down. He's dressed in dark jeans and a white cotton T-shirt beneath a leather jacket. The shadows around him seem to move strangely, as if he's a magnet they're attracted to. It takes me back to the moment in the locker room last night. I convinced myself I imagined him. I convinced myself the threat in Evie's was related to the bartender, not me.

But here he is again. And there's something not right about him.

"Stay away from me," I say.

Raising his hands in surrender, he opens his mouth to say something, but I spin on my heel, adjusting my laptop bag and shooing away the bird blocking my path. Seconds later, I emerge from the dark alley into the morning sun.

I hurry down the central path between seminar buildings. There are more people here, coming from all points of campus on their way to the same early class. The tension starts to ease from my body.

Until I see a face covered in blood peering blankly from a dark window of the science building.

I rub my eyes, then look again. There's no one there. Still, I quicken my pace. I need to pull myself together.

My heart beats fast as I take my seat near the back of the tiered hall, where Professor McNeil starts to drone on about the binding nature of business agreements. When I open my laptop, I see the story about the seven-car pileup. It's accompanied by the image of a businessman with graying hair and a blue suit. A billionaire named Richard Livingstone—he tends to appear on the news from time to time thanks to a series of alleged tax evasions.

I close the page and pull up the email from Devils Inc. again. A horrible sense of dread creeps over me when a search for the firm reveals no results.

I go back to the email. This time, I notice the company name is hyperlinked. I hover the mouse over it for a second. Then I click it.

Bright red floods the screen as "Devils Inc." curls across the page as though someone is writing it, followed by "Experts in soul-trading and moral defense." I click on "Learn more. . ." and start to read the writing below.

Have you broken a divine law? Are you worried your bad deeds outweigh your good? Or are you rotten to the core?

Do you worry that at time of judgement, you will be denied access through those pearly gates?

Or are you simply down on your luck and searching for an investment in your soul?

Well, Devils Inc. can—

"I've been looking for you," a voice rasps in my ear.

I look over my shoulder, irritated at being disturbed.

And I suck in a breath.

A man sits there in a tattered blue business suit. Sallow skin hangs from one side of his face, exposing bone, and his graying hair is matted with blood.

I blink hard. He doesn't disappear.

"You're Rachel, right?" he says, his pale lips twisting into a smile.

The girl on his other side doesn't react. She doesn't seem to notice him at all.

"Pleased to meet you," he rasps again. "I'm Richard—"

I slam my laptop closed, tuck it under my arm, and barge out of the lecture hall, away from that . . . thing. I hear people murmuring, but I don't care.

This can't be happening. This can't be happening.

I don't look to see if he follows. I certainly didn't need him to introduce himself. He was the semi-famous business guy, Richard Livingstone, the one who the news said was involved in the accident.

And he was dead.

Chapter Six

We learned about a principle called Ockham's Razor in class once. It's the idea that the simplest explanation is often the most likely. In the past twenty-four hours, I've been visited by an Omen, an Angel, and a dead guy.

So come on, genius . . . what is the simplest explanation for that? Hallucinogens in the cocktails last night? Some kind of fever?

No. All leave too many questions unanswered.

But what does that leave? That this is actually happening?

Shit.

When I reach the square, I rub my face and take another deep breath. I just need to head back to my room, call Josie, and talk this all through. It'll be fine.

The square is completely empty; no noise comes from the food hall behind me, and the ten long stone steps that lead down to it don't have their usual crowds of freshmen drinking cans of soda between lectures. As I reach the center, a cloud passes overhead. The hairs on my bare arms stand on end.

"Rachel . . ."

It's the dead guy—Richard Livingstone. He's followed me out of the classroom.

"Rachel," he says, staggering forward, his hand extended. "A pleasure—"

Before I can run, two more figures stagger out of the shadows. A hunched old woman in a torn floral dress, and a young blonde who would be attractive if she didn't look so . . . deceased.

"There she is!" says the old lady. "There she is!"

I spin to the third exit by the glass-walled student work zone only to find Crow blocking my path at the top of the steps, the cloudy sky behind him making for a moody backdrop. The corner of his lip curls up.

Shit.

The two women across the square clamber down the steps toward me while Richard clamps a bony hand on my shoulder.

With a cry, I bend forward and flip him onto the pavement.

"Bitch. I was only being friendly," he spits through bloody teeth as he jerks upright. "Don't turn your back on me."

He grabs at my ankles, but I sprint toward the library that dominates the square's fourth side, staggering to a halt as a stocky guy with a ginger beard limps out from behind it. He's wearing torn board shorts. A bone juts out from his leg.

Adrenaline takes over. I throw a fist into his face, feeling his nose crunch against my knuckles before he staggers back. Right into two men in suits.

What the hell is going on?

They push him back toward me, but I side-kick him in the chest, and he takes out one of the suits as he falls. That only leaves the other. I punch him in the neck when he surges forward, then knee him in the groin. He doubles over just as a hand clamps on my shoulder, and the heavy scent of floral perfume and blood floods my nostrils.

DEVILS INC.

I send that little old lady flying. She lands on her back, a startled expression on her bloody face. She looks a bit like my grandma.

"I'm so sorry, ma'am," I say, raising my hands.

She jerks upright, popping a dislocated arm back into her shoulder. "You kids today! So violent. It's all those video games." She stumbles to her feet, her expression now murderous. "Someone ought to teach you a lesson."

When I lurch back, I hit something solid.

Heart leaping, I turn, putting my full force behind my fist, but Crow catches it. His palm is rough and warm, and I feel the strength in his arm.

Behind him, Richard Livingstone stumbles back to his feet.

Crow raises an eyebrow. We're both breathing fast, though his eyes hold amusement rather than the horror that must emanate from mine. I stare up at him, dumbfounded. Then he nods at something over my shoulder and releases my fist.

As Crow grabs Livingstone by the neck, I spin around and block the incoming swipe from the old lady. I wince as I kick her frail form into Beardy, sending both of them toppling down again.

I chance a glance over my shoulder to find the remainder writhing on the ground. Crow stands a couple of feet away, wiping his hands on his jeans before studying a bloody mark on his white T-shirt.

"That's going to leave a stain," he grumbles.

Before I can say anything, Livingstone grunts and pushes himself on all fours. Crow kicks him in the face with a heavy black combat boot, then pulls a set of car keys from his pocket.

"Come on, little Demon. Let's get you out of here," he says, stepping over the corpses. "Unless you'd rather stay?"

I glance at the groaning old lady, who sits up and straightens her wig.

"They won't stop coming after you, you know?" he adds in a singsong voice without looking back to see if I'm following him across the square.

One of the suits narrows his gaze on me. I watch him pop a bone back in his arm, then look to Crow again.

Crow is the lesser of evils.

Probably.

Reluctantly, I jog after him, skirting past the crumpled form of the blonde woman in the raggedy dress at the bottom of the opposing steps. Crow stops at the top, something unreadable in his expression.

"What are you doing?" I say.

He brings two fingers to his mouth. Then he whistles.

The sky behind him darkens as the air fills with the sound of flapping wings. I duck, hands over my head, crying out as cold air and black feathers brush my forearms.

"WHAT ARE YOU DOING, YOU BAST—?" I start to yell.

Then they're gone. Descending onto the weird zombie guys instead.

"What. The. Hell?"

Crow's grin widens. "Can't kill the dead. But you *can* keep them busy."

Didn't Gabriel say something about Crow and his birds last night?

Heart in my throat, we walk away from the crow-versus-zombie carnage happening below and head to the campus parking lot. I flex my fingers, knuckles bruised from the fight.

"Couldn't you have just done that crow attack thing from the start?" I ask.

"Aye. But where's the fun in that?"

"Fun!"

He shrugs. "I was curious to see how you'd fare," he says. "Something similar happened when they recruited this jock five years ago. *Huge* guy. They wanted him for security." Crow chuckles. "He threw his iced latte at one of the souls, tripped over his shoelaces, and then just lay there on the floor waiting for someone to rescue him."

There's too much buzzing panic coursing through my system for me to find the right response. All I mange is: "Dick."

His laughter increases.

When we reach the parking lot, he points to a black Mini Cooper in the shadow of a tall tree. It seems a little quaint for him, but I make no comment.

"Get in then," he says, a smile still dancing around his full lips as he opens the driver's door and climbs inside.

Before I can change my mind, I get in the car, close the door, and fold my arms across my chest. Crow twists the key in the ignition.

"Good choice," he says as he reverses.

"Where are we going?"

His eyes glint. "Devils Inc.," he replies.

Chapter Seven

As we leave campus, I can still see big black birds plummeting in and out of the square. They look like they could be fighting over a dropped sandwich. But they're not.

They're fighting over zombies.

I should be scared. That would be the logical response. Truth be told, my body emulates something like fear. My palms are clammy, my heart beats fast, and my body is so full of energy I find myself tapping my foot. It's not fear though. It's adrenaline. I'm pumped up. I haven't had a fight like that in . . . well, ever. What with my opponents being dead and all.

As Crow drives toward the center of town, my brain kicks violently into gear, screaming that I'm in a car with a strange creep who controls birds. I think he notices the change because I see a quirk tug at the side of his lips out of the corner of my eye.

"What the hell is going on?" I demand.

"I was wondering how long it would take you to freak out," he says.

"Yes, well. Now you know," I snap.

As we pass Evie's Garden Bar, Crow waves at someone—or something—in the alley by Apocalypse. But then we're passing by the small church at the end of the street and turning onto the road leading to the freeway.

"I told you, there was a seven-car pileup this morning," he says.

"Oh. And that explains everything."

"It does, actually."

"Right. So there was an accident on the freeway, some people died. And the logical next step in that story is that they came back to life again to attack me on campus. How obvious. How—oh, shit!" I look over my shoulder as we take the on-ramp. "We should tell someone. What if they attack someone else?"

"They won't. No one else can see them," he says. "Just you. And they didn't come back to life. They're dead."

"They didn't seem dead."

"Really? See a lot of people with protruding bones and hanging flesh, do you?" He raises his eyebrows, gaze still fixed on the wide road ahead. "Definitely not recruited for your brains, eh, little Demon?"

At that, all I can do is splutter.

He laughs. "I forgot how fun these little jobs were. Fun for a while, anyway. I'm going to need you to suspend your disbelief soon, or it's going to get boring."

"Oh. Well, I'd hate that. For you to get bored."

"You might." He catches my eye. "I'd have to find some other way to amuse myself."

I stiffen. I jumped into a car with this guy because he helped me out, but what do I actually know about him? He's been following me, I might have seen him creeping around the locker rooms, and he showed no restraint when it came to exhibiting violence.

He's strong too. I felt it when he caught my fist.

"Are you threatening me?"

"I told you last night, that's my job."

I glance out the window, then at the door handle. The traffic means we're moving slowly—I could probably make a run for it.

The locks click.

"Unlock the doors," I say.

He holds my gaze a moment longer. "Just messing," he says, turning his head back to the cars in front of us. "I'm not a threat to you. Not on this contract, anyway. I just meant I might ditch you. You're not exactly worth very much."

"Excuse me?"

He laughs again. "There you go. You're still amusing. You'll be fine."

I take a deep breath, close my eyes, and lean back against the headrest. "You're a dick."

"I know."

We fall into silence, and it gives me a chance to get my thoughts in order.

Everything about this guy screams untrustworthy. But ever since last night, things have been weird. A mysterious guy claiming to be an Angel somehow got into my room, I've been offered a mysterious internship, and—oh, yeah, I was attacked by dead people.

I glance at my knuckles, which are pink from the fight. If it was some kind of prank, there's no way it would have gone this far.

So what does that mean? I've actually sold my soul to the Devil?

And I was worried about telling my parents I wasn't sure about law school. . .

"Is this real?" I say.

"Aye."

"Seriously?"

"Uh-huh." Crow taps the steering wheel with his thumbs, apparently without a care in the world.

"Right. So then how does me signing away my soul equal dead guys coming after me?"

"Some smart-arse created an app," he says.

"Can you stop speaking in riddles, *please?*"

He shifts on his seat, head brushing the ceiling as he rummages in his jeans pocket. A moment later, he produces his iPhone.

"What am I supposed to do with this?" I say when he hands it over.

"There's an app on the home screen," he says. "Afterlife."

I find the icon—a black "A" on a white background—and tap it. A white screen materializes.

Hello, recently deceased! What are you looking for?

Below are four black buttons. They read, "MORAL DEFENSE," "SOUL INVESTMENT," "SOUL RATING," and, "OMENS."

I must be pulling a "what the hell?" face, because Crow chuckles.

"It's like one of those insurance comparison apps," he says. "You know? Where they compare prices across all the companies and give you your best options?" He snatches it from me and taps the screen a few times, one hand resting on the wheel. "It asks you a series of questions based on what you're looking for—whether you're good or bad, where you're based, where you died, etcetera. Then it shows you your best bet," he says. "Here."

He hands it back, and I almost drop it. There's a map on the screen now, one with moving red, white, and black dots intended to represent "Ethereal forces near you." But that isn't what catches my attention. There's a pair of dots—one red, one black—approaching downtown Los Angeles. Next to the red dot is a photograph of me.

"What the hell is this?" I say, zooming in on a picture taken from my Instagram. It's from last Halloween when Josie persuaded me to dress up as a "slutty Demon" and be her date to one of the sorority parties. I'm wearing red latex and horns while prodding a keg with a plastic devil's fork. Josie's in the background attempting to play beer pong with her cat ears askew.

"Don't worry. You can change your profile pic," he says.

"Yeah. Because that's what's concerning. Not the incredible invasion of privacy." Although, I take note of where the "UPDATE PROFILE" button is before reading the rest of my bio.

Name: RACHEL MORTIMER
Company: DEVILS INC.
Level: INTERN
Active Cases: 0
Cases Won: 0
Cases Lost: 0
Soul Investments: 0
Reviews: 0
STATUS: ONLINE

"Like I said, some smart-arse created an app," says Crow. "When you die, it's automatically installed on your phone so you can check out nearby services after the whole 'welcome to death' spiel."

I frown. "What's that got to do with me?"

"Well, you were nearby. And you don't have any cases at the moment, so you were an obvious choice. Not to mention, most of the lawyers at Devils Inc. have set themselves to unavailable. They're predicting the death of a high-profile politician soon, and neither side wants him." He waves a hand in dismissal. "I can't be arsed to explain it all to you, little Demon. Not my job."

I open the window, letting in a soft breeze, the scent of car fumes, and the screech of a red Lamborghini as it overtakes us. Then I dangle his phone out the window.

"I swear to god, I'll drop this if you don't make it your job," I say.

He doesn't look particularly concerned. "Swear to god, huh?" He chuckles, then glances at me. "Okay. Calm down."

I'm tempted to do it just to spite him, but who knows how dangerous omens are. Slowly, I put the window back up.

"Go on then," I say.

"Well . . . everyone wants to go up when they die, don't they?" he says.

I look at him blankly.

"You know, *up*. Heaven. Paradise. Through the pearly gates. Whatever. . ." He pulls into a parking spot on a street of expensive-looking office buildings. After shutting the engine off, he turns to look at me, resting an arm on the back of his seat. "But only 'good' people are meant to go up. And 'bad' people are meant to go 'down.'" He points to the gearshift. "You follow?"

I look at him, perplexed. "Well, yeah. I suppose. But I don't see what it has to do with me."

"Well, good and bad can be pretty arbitrary when you come to think of it. Right?"

"I guess."

"And it's not as if the higher-ups *or* lower-downs left comprehensive legal guides. A lot of it is open to negotiation. There are frequent loopholes. And some souls are more . . . desirable than others. Sometimes, 'down there' doesn't want a bad soul. And sometimes, 'up there' doesn't want a good one."

"What do you mean, *desirable?*"

He blows out hot air. "I hate explaining things."

"I don't know why," I snap. "You're so good at it."

He climbs out of the car and makes a show of stretching on the sidewalk. Then he nods to the massive skyscraper to our left. It's made of shiny black glass.

"They'll explain it for you. Welcome to Devils Inc., little Demon. Ready to go in?"

41

Crow leans against the top of the Mini Cooper, absently studying his blunt fingernails. I don't move from the passenger seat, my mind still struggling to make sense of his shitty explanation of what's going on. Outside, suited people carry paper coffee cups and laptops through the revolving glass doors.

"Sometime today," says Crow. "I'm contracted to deliver you, little Demon. I'll throw you over my shoulder and carry you in if I have to."

I snap out of my blank stare and turn to look at him.

"You will not," I say.

"Oh, I will."

I arch an eyebrow and call his bluff. "Do it then."

He holds my gaze. Then he pushes off the car and walks around to my side. And—oh, shit, he's not bluffing . . .

Hastily unfastening my seatbelt, I clamber out with as much dignity as I can muster.

"I was coming anyway," I say.

He chuckles as he closes the passenger door.

Something catches my eye on the phone map as we start to walk down the palm tree-lined boulevard. The buildings on either side of our dots are labeled. One has the Devils Inc. logo hovering above it; the other says "Halo Corp."

I've seen that logo before too.

I touch my jeans pocket, feeling the edge of the business card that weird dude Gabriel gave me.

He said he was an Angel. . .

Holy shit.

I look up to study the two skyscrapers in a new light. They face each other like they're in some kind of standoff. Unlike Devils Inc., the other building is bright white, its many large windows reflecting the blue sky. The top floor seems to be made of mirrored glass.

"What's in there?" I ask, handing back his phone.

He follows my gaze across the street. "A load of stiffs."

"Oh, that's so informative."

He smirks. "They're Devils Inc.'s main competitors. You met one of them yesterday, I presume? A skinny redhead who walks around like he's got a stick up his arse."

"You know him?"

"Aye. I know him." Something in his eyes darkens as he stares at the building. Then he heads for Devils Inc. "Come on."

I pause. I may have taken the ride with Crow to escape the zombies, but now I'm out of harm's way, is this really a good idea? Jonathon used to always say big companies would suck out your soul eventually. If everything I'm being told is true, this place does that in a literal sense. It might be true that I need an internship, but am I this desperate? Finding a coffee shop, getting a much-needed caffeine boost, then heading back to campus might be a more sensible option.

"Tell it to me straight—why should I go in there?" I ask.

He turns to face me. "Because the dead guys'll keep coming for you?" he offers. "Because they've actually accepted you onto their internship program, and you can't afford to be picky? Because they own your soul now?" He turns and carries on walking as though confident I'll follow. "Take your pick, little Demon."

I fall into step beside him. "They don't really think they own my soul, do they?"

"You really should have read those terms and conditions."

We approach a revolving door made of tinted black glass. Crow stops, giving me a moment to take in the horned obsidian goat's head hanging above it. Its eerie ruby-red eyes give me the serious creeps.

"What were you and him talking about, by the way?" he asks with forced casualness. It's a new tone for him.

I think back to what Gabriel said. He mentioned saving my soul if I secretly passed him information. It all seemed like bullshit at the time. But on the off chance it's real and I *have* accidentally promised myself to Lucifer, perhaps it's a good idea to keep that particular conversation to myself. . .

"Something about being an Angel. I was just trying to get him out of my bedroom, to be honest," I say.

As Crow holds my gaze, the gold flecks near his pupils seem to glimmer. Then he shrugs.

"I don't blame you. Dull guy." He steps toward the revolving doors. "Gabriel in a girl's bedroom. That must be a first."

He halts, and I almost walk into his back.

"Best not to mention him when you get inside though," he says.

"Why not?"

"Just trust me on this one."

Before I can tell him how little I trust him, we're entering the lobby of Devils Inc.

Chapter Eight

The lobby is huge—about half the size of a football field—and I pause a moment to take it in.

The floor is made of black marble. The walls are black, too, with bronze plaques at regular intervals. To the right, people sit in throne-like chairs having what looks like serious conversations over circular black tables. The whole space is cold and strangely lit by small red bulbs in the ground.

"Come on, little Demon," says Crow. "Let's get this over with."

He walks toward a black marble reception desk. Another huge obsidian goat's head protrudes from the wall behind it, but that's not even the largest decoration in the room. In the center of the space there's a stone statue of an athletic man with horns. He has a pointed tail curling down one of his muscular thighs, a snake twisting around one arm, and he's holding a long black Devil's fork.

Lucifer.

His red eyes seem to look right at me.

"Not exactly subtle," I say under my breath. "Don't people get freaked-out seeing some big-ass statue of Satan in the middle of reception?"

"Aye," he agrees. "This place has always had a bit of an issue with its public image. The PR department is working on it."

As we pass by, a strong whiff of egg overcomes me—one that reminds me of when Lucas throws his lactose intolerance to the wind and gets his hands on the cheesy hot dogs from Diablos. And it's seriously unpleasant.

"Did you just fart?" I ask him.

He laughs. "You'd know if I did." When I simply stare at him, he points to the yellow base of the statue. "It's the rock!"

"Sure. Blame it on the rock."

He continues to laugh, which attracts the attention of those loitering in the lobby. As I catch the eye of one of them—a slender guy in black, with floppy dark hair and tattoos—I wish Crow would shut up. The guy smirks at me in a predatory way.

"It's brimstone," says Crow, oblivious to my discomfort. "You know, sulfur? They'll tell you it was mined from Hell."

We're at the desk now. Crow leans on the marble surface and clears his throat to get the attention of the receptionist, who's kicked back with her boots up. Although her black hair is shaved close to her head on the sides, it's long on top, swooping down to cover one eye. A black snake tattoo coils around her neck and disappears into a black blazer with "Devils Inc." embroidered in gold on the pocket.

Ignoring us, she continues to peel the skin off an apple with a sharp blade.

"Adalind," says Crow. "Pleasure to see you again."

She looks up slowly, her silver nose stud catching the light.

"Oh. It's you," she says. Her face wrinkles as though she smells something unpleasant.

"How's life on reception treating you? Good, I hope?"

She stares at him, her delicate features devoid of any emotion. As the awkward silence stretches on, I'm not quite sure what to do with myself. Crow breaks first.

"Got a delivery for you," he says, nodding in my direction.

"I'm not expecting a delivery," she says, but she slides her gaze over anyway.

A cold feeling jolts through me when our eyes meet. Underlined by thick black liner, hers don't look quite . . . human. The pupils are slit-shaped rather than round.

They're also filled with complete and utter disdain.

Without saying a word to me, she looks back at Crow. "Tracking number?"

Crow pulls his cell out of his pocket, taps the screen a few times, then slides it over. With another heavy sigh, she swings her legs off the desk, drops her blade, and leans toward her keyboard to type something into the computer.

Crow drums his fingers impatiently against the counter. "Sometime today."

She makes a point to move slower, taking a bite of her apple and munching it.

Both of them ignore my presence.

If it wasn't for the whole zombie thing earlier, the weird, intrusive Afterlife app, and the fact I really need an internship, I'd be out of here. As it is, I sigh and flick my gaze up to the TV screens around the horned goat's head.

Some of the monitors show the day's news, the big local story being the pileup on the freeway. Others loop through weird charts and images. One is a line graph titled "SUCCESSFUL MORAL DEFENSES." Another is called "SOUL RATINGS" and provides a table of names with plus and minus numbers in the adjoining columns. Another displays the map from the Afterlife app, centered on Los Angeles.

"*This* is the intern?" says Adalind finally, bringing my attention back to her and Crow. Although her tone is annoyed, her eyes hold a new glimmer of interest. "She's not expected until this evening. You'll have to bring her back later."

"Yeah, not happening," says Crow. As he leans over the reception desk, his leather jacket squeaks against its surface. "Want me to take her upstairs for you? I'll do it for a price."

"Your kind make me sick," she seethes.

"I know. But you need my services."

After a tense moment, she reaches for a black tablet and slams it onto the counter.

"Sign in," she says, "then take her through. Top floor. I'll try to arrange for someone to take her off your hands."

"Wasn't so hard, was it?" he says as he squiggles his finger across the screen. Then, without another word to Adalind, he walks toward a bank of six elevators.

I follow but feel Adalind's strange eyes on my back as I do. I turn around, expecting to meet her surly gaze, but instead, she's looking at my feather tattoo. Realizing I've caught her, she hurriedly goes back to dismembering her apple.

Chapter Nine

"What's her deal?" I say as the elevator doors slide open.

Inside, Crow pushes one of about two hundred buttons, then leans back against the mirrored wall, arms folded across his chest. Floor zero is right in the center of the keypad. This place must have a whole load of levels belowground as well.

"Adalind's?" says Crow.

"No. Mother Teresa's," I reply, leaning in the opposite corner. When he doesn't reply, I huff, "Yes, Adalind's. She seems to really hate you."

He shrugs as the elevator hurtles upward. "Aye, she's a real xenophobe—"

"Don't tell me it's because you're Scottish."

His low chuckle vibrates through the enclosed space. "She's just like that. Rumor has it, she used to have one of the top jobs here. But she screwed it up, got a major demotion, and now she works reception. And, as you could probably tell, she's pretty pissed about it."

The elevator pings, and the doors slide open, revealing a frenzy of people in black blazers balancing stacks of paper and coffee cups as they hurtle about. It's so busy I can barely see the view of Halo Corp. through the tinted glass windows beyond.

A girl with sleek black hair and a headset almost knocks me over as she barges past us into the elevator.

"—told me to check out the Purgatory Vaults," she says. "Something about some scrolls, but I don't see why—"

"Woah, steady on," says Crow as we step out.

She scowls at him as the doors close. When other people register Crow, they also start to give us a wider berth.

"There's more to it than that," I say. "Everyone seems to hate you."

"And here I was thinking I was a pretty likeable guy," says Crow.

The hallway spits us out into a huge office with garish red carpet and uniform rows of black desks. As we head through the chaotic hub, I notice loud, brightly colored graffiti everywhere—a green serpent coils around the elevators behind us, flames lick the filing cabinets, and cartoonlike depictions of torture cover the backs of every desk.

It smells like coffee and sweat, and there's a distinct lack of air-conditioning. I tuck a strand of hair that's started to stick to my forehead behind my ear.

People stare at us as we pass, eyeing me with curiosity and Crow with visible distaste.

"What did that receptionist mean when she said, 'your kind'?" I ask.

At the end of the open office is a hallway leading to small, dingy room with a poorly equipped kitchenette on one side. A note pinned to the fridge says, "USE MY MILK AGAIN, AND I'LL FLAY YOU ALIVE." A collection of shabby black and red armchairs and a scuffed black table have been pushed next to the window.

Crow drops down into one of the chairs, instantly at ease, manspreading as though we haven't just passed twenty people who seem like they'd happily kick him in the balls.

"I'm an Omen," he says.

"And that means?" I reply, sitting in the armchair beside him, tucking one leg beneath me to stop our knees from brushing. A stack of newspapers has been dumped on top of the table, and someone has graffitied the president with Devil horns and a moustache.

Crow groans, tilting his head back then rubbing his face. "What's with all the questions? I can't take it anymore."

"You know, if you actually told me what was going on, then I wouldn't have to ask," I say, irritation rippling through my body. I look around. "Why have you brought me to some shithole office kitchen? I thought this was about an internship?"

"Aye. This is the interns' floor. I'm just babysitting you until someone takes you off my hands," he says, still staring at the low ceiling. "Someone else will explain it."

"That's it! I'm out of here." I stand abruptly, knocking his outspread knee.

Suddenly, he grabs my wrist, reflexes faster than I imagined. Reflexes of my own kick into gear, and I grab his neck, pushing him back into the armchair and resting my knee between his legs.

His eyes widen. Slowly, he releases his grip on my wrist and puts his hands behind his head, raising an eyebrow in challenge. Amusement glimmers in his gray eyes.

"Have your way with me if you will. I like it rough," he says.

I hold his gaze a moment longer, then let him go. "You're a dick."

He grins, hands still behind his head. Then he shakes his head.

"Go on then. What do you want to know? Why everyone hates me?"

"It's becoming easier to figure out," I say.

"As I said before, I'm an Omen."

I sit back down.

"I work for a consultancy firm called Omens Limited," he says. "We do contract work for both sides—for Devils Inc., and"—he gestures to the glinting white skyscraper across the road—"Halo Corp." He shrugs. "People don't like that we flit sides. Think we should choose an allegiance."

"Why don't you?"

"Tried that once. Pays better not to," he replies. "Plus, they like me even less over there." Something dark flits behind his eyes before he masks it with another smile.

"So you were paid? To what? Follow me around? Piss me off? Bring me here?" I pause. "That *was* you in the locker rooms yesterday, wasn't it?"

"Aye, that was me."

I stiffen. Despite everything that's happened, I was still persuading myself I imagined the shadowy man in the mirror. The thought that Crow might have been there while I was showering is too creepy.

"That's not okay," I say. "How long were you in there?"

"Calm down," he says. "I *did*n't see anything. I *did* hear a pretty off-key rendition of that Fleetwood Mac tune blaring through the walls though. Wasn't too keen to get any closer to that."

Heat floods to my face. "Why were you following me?"

"The sides have a recruitment agreement in place. They're allowed to recruit mortal souls to work for them, but they have to give at least twenty-four hours' notice prior to presenting the mortal soul with the agreement. You know, to give the mortal chance to turn it down?"

"Are you talking about this Wi-Fi thing again?"

"Now you're getting it."

"You didn't give me notice. . ."

"The ladders you walked under on the way to class, the crows, the black cat, the flickering lights. . ." He lists the items on his fingers. "I broke a shitload of mirrors too. And that ominous feeling you've had building in your chest for the past twenty-four hours?" He shifts forward in his seat, eyes glinting. "That was me."

"Oh, right. Of course. No written notice, but a bad feeling and a series of minor annoyances? That will really stand up in court. Seems more to me that you're listing things I could use to file a restraining order against you."

"It stands up in *our* court. And your laws don't apply to me."

I shake my head. "Whatever. So Devils Inc. paid you to come and bring me in?"

"Well, that's the interesting thing," he says, leaning closer. "I was sent the contract about the job for your soul through the Afterlife app. Anonymously."

"Is that unusual?"

"For this kind of job, aye."

I frown, thinking about the veritable inbox of rejections I've accumulated. This year hasn't been going well. My grades aren't great, and my professors say I'm not applying myself. I'm pretty sure boxing and binge-watching movies aren't particularly attractive extracurricular activities on a résumé either. Actual law firms don't seem to want me. If this is real, and Devils Inc. could have any lawyer in the world, why would they head-hunt me?

Crow holds my gaze, his expression intense. My pulse quickens.

Then the spell breaks, and he looks at something behind me.

"Adalind," he drawls. "They actually let you leave reception, huh?"

"Shut it," comes the crisp reply.

Adalind has arrived wearing the same deadpan expression. Her piercings glint in the sunlight coming through the tinted window.

"We're not paying you any more for this job, Omen. You can see yourself out." Then she looks at me with her strange, inhuman eyes. "Let's get this over with, shall we?"

She swivels on her black boots, then marches back down the hallway.

Crow shrugs. "Good luck, little Demon," he says. "I'm sure I'll be seeing you around."

Chapter Ten

Adalind leads me away from the kitchenette, a black file in one hand. Now she's standing, I realize she's shorter than me, but despite her athletic build, she seems to trudge rather than walk, as though her black combat boots are too heavy.

"That guy's an asshole," she murmurs to herself.

"Yeah," I agree under my breath, fighting a strange urge to look over my shoulder and catch his eye.

"One day, I'll enjoy playing with his entrails."

Torn between a fear she's deadly serious and an odd desire for her approval, I end up making a weird noncommittal noise as we turn right and start to walk along the black meeting room-lined wall of the open office.

Truth be told, I'm uneasy at being parted from Crow. The guy may be an asshole, but he's seen me through all this weirdness so far. What's that saying? Better the devil you know. Or Omen, in this case.

Now the adrenaline from the fight has worn off, my hangover is starting to creep back in, as is the dry mouth. From Adalind's stormy expression, it's doubtful I'll be offered a glass of water. As if in answer to my question, she scowls at some blond guy passing by and causes him to spill his cup of coffee.

Yeah. I definitely prefer Crow.

"So I got an email about an internship?" I say.

She pinches the bridge of her nose. "Yes. I'm aware. I sent it." She sighs. "Always stuck with the shit jobs. "

"So are you giving me an interview or something?" I ask as we walk past numerous deceased plants and meeting rooms graffitied with cartoon Devils.

Without answering, she stops in front of one. A plaque reading "Meeting Room M:25:46" is pinned to the black brick.

"Go inside and take a seat," she says, voice flat.

I do, stepping past her to sit at one of the six plastic chairs around a black circular table. A bulky old-school TV on wheels dominates one side of the small room, and Adalind slumps into a seat in front of it, dropping her black file onto the table. "Rachel Mortimer," reads the label on the front.

She flicks it open, sighs, then pulls out a sleeved disc. She sticks it into the DVD player and presses play.

"What—?"

"Shh," she hisses.

The TV turns on.

"Devils Inc. Recruitment Introduction" flickers in white letters before fading into a shot of a prestigious office. There are bookshelves full of dusty tomes interspersed with decanters of deep red and honey-colored liquid. The most prominent feature in the room, however, is the intimidating mahogany desk. And the man sitting behind it.

Ostensibly in his thirties, he's tall and slender, with sharp cheekbones and a mop of fiery red curls. He wears a black suit, but it's different than what I've seen the other employees wearing—more expensive.

He shuffles some papers on his desk, then adjusts the cuffs of his sleeves. As the camera zooms in, he looks up with a wicked smile that doesn't quite reach his black eyes.

"Hello . . .?"

He pauses as if waiting for something.

"Rachel Mortimer," drones Adalind, making me jump.

"Welcome to Devils Incorporated. I'm Mephistopheles, and I run the soul recruitment program for our Dark Lord and founder, Lucifer. At precisely—"

"Seven minutes past nine," Adalind interjects, feet now resting on one of the plastic chairs.

"—at the location—"

"Evie's Garden Bar—"

"—you entered into a contract with our organization and promised your immortal undying soul to us in exchange for—"

"Free Wi-Fi," supplies Adalind.

Mephistopheles's smile widens. "Congratulations! I hope you reveled in the earthly pleasures our organization arranged for you as compensation for your soul."

My mouth drops. These people aren't seriously trying to tell me the Wi-Fi I used to send an application to a stupid firm that auto-rejected me is a divine pleasure to be exchanged for my soul, are they?

"Erm—" I start.

"Shh," hisses Adalind.

"But now, it is time for your side of the bargain. It is time to join us here at Devils Inc., where you will serve until Judgement Day—at which point, of course, your soul will come down to the depths of Hell for all eternity."

I glance at Adalind for some sign that this is a funny initiation joke, but she's staring disinterested out of the window. The forked tongue of the snake tattoo on her neck winds down her shoulder to poke out of her sleeve.

"Now," drawls Mephistopheles, bringing my attention back to the TV, "you're probably wondering what it is we do here at Devils Inc. So let me fill you in." He rises to his feet and strolls over to the bookshelf, which he leans against in a faux casual pose. "We run the show up here during our Dark Lord and founder's absence from earth so only the very best souls make their way down to Hell. Among the many teams that exist within our organization are a few that will be of particular interest to our new recruits."

He reaches for one of the decanters on the shelf. Slowly, he pours red liquid into a small crystal goblet. It could be red wine, but it has the thick consistency of blood.

"Our Soul Investments Team works hard to identify souls that might be of interest to our Dark Lord and founder," he continues, putting the cork back in the decanter. "Our Soul Recruitment Team works to lure them in. Our Legal Team oversees the entire operation, making sure that when there is a legal dispute with our main competitor, Halo Corp., Devils Inc. wins. And, of course, our military program allows us to build our army in preparation for the Final War to come once the Revelations Clause is exercised. It is a great pleasure to welcome you to our—"

He pauses again.

"Legal Team," says Adalind, stifling a yawn.

"—where you will serve as—"

"An intern."

He raises his glass. "Here's to an eternity of servitude to the Devil," he says, taking a sip. When he pulls the goblet away, his grinning lips are stained red. "Any questions?"

Chapter Eleven

"Um, yeah. I have a few," I say when another long pause suggests we're still in the ask-and-answer portion of the video.

"Then your assigned Devils Inc. mentor will be happy to answer them," Mephistopheles drawls.

I look at Adalind, who's still staring moodily out of the window. She looks like she's just waiting for someone to ask her a question so she can immediately kill them.

"As for me," Mephistopheles says, "I'll be seeing you in Hell. Until then . . ." He raises his crystal goblet once more, then gulps down the rest of the viscous red liquid.

The scene fades to white noise.

Adalind sighs heavily, then turns off the TV. She folds her arms across her chest before lazily turning her attention my way. "What?" she says.

"Is this some kind of joke?"

"Do I look like I have a sense of humor?" she asks. Her eyes are blank, and her pierced nose is raised in challenge.

I pause. "No."

She places the black file back on the table, flips it to the front, and slips a flat black cell phone from the front sleeve.

"This is your company phone," she drones, sliding it across the desk. "The Afterlife app is already installed. You can access your profile now. You might want to change your status to offline to stop any unwanted soul attention until your training."

When I don't take it, she slips something else out of the pocket. "This is your Devils Inc. access card," she continues, sliding over a black piece of plastic emblazoned with devil horns. "It'll get you into the places in the building that an intern is allowed to go. Which are not many."

She runs a hand through her black hair before pulling a piece of paper from the file. "And this is your contract, which states the terms and conditions of our compulsory internship offer." She glares at me. "Go on. Take it."

Jaw set, I lean forward across the table and drag the three items toward me. The top few lines of the contract catch my eye instantly. *"By accepting the terms and conditions of our free Internet service, you hereby sign away your immortal soul to the Devil and agree to be called upon, at any time, to enter into his service."*

"You'll come in on Monday evening at seven and not a moment sooner." Adalind's monotonous voice takes my attention from the paper.

"In the evening? That seems a bit late."

"We offer a twenty-four-hour service. I don't make the rules. If you have a problem with your working hours, then feel free to send your complaints to I-don't-give-a-crap at Devils Inc. dot com. In the meantime, I'll arrange for someone to run through your training. Which will be a pain in the ass since we're extremely busy at the moment." She arches a pierced eyebrow. "Any questions?"

It's a challenge rather than a genuine offer. Still . . .

"And if I don't accept it?"

"You'll be transported to Hell."

I stare at her. "This is ridiculous. You seriously expect me to believe this is legally binding?" I glance at the piece of paper, scouring my mind for anything I've learned about contracts in my business law class. "It's . . . it's too vague."

"It's not."

"It's fraudulent!"

"Everything looks clear and accurate to me."

"An agreement needs to be made by consent of both parties. I didn't know what I was signing."

She shrugs.

"Well, what about the fact exchanging my immortal soul for a service makes the object of the contract illegal itself?" I declare.

Adalind exhales sharply through her nostrils, then leans forward. She taps the bottom of the contract: *"This Soul Agreement between Rachel Mortimer and Devils Inc. shall be governed by and interpreted pursuant to Ethereal Law."*

My mouth feels dry, and I swallow as I stare at the piece of paper. I have trouble enough understanding California State Law. I have no idea what rules these people are following.

I blow out a long breath. Then I decide to make lemonade out of evil lemons.

"Will it count for university credit?"

She shrugs. "I guess. Now, we're done. I have more important things to be doing," she says, marching out of the meeting room.

I want to tell her I have things to be doing too—such as class, and meeting Josie and Lucas for lunch, and rationalizing this completely crazy morning, and sleeping off this appletini-induced hangover. But my head throbs, and right now, I just want to get out of here.

Hands slightly shaking, I fold the contract and put it in my jeans pocket along with the new cell and access card. My fingers brush against the Halo Corp. business card as I do.

It's not until I've finally made my way back outside that I realize I don't have a ride back to Trinity Falls. I curse, pulling out my cell and leaning against the obsidian black wall. Lucas has a car, so I open up our group chat with Josie to see if they'll come pick me up.

There are about a million messages waiting for me. Josie was bored in her theology lecture, Lucas thinks the guy playing Doctor Faustus is hot, they both think my lack of response to their messages means I've died, and Josie is heading to Apocalypse for some kind of interview for the bartender job.

I finally reach the part about their current whereabouts: Lucas has ditched us for lunch in favor of grabbing a hot dog with the guy playing Faustus, and Josie's at an impromptu Wicca meeting due to one of the girls sensing bad energy on campus yesterday. I always thought that spiritual-type stuff was a load of bullshit, but there definitely *has* been bad energy on campus, and his name is Crow.

I let them know I'm not dead *(Just potentially bound to Hell!)* and trudge toward a bus stop down the street, which has been graffitied with devil horns and halos. Apparently, there's an hourly bus.

I'm just settling onto the edge of the metal bench when a beeping horn makes me flinch. Crow's black Mini Cooper is coming down the road. I smile and wave as it slows. Maybe Crow isn't such an asshole after all.

But just as I walk toward the curb, he speeds up again, hurtling out of sight.

Anger surges through my body.

"Dick!" I growl, but I don't have long to seethe.

A slender figure stands across the road, face hidden in shadow. When he steps into the light, the sun turns his red hair almost golden.

Gabriel.

It's clear he wants to speak to me, but, hell, I've had enough. When the bus rolls up with a gasp of hot, smelly air, I get ready to make my escape. As I'm about to step aboard, however, a hand grabs my shoulder and pulls me back to the sidewalk.

Gabriel. How on earth could he have crossed the road so quickly?

"Can I help you?" I sputter, still in shock.

"We can't be seen. We don't have much time."

He spins on his heel just as the bus doors close again.

"Come. I want to show you something."

Chapter Twelve

I watch Gabriel as he speeds across the wide street toward Halo Corp., fists clenched and gaze swinging from side to side as though he's about to be ambushed. Then I blow out hot air. While I suppose I could go and get a Coke or something, that's not going to fill the hour I'll need to wait for the next bus.

Reluctantly, I follow him into a small alley. If this is what he wants to show me, I'm underwhelmed.

"How did you get across the street so quickly?" I ask.

Lowering his head, he clasps his hands together. "I used a small Miracle. Which will be fine. They're not usually tracked. Not small ones. Probably. And anyway, I had to show you. It's important. What else can I do . . .?" His voice drops as he continues to mutter to himself, something about how all will be forgiven when he's saved the world, and how much of a pain in the ass it is that it's fallen on him to deal with pesky mortals yet again.

"You know I can hear you, right?" I say.

He glowers at me, lips pressed into a thin line, before he gestures that we should go deeper into the alley. We do, although soon, the path forward is blocked by the signs of construction.

"Where are you taking me?" I ask.

"The Purgatory Vaults," he replies, ducking under some scaffolding. "Hurry."

"The what now?"

"Purgatory Vaults," he repeats, then he starts up his muttering again as he leads me to an abandoned building.

"You realize that's not an explanation, right?" I say.

"Do all you mortals have to be so tedious?" he snaps, pulling a leather wallet from his jeans pocket. "I'll explain when we get inside."

He slides out a plastic keycard that, apart from being white, looks a lot like the one Adalind gave me. He flashes it at the keypad next to the door, there's a beep, and it creaks open. After one last look over his shoulder, he pushes his way inside.

"Come on then," he hisses.

Dim automatic lights flick on, revealing what looks like a subway station. The walls are concrete, the floor is covered in patterned linoleum, and there's a ticket machine with an "out of order" sign. Just ahead, steps lead down into a mouth of darkness.

"Are we going somewhere?" I ask, prodding a dead rat on the floor with the toe of my Converse. "Because, hate to break it to you, but it looks like the trains are out of service."

"No. We're here to prevent the Apocalypse," he says, then sighs. "Just . . . wait here a moment."

Gabriel approaches the broken machine, pushes a few buttons, and seconds later, it shudders to life, spitting out two tickets. Then he hurries down the steps, his smart shoes clicking against the linoleum.

"The Purgatory Vaults are this way." His voice echoes as his red head disappears into the shadows. "Come on."

I linger at the top of the steps, breathing in the dank air as I weigh up my options. This time yesterday, I would never have even considered following some strange guy down into the depths of an abandoned train station. Or vault. Or whatever. But yesterday, he said he'd help me, and if I've actually signed away my soul to Devils Inc., I need all the help I can get.

My gut feeling about him is that he's okay, if a little odd. Plus, according to him, he's an Angel. Which is admittedly becoming easier and easier to believe.

I find him waiting for me by a set of turnstiles at the foot of the stairs. He passes me one of the tickets—pulling away quickly when my finger brushes against his—then inserts his and steps through the metal barrier. I do the same.

"So what *are* the Purgatory Vaults?" I say as we head through an arched door leading into a bright hallway. As we walk, we pass by a series of ornately framed paintings that give this the air of a museum or gallery; I recognize depictions of the Garden of Eden and The Last Supper, and—if the way my companion scowls is any indication—an oil painting of the Angel Gabriel.

"There are a number of contracts in place between our two companies to stop things from getting out of control," he says. "One of these contracts led to the implementation of the Purgatory Vaults. There are certain biblical artefacts that both sides believe they have a claim to. The use of any of these would give an unfair advantage to one side."

We stop at a metal door.

"So an agreement was made to store them in a high-security room placed in between the two organizations. Both sides can monitor the artefacts, but neither side can use them without filing the correct paperwork."

"It doesn't seem high-security," I say. "We've literally just walked in."

"Well, it's lunchtime," he explains.

"So?"

His cheeks pinken, and he hurriedly averts his gaze to the silver watch around his wrist. "I gave the security guard some vouchers for a free meal at TGI Fridays and said I'd cover his shift."

"How dastardly of you," I tease.

But he doesn't seem to see the humor. "It had to be done," he mumbles to himself. "It's important. All will be forgiven. All will be forgiven." He continues to mutter as he flashes his access card again.

A loud sound echoes around us as the seal around the metal door releases.

"Why did it have to be done?"

He turns his head, the expression in his ice-blue eyes deadly serious.

"Because someone has triggered the Apocalypse," he says.

Chapter Thirteen

"The *Apocalypse?*" I repeat.

But Gabriel has already slipped into the Purgatory Vaults. With a frustrated sigh, I follow, only to find my questions immediately knocked out of me.

"It's quite something, isn't it?" he says, and for a moment, the worry in his voice is replaced with pride.

If I thought the hallway felt like a museum, it's nothing compared to this. In the middle of the room, surrounded by more glass display cases than I can count, is a bench with two huge stone wings—one white, one black—curling out from either side. What's more, the ceiling is painted in two halves. The patch above Gabriel and me depicts a blue sky scattered with fluffy blue clouds, but then it transforms into hellish depictions of fireballs and darkness.

Directly opposite us is another high-security metal door.

"Yeah. But you mentioned something about an Apocalypse?"

He sighs and shuts the door behind us. "You mortals have no appreciation for fine things."

"And you Angels have no manners," I mutter.

"Pardon?" he says. When I don't elaborate, he checks his watch again, then starts to cross the room. "This way, please."

We weave through the display cases, each with a bronze plaque detailing its contents: a slab of stone labeled as Moses' Tablet, a rotten piece of wood from Noah's Ark, and a small withered plant that apparently had something to do with a guy called Jonas.

I pause when I reach a case near the stone bench. It's cordoned off with crimson rope and has a piece of paper taped to the glass. *DO NOT REMOVE. WILL DISINTEGRATE.*

A single apple—a couple of bites missing—floats inside.

"The Apple of Knowledge," reads the bronze plaque.

"The forbidden fruit from Eden, passed by the Serpent to Eve, who took a bite and persuaded her husband to do the same. Source of sin. All parties punished for breach of verbal contract. One bite will instill great knowledge—"

"Stop dawdling," says Gabriel.

He's stopped in front of another glass case. Behind him is a chair, a newspaper, and a half-eaten sandwich I guess belongs to the security guard now enjoying a big juicy burger at TGI Fridays.

My stomach grumbles, and a look of horror crosses Gabriel's face.

"Is this stuff for real?" I say in an attempt to distract him from my bodily noises.

"Yes," he says, eyes glinting with eagerness. "I've always found it fascinating in here. I applied for a position to oversee it once, but . . . after the incident with . . . well . . ." He becomes interested in the fire of the mural overhead.

"After the incident with what?"

His cheeks are pink again. "Never mind."

Realizing there are more pressing matters than whatever the guy Crow referred to as a "stiff" considers embarrassing, I press on.

"So what's in this one?" I peer inside. There are four spotlights, but whatever they're highlighting must be small because I can't see anything.

"Nothing," he says like I'm a complete moron. "It's very obviously empty."

I fold my arms across my chest. "Right. Like *obviously* you're an Angel, and I *obviously* signed away my soul to the Devil for free Wi-Fi, and I *obviously* was attacked by dead people who were *obviously* driven away by a man who can *obviously* control birds—"

His eyes narrow.

"—and now I'm *obviously* destined for Hell while *obviously* standing a room that has the apple from Eden in it. *Everything about this situation is so completely obvious.*"

I exhale, breathing out my growing rage, and lean against the case, ignoring his look of disapproval.

"So please tell me, *obviously*, why are you showing me an empty display case?"

He seems nervous, although I'm not sure if it's because he thinks I'll start yelling again. "Well . . . because it's empty. That's the point. Are you familiar with the Book of Revelation?"

I shrug. That's more Josie's area than mine. "That's the one that talks about the end of the world, right?"

"Yes. Revelations talks of a scroll. Nowadays, for legal purposes, there are four of them—one for each of the Horsemen. Each is bound by a wax seal, and if you're familiar with Revelations, you'll know that when each seal is broken, it will trigger the Apocalypse."

When I only look at him blankly, he continues.

"This case displayed them."

"Oh." I start to see why he's worried. "Where are they?"

"They were checked out a few days ago for maintenance. And they have not yet been returned. Which is *very* bad news indeed." He shakes his head. "If they're delivered to the Horseman brothers . . ."

I tuck a strand of hair behind my ear. "Why don't you just ask the person who checked them out to return them?"

"I can't. Obvious—"

He shuts his mouth when I give him a withering look. Regrouping, he pulls his phone from his pocket and taps it a few times. There's a table on the screen, some kind of logbook.

"What am I looking at?" I say.

"The name of the person who checked it out."

I scan the table. *"Dover, Ben"* is listed beside *"Apocalyptic Scrolls."*

"Dover, Ben?" Something stirs in my mind—memories of a prank Jonathon taught me once. "As in, Bend Over. You've been fake-named."

"Yes. I agree," says Gabriel. "But none of the higher-ups will give me the time of day to explain."

I glance around, noting a security camera camouflaged among the mural's dark clouds. "Have you checked—?"

"Of course I've checked the security footage!" says Gabriel. "Wiped. And the security guard says nothing unusual happened that day either." He shakes his head. "So it falls to me."

"What does?"

"Saving the world! Don't you see what has happened here?" he snaps. "Someone has stolen the Revelations Scrolls! And if we don't get them back before they are delivered to the Horseman brothers, the world ends."

"Excuse me, 'we'?"

"Well, I can't do it alone!" He looks at me sideways. "Though I wish I could."

I raise my hands. "Hey. I didn't ask to be included in your weird end-of-the-world plan, buddy."

"It will be dangerous," he continues as though I didn't speak. "But I need you to be my eyes and ears in Devils Inc. This has their name written all over it."

"Why me?"

He glances at me incredulously. "You have access to the building, and you signed your soul away to the Devil in exchange for free Wi-Fi. As a law student, no less."

"There's no need to be an ass."

He gives me an unimpressed look before sighing again. "Look, help me track down the scrolls before the Apocalypse, and I'll help save your soul from an eternity in Hell," he says, then he holds his hand out stiffly for me to shake. "Do we have a deal?"

I stare at his outstretched palm. After everything I've seen today, the damnation of my soul is starting to feel a bit too real. If I help Gabriel, I could still meet my pre-law program's internship requirement, which would keep my parents off my case.

Two evil birds, one stone.

"Okay, deal," I say.

His grip is firm as he shakes my hand once. Then he wipes his hand on his jacket as if he's touched something filthy.

"Excellent," he says, walking past me toward the door. "Shall we go?"

I follow him back through the Purgatory Vaults, coming to a halt when he stops in the part that looks like an abandoned station.

"So what do you need me to do?" I ask.

"Complete your training. Report to me if you hear anything weird. I'll be in touch."

I glance at the doors. "You couldn't give me a ride home, could you?"

He looks vaguely horrified. "I don't have a car."

I sigh. "Okay. Well, I guess I'll be seeing you then."

I head back to the graffitied bus stop and check my cell for the time. Josie must be heading to Apocalypse for her bartender interview now. I send her a quick message to wish her luck.

Then I close my eyes to block out the midday sun. It's making my headache infinitely worse.

It has been a weird morning. And if what Gabriel said is true, things are about to get worse. I've signed away my soul, and the only way to save the world is to stick out an internship that might be literal Hell.

PART TWO
APOCALPYSE

"APOCALYPSE" Employment Terms and Conditions

Dear Josie Bishop,

We are delighted to offer you the position of **bartender** *at "Apocalypse" commencing on Saturday 21 March.*

Please find the terms and conditions below. And feel free to stop by for a drink on us this evening to celebrate!

Yours Devilishly,
Darius, Felix, Will, and Chris Horseman
Apocalypse Co-Founders

This employment contract ("The Agreement"), dated Friday 20 March, is between **Josie Bishop** and **The Horseman Brothers.**

Job Title and Description

1. The initial job title of the Employee will be the following: **bartender**

2. On entering The Agreement, the Employee agrees to carry out duties such as serving drinks, training, cleaning, and other Apocalyptic tasks as determined by the Horseman Brothers.

Renumeration and commencement

1. Employee will be paid $22 per hour for services.
2. Job will commence imminently.

Termination

1. The Horseman Brothers retain the right to terminate The Agreement, with no notice, on the occasion of the Apocalypse.

Job Benefits

1. The Horseman Brothers may offer free drinks, training, and escape from Judgement at their sole discretion.

I hereby agree to the terms set forth in this agreement:

Name: _____ Date:_____

LAUREN PALPHREYMAN

Chapter Fourteen

Josie's day so far. . .

It's a beautiful morning, and with my interview at Apocalypse this afternoon, my day can only get better. Rays of sun shine onto my patchwork bedspread as if they've been sent down from Heaven itself. Despite dancing the night away and drinking a zillion appletinis, I'm feeling fresh as a freaking daisy.

I leap out of bed, wrestle my hair into a hairband, and pull on my sneakers. Then I slip in my earbuds and head out for a run. As I reach the bottom of the stairs, I see someone has left a ladder right over the exit. Ha! Not today, Satan! No bad omens are going to ruin this glorious morning.

It's way too early for Lucas, but I might catch Rach on her way to class. I hope so—I want to tell her about the seriously fine gentleman I met at Apocalypse last night. His name was Darius. I'd have taken the bartender job just to gawk at him, but the pay is great too.

"Hey, girl!" I yell as I jog past Lisa, one of the girls from Rachel's block who is also in my Wicca group. I back up and pull out one of my earbuds. "How's it going?"

"Josie! Meetup today at lunch," she says, jogging in place. "You in? Cassie sensed some bad energy on campus last night."

"Count me in!"

"Great! See you then!"

We both turn and continue our run. As I slip my earbud back in, I catch the cawing of a crow. I look up to see one perched on the sign of Trinity Falls Campus Gym.

One crow.

One for sorrow.

There's some bad energy on campus, all right. Didn't Rach say she broke a mirror yesterday? I cross myself.

Almost instantly, another crow joins the first. I let out a breath.

One for sorrow. But two for joy.

I continue my jog. At the campus square, students mill around with coffees and smoothies. But there's no sign of Rach.

Ah well. I'll catch her later.

I jog down the steps on a renewed mission for an ice-cold smoothie, but then I stop. I have the strangest feeling someone is watching me.

As I'm squinting into the shadows, a small feather floats in front of me. I smile. Grams always used to say that was a sign a Guardian Angel was watching over you. I catch it in the palm of my hand, make a silent prayer to thank the Lord for this beautiful day, then blow, watching it dance away on the warm breeze.

Perhaps there is someone watching me after all.

Inside the food hall, there's a serving station where Martha doles out pancakes and crispy bacon to the few early risers lined up by the mirrored wall. Next to it is Lazarus Coffee, which has a much longer line. The closed deli area on the left won't open until lunch, but that isn't what I want. I want the colorful fruit and a large, vibrating blender.

At the counter, I select a strawberry and watermelon smoothie, then wait. As I do, something catches my eye on the linoleum floor.

"Drop this?" I ask the smoothie guy.

"Nope," he replies brightly, handing me my drink. "But find a penny, pick it up . . ."

"All day long, you'll have good luck!" I finish with a grin, pocketing it as I make my way toward the exit.

That's when I hear a sharp noise over the cutlery and conversation. A crack snakes along the mirrored wall.

"Holy macaroni," I say, reaching for a packet on the table and throwing salt over my shoulder for more luck.

A torrent of creative cuss words comes from behind me. Heart jumping, I spin around to find a tall dark-haired guy in a leather jacket. He's rubbing his eyes like there's no tomorrow.

Or like someone just threw salt in them.

"Oh, my God! I'm so sorry!" I say. "I didn't see anyone behind me. Are you okay?"

"Okay? What the hell!" he says gruffly, and I try to place the accent.

He blinks a few times before his eyes focus on my face. They are both a little red due to the recent salt incident, but his irises are a cloudy gray. He's pretty hot in a bad-boy kind of way, with broad shoulders and a rugged jawline covered with day-old stubble. He looks familiar, too, even though I don't think I've seen him on campus.

"Do I know you?" I ask.

"I'm the guy you just hit in the eye with salt!" he says, incredulous.

Scottish. The accent is Scottish.

"You know what? It's not worth it," he mutters, turning toward the exit. "I only took the job because I was on campus for the other one anyway."

"What's his problem?" I mutter under my breath as the double doors swing behind him.

Then I shrug and slurp my smoothie.

What a beautiful morning.

***

Theology. Yawn. But at least Lucas keeps me entertained with updates on his new crush from his theater class and his excitement about me scoring the job at Apocalypse. I know it's because he thinks I'll make him free drinks—and I will as long as it isn't a problem with the owners. I'm broke AF at the moment, and I don't want to be any more of a strain on my mom, who is working her ass off in shitty jobs just so I can be here.

Rach is in on all of these texts, but I don't hear from her until I'm heading into the glass-walled work zone to meet the girls. As I plop myself down in one of the pink beanbags in the corner and straighten my long tribal-patterned skirt, I can't help but notice a weird amount of crows hanging about the square. They're everywhere—perched on the old tower, on the sign for the library, and milling about on the stone steps.

Seriously weird.

I go back to my phone and message Rach. It's a relief to hear from her, honestly. She's been quiet lately, spending loads of time alone at the gym. I think it's because the anniversary of Jonathon's death is approaching. I'm an only child—unless you count my asshole half-brother Nathan, which I don't—but still, I can't imagine losing a sibling. She won't talk much about him, but I get the impression they were close even though her parents favored him.

The meeting starts, and I brighten, putting my phone away.

If I get this Apocalypse job, I'll cheer her up with free drinks and dancing.

After we send good vibes out into the universe, I flick on some mascara and adjust the big, blocky red beads of my necklace so they hang right over my black strappy top.

Bartender interview-ready? Check!

But no, something is missing. Then I smile, pulling out a small bottle of perfume from my purse. I spritz myself with the incense-y sandalwood scent.

Hot co-founder of Apocalypse-ready? Check!

Waving bye to the girls, I make the ten-minute walk to Trinity Falls' main drag. When I reach Apocalypse, the usually bright neon sign is turned off.

Steeling myself to go in, I look around. The woman who works behind the bar at Evie's stares at me through the glass. I smile and wave. She turns away, an odd expression on her face.

I shrug. Then I take a deep breath and knock on the wooden door.

Moments later, it swings open.

"Josie, you made it," Darius says.

Just like last night, he's drop-dead gorgeous, with dark skin and short, curly black hair. Today, his white shirtsleeves are rolled up, revealing the tattoos on one of his forearms. The most prominent is a scythe with black flowers curling around the handle. His eyes are dark and endless. But there's something else too. Something that makes my blood run hot and cold at the same time.

I can't even deal with how hot he is. And young for a co-founder of a club.

"Darius," I say, heart thumping as I try to act breezy. *Get it together, girl.* "So great to see you again! So you have a job opening?"

His smile widens. "Yes. One of my brothers recently received an unexpected summons," he says in a low British drawl. "And we believe it will be keeping us busy for the foreseeable future. So, please, come in, let me tell you all about it."

He takes a step back into the shadow, then pauses.

"Oh, and by the way, my brothers call me Death. Just a little nickname. Silly, really. But don't let it bother you."

"Death?" I repeat, glancing at the horseshoe above the entrance. "Ohhh." I laugh. "Like the Four Horsemen of the Apocalypse, right? Cute."

"Yes. Exactly. Now, please, follow me. I'll go over the role, and then you can sign the contract."

Chapter Fifteen

When I finally get back from Devils Inc., I kick off my sneakers, gulp down the glass of old water on my nightstand, then collapse onto my unmade bed. My head thumps, and I'm not sure if it's thanks to dehydration, heat, or sensory overload.

I push myself upright against the chipped wooden headboard, my eyes drawn to the stack of books on my desk—still in alphabetical order, thanks to my odd new ally. Then I empty the contents of my jeans pocket onto the crumpled sheets: the Halo Corp. business card, the company cell from Adalind, and the contract.

I unfold it, pressing it against the mattress. And there it is, Section 666 of Evie's Garden Bar Free Wi-Fi Terms and Conditions. It outlines how, if I accept, my soul belongs to the Devil. And there, below it, is my time-stamped acceptance. There's also a clause above it about how I agree to be transported to Hell imminently if I fail to comply with the company's rules and regulations, and that includes a ban on insider trading. There's also a section detailing the things that constitute twenty-four-hour notice before being given the agreement.

Apparently, omens of the sort Crow sent do count. Well, that's complete bullshit. If he really wanted to warn me, he could have told me straight-out what was coming. But he didn't. And then today, he just drove off and left me to stumble into another ridiculous agreement.

What a complete and utter dick. I'd like to give that Omen a piece of my mind.

I jump up and grab my gym bag. I need to punch something. As I swing it over my shoulder, though, my cell buzzes.

"Hey, girl!" Josie says as soon as I pick up. "You won't believe the day I've had!"

"Ditto," I say, heading to the window.

"Oh, really? Tell me!"

"You first," I say, unsure how I would even start to explain my morning without her thinking I've lost my mind. She's already worried about me because of the whole Jonathon thing.

"Well, you're speaking with the newest bartender at Apocalypse! And, babe, you would not believe how hot the club owners are," Josie continues. "They're half-brothers. And Darius, the guy who did the interview . . ."

As she continues to speak, movement catches my eye outside between two concrete dorm blocks. The very dead Richard Livingstone staggers out of the shadows, phone in hand, business suit practically torn to shreds by Crow's birds.

"You've got to be kidding me," I mutter.

"I know, right!" continues Josie as the zombie asshole below checks his cell, then looks up. "They're totally committed to the Apocalyptic aesthetic. Darius asked me to call him D—"

"Josie, I'm so sorry," I say as Richard's eyes meet mine. *Shit.* "I've got to go."

"Oh. Okay." Josie sounds disappointed. "Why?"

"Someone's at my door," I say—not untruthfully, as Livingstone is currently staggering into my building.

"Well, meet me and Lucas at Apocalypse tonight? Darius said drinks were on the house!"

"Yep. Sure. See you tonight!" I hang up the phone.

Shit. Shit. Shit.

I did want to beat the crap out of something, but this wasn't quite what I had in mind.

I look around my small room, searching for something to use as a weapon. My boxing trophy? My lamp? My humongous business law textbook? Then my eyes catch on the small black cellphone on my bed, courtesy of Devils Inc.

That damned Afterlife App. That's why Richard is here.

I grab my phone, heart in my throat, and see a push notification informing me there's a potential client in close proximity.

"Thanks for the warning," I grumble. Adalind said I needed to set my status to offline to stop the dead from coming to me.

Tapping the icon, I scroll down the page of my bio, past my profile pic and a section where I can add a description.

I hear movement outside my door. Footsteps.

Shit.

And then I see the status bar in the top right-hand corner of the screen. I slide it to "Offline."

There's a pause.

Then the footsteps retreat.

Exhaling, I fall back on my bed, cell still in hand.

I can't believe that actually worked.

I can't believe there's an app for the newly dead.

I can't believe this is my life.

I bring up the map with the dots from earlier. There's a search function at the top, and I type in "Crow" to see where that asshole is at the moment.

The screen zooms in on a small black dot. I zoom closer to see he's currently at The Hills Luxury Lodge on the outskirts of Los Angeles.

I tap on it to find that it's a retirement home.

Seriously? Terrorizing the elderly? Does this guy have no morals at all?

To distract myself from messaging him about how he's an ass, I click around to read more about Afterlife instead.

As soon as I click on the "About" page, my heart stops in my chest. Suddenly, the reason for the strange interest in my tattoo becomes evident.

The "L" of Afterlife is represented by a long, elegant peacock feather. The exact peacock feather I had inked on my shoulder to memorialize my dead genius brother. Every flourish, every barb, every bit of color is identical. This can't be a coincidence. I designed the tattoo myself.

But why would it be here?

I run my trembling finger over it, heart beating hard against my rib cage as questions I should have thought of hours ago crash into my mind with the same force as the car accident that took him from me.

If all of this is real, then what happened to Jonathon after he died? Is he still here? Can I find him?

And what has he got to do with Afterlife?

***

I spend the rest of the afternoon trying to find out more about the app and Jonathon. Searches for him come up empty. *User not found.*

Fumbling for Gabriel's business card, I key his number into my phone and pace around as it rings. He doesn't pick up until my fourth attempt, and he doesn't give me a chance to speak.

"You can't call me," he hisses. "Not here. It's too dangerous. If we need to be in touch, then I will contact you."

He hangs up.

I instantly redial, but this time, it goes straight to voicemail. I let out a strangled noise of frustration and hurl my cell at my mattress, watching it bounce across the comforter. Then I grab the Devils Inc. phone and search for Crow again. He's still at the retirement home, probably scaring old ladies with crows during bingo or something.

My thumb hovers over the "Message" button by his name. Then, before I can talk myself out of it, I push it and key in a quick request: *It's Rachel. I need to talk to you. Can we meet?*

I don't like this guy. I don't want to need his help. I don't want him to think I've even thought about him for a second. But Jonathon is more important than my pride. I need to know what happened to him after he died. I need to know why the feather that bonded us after his death is part of the Afterlife app. I need to know if he's still here. And I think Crow knows more than he's letting on.

Sucking in a deep breath, I push "Send."

I stare at the white chat box waiting for a response. A couple of minutes later, a little check mark appears indicating Crow has seen the message.

I wait a few minutes for his reply.

Then a few more.

Then a few more.

It doesn't come.

I sit on the edge of my mattress and put my head in my hands. Sure, he helped me fight off those zombie things earlier, but then he deserted me on the sidewalk. I really am just a job to him, aren't I?

I spend the next couple of hours in the gym imagining Crow's smug face beneath my fists instead of the crimson punching bag: his hard jaw, his stupid smirking lips, his cloudy gray eyes.

It's not until I'm back in my dorm, freshly showered, that the Devils Inc. phone buzzes on the desk. The map is still zoomed in on Crow's little black dot, which now moves down the freeway toward Trinity Falls. What's more, there's a notification lighting up my inbox. I feel a jolt in my chest as I pick up the phone and tap on it.

Missing me already?

A wave of irritation washes over me, but it's accompanied by relief.

No, I reply. *Can you meet me tonight?*

I see that he's typing. Then . . .

Sure. Where?

Although I'm surprised by his easy compliance, I bite back any gratitude. After everything that's happened, the *least* he can do is give me a proper explanation. I check the time. It's almost seven, and I said I'd meet Josie and Lucas in the food hall before we went out.

Do you know Apocalypse? The club opposite Evie's? I tap in.

I wait a few moments for a response.

I'm familiar. Great place to pick up girls.

I grit my teeth. *You're an asshole.*

I know, he replies almost instantly. *See you tonight, little Demon.*

Chapter Sixteen

A warm dusk has settled over Trinity Falls by the time we leave the food hall.

Josie wears a long-sleeved green dress, hoop earrings, and her most expensive perfume, while Lucas wears chinos and a pale pink shirt. I opted for a black dress and flat but stylish boots. After the day I've had, I'm not risking having to fight dead people—or Omens, for that matter—in heels. But it doesn't mean I can't still look good.

Josie describes the hotness of Darius in intense detail as we head toward Apocalypse, but I'm distracted by thoughts of how I'm going to wring details out of Crow.

"He has these, like, infinite eyes or something," says Josie. "And—"

"You know you can't sleep with him now he's your boss, right?" says Lucas, raising an eyebrow at Josie over his glasses.

"Oh, damn," says Josie, face falling. "You're right. I never thought of that."

Lucas chuckles. "Then again, a bit of forbidden romance never hurt anyone."

"Now you're talking," says Josie. "Come on! Darius said he'd put our names on the list."

The buzzing neon sign of Apocalypse casts a flickering blue light onto the sidewalk. Josie bypasses the gathering line and goes to speak to the tall Hispanic woman running the door. Holding a clipboard, she wears red lipstick, leather pants, and riding boots.

While they talk, I stare up at the sign overhead. The name of the club suddenly feels ominous given everything that's happened today.

"Do you know if Josie's signed a contract with the club yet for the bartender position?" I ask, suddenly uneasy.

Lucas looks up from his phone. "Yeah. She said it was all sorted. Why?"

"I dunno. I just have a feeling."

"I think you just need to—"

"Do *not* tell me I need to get laid," I say, pointing a finger at him.

He laughs and raises his arms. "Just sayin'."

Josie beckons us over—much to the displeasure of a group of girls at the front of the line.

Lucas and I follow Josie as she struts ahead down a long, dark hallway. Along the black walls are neon-blue lights; I spot a bow and arrow, a sword, a pair of scales, and a scythe. They buzz as we pass.

"Do you have the job contract you signed?" I ask her, raising my voice over the pulsing music coming from the club downstairs.

"Not with me," she says.

"Was there anything weird in it?"

She gives me a puzzled look. "Yeah, the fact that it pays twenty-two dollars an hour! And that's not including tips." She pauses. "But I guess it was kinda . . . playful."

We start to descend into the main room, Lucas trailing behind as he taps out another message on his phone.

"In what way?" I ask.

"Well, it's like I said before." Josie pauses in front of the wooden door at the bottom of the stairs, absently running a finger over the silver horseshoe nailed to the center. "They're pretty committed to their aesthetic," she says, then she pushes open the door.

Apocalypse's dance floor is a blur of noise, colorful dresses, white smoke, and flashing blue strobe lights. A crush of students dance to a penetrating beat that seems less like music than something intended to make your whole body vibrate. Just beyond them, some blond guy kneels on the bar, white shirt flapping open as he pours a bottle of alcohol down his chest. Some random guy laps it off his abs while a surrounding crowd whoops and cheers.

I've been here a few times before, but I've never really thought of it as having much of an aesthetic—unless "loud and seedy" counts. Then again, the only times I've ever wanted to come here have been after I've had a few too many appletinis.

As I look at it soberly, however, I notice that the booths built into the sides of the club look like stable stalls, the neon-blue signs on the black brick walls are shaped like trumpets, and the DJ on the raised deck in the corner shouts about how we need to party like it's the end of the world.

My unease grows.

As we reach the bar, I note there are silver symbols adorning its edges: a scythe, a bow, a pair of scales, and a sword. The same ones as in the hall. And the symbols are repeated on the trembling glass shelving in the middle of the island. Beyond the bar is a double door marked "No Entry." The word "APOCALYPSE" flashes in blue lights above it.

"That's Chris," shouts Josie, pointing up at the blond guy on the bar's obsidian surface. In riding boots and leather pants, he looks like a character from a debauched high fantasy story. "Or, as his brothers call him while at work, Conq . . ."

"What?" I yell, hardly able to hear her over the pulsating music.

"And this is—"

"William." A deep voice cuts through all the chaos.

Turning, I find myself face-to-face with a tall man with neat black, slicked back hair and cool blue eyes. He's dressed much like Chris, but his shirt is buttoned up to the collar. He looks like a gentleman about to go on a late-night hunting trip.

"Josie, so nice to see you again." His accent is British and as smooth as silk. "Can I get you and your friends a drink?"

"Yes!" says Lucas, barging forward.

William's smile widens. "Excellent."

Lucas and Josie attempt to make conversation with each other over the music as he takes our order. I keep my eyes on William. With long, slender fingers, he pulls down a bottle and starts to mix our drinks. As he does so, he leans over the bar to whisper something to a woman in a red dress. A hard look crosses her face, and she marches forward, pushing apart the crowd to confront the man who just lapped alcohol from Chris's chest. Chris grins boyishly and jumps back behind the bar.

The woman at the door comes to remove the fighting couple from the bar. She throws a pissed-off look at William before marching them out.

I turn to ask Josie and Lucas if they saw what just happened, but before the words are out, I spot a familiar someone slurping a Coke through a paper straw. Despite being in a hot, dark club, he wears a blue beanie and shades. He's also ditched his white blazer for a baggy azure sweater.

Gabriel.

This can't be good.

"I'll be right back," I yell in Josie's ear before pushing my way toward him.

Gabriel glares at me over his shades I approach.

"I have *so* many questions," I say. "Like, one, what on earth are you wearing?"

"I'm undercover," he says. "Now, go away. We can't be seen talking."

"Can you even *see* anything?" I ask, peering into his dark lenses.

"Yes. I'm an Angel."

I stare pointedly at the strand of red hair peeping out from beneath his hat.

"Stop that," he says, tucking it away.

"Aren't you hot?"

"Not really." He shrugs beneath his big baggy sweater. "I don't really feel temperature."

"What are you doing here?"

"I told you earlier. If someone wants to trigger the end of all days, it's likely they delivered the scroll to the Horseman Brothers. You know, the Four Horsemen of the Apocalypse? I thought you said you were familiar with the Book of Revelation."

My eyes go back to Chris and William shaking drinks behind the bar. Then I glance at the stable-like booths and think back to the fact Josie said the owners were half-brothers. Right on cue, the DJ shouts something about it being the end of the world and everyone being invited. The crowd cheers.

"Oh, *shit,*" I say. "Are you telling me the *actual* Four Horsemen of the Apocalypse own this club?"

"Yes!"

I grab his arm. "My friend Josie just got a job here!"

He frowns. "They're taking on staff? That's most unusual."

"She said something about there being a job opening because the co-founders thought they were going to be busy," I say, voice hoarse. "Something about one of them being summoned."

Gabriel's face darkens. Then he pushes his shades back up his nose.

"Then I was right," says Gabriel. "It's started. The Apocalypse."

"What about Josie? I need to—"

"You can't say anything to Josie, Rachel. It's against Ethereal law to talk about our world to a mortal—you'd be in breach of your Devils Inc. contract. I'll figure something out. She could be an excellent source—"

"A source? She's in *danger*."

He opens his mouth to say something else, then shuts it, his gaze fixing on something at the other side of the club. Suddenly, he crumples his Coke can between his slender fingers.

"I have to go," he says.

"Are you serious? You can't just drop that bombshell on me and—"

But he's already dropped his can and headed for the door, cutting through the crowd that seems to subconsciously part as if he's Moses, and they are the Red Sea.

It's not the weirdest behavior he's exhibited, but I'm curious to see what spooked him.

And I spot it—or, rather, *him*.

Crow is making out with a blonde girl in one of the stable booths. Something clenches in my stomach.

"I saw that guy earlier today," says Josie, appearing beside me to thrust a drink in my hand. "In the food hall. Accidentally threw some salt in his eye, actually . . . He was pretty *salty* about it."

"You've seen him before?" I say.

"Yeah. You know him?" She looks at me intently. "Oh, no. You like him. Sorry, babe. Looks like he's taken."

"What? No. Gross." I shake my head a little too vehemently. "He was at that law internship interview I went to this morning." I may have skipped a few key details when I told Josie about my morning over dinner, but I did fill her in that I had an internship.

Rage pulses through my veins. Not because he's making out with some girl—as if I would I care about that—but because Josie

95

must have been another job. If so, he didn't do a great job of giving her twenty-four hours' notice either.

Josie misinterprets my anger and says something about there being plenty more fish in the sea before telling me to come hang out with her and Lucas.

"I'll come find you in a bit," I say, forcing a smile. "Just give me a minute. I want to talk to him about a work thing."

She agrees and starts to leave, but then I call her back.

"Oh, Josie?"

"Yeah?" she shouts over the music.

"Don't go anywhere alone with Darius."

I'm not sure if she heard me; her eyes look a little vacant. "Yep! See you soon, babe!"

As she heads through the flashing lights, I turn back to Crow, who unlocks his lips from the blonde long enough to give me a wave. He whispers something in the girl's ear. She turns to stare at me, outrage plastered across her delicate features. Then she turns back and slaps Crow in the face before storming off.

As satisfying as that is to watch, it doesn't quell my irritation. Particularly as it doesn't seem to bother Crow in the slightest. The asshole smiles as he beckons me over.

The blonde scowls at me as she marches past.

"Pervert," she hisses.

"Excuse me?" I say.

She keeps going, hands clenched at her sides.

As I slide into the horseshoe-shaped bench, the black-and-white leather cushions stick to my bare thighs where my dress rides up. When my knee accidentally brushes against Crow's, I jerk it back. Though we're still in the crowded club, the booth feels private; the walls dividing the stable stalls are high and black.

He still has one arm casually draped over the back of his bench, though there's an angry mark on his cheek.

"What did you say to her?" I ask.

"I said you were my girlfriend and you liked to watch," he says. "Then I suggested we have a threesome."

"Ugh. You're disgusting."

He shrugs, smiling. "Got rid of her, didn't I? Isn't that what you wanted? For us to be alone?"

I stare at him. "Yes. But you could have just asked her to leave."

"Aye. But she wouldn't have."

"Oh, really? And why is that?"

He leans across the shiny black table as if he's about to tell me a secret. "I'm a good kisser." When I simply snort, he leans back. "Don't believe me? You can try me out for yourself."

"I'd rather gouge out my own eyeballs with a spoon."

"Aye? Lucky for you, I think they have a room in Hell where you can do just that." He shifts forward again. "Unless, of course, you've sorted an alternative arrangement." His eyes flick to where Gabriel was standing earlier. "If Devils Inc. found out you were consorting with a certain stick-up-his-arse Angel," he continues, "you might find yourself there sooner than expected."

The air in the stall suddenly feels very still. I lean forward, bare arms sticking to the table where someone has knocked over a drink. I'm close enough now that I can feel his warm, slightly beer-scented breath on my skin.

"And you're going to tell them?" I ask.

"I could. People would pay for a secret like that," he says.

"Is that why you agreed to come. To threaten me?"

He holds my gaze for a long beat. Then he shakes his head and leans back, taking the tension with him.

"No. I came here because you asked me to. Don't worry. Your secret's safe with me, little Demon."

"Then what the hell was the point in all that?"

He shrugs. "I was curious."

"Curious?"

"You attacked me earlier when I was winding you up." He turns the beer bottle between his thick fingers, fiddling with the label. "I wondered what you would do this time."

I rub my forehead. "God, you're annoying."

He chuckles. "Aye, maybe. I can't help it. I'm bored."

"You're actively trying to piss me off because you're bored?"

"You try being immortal. Well . . . you'll see." When I do nothing but glare, he sighs. "Is that why you asked me here then? To have a go at me about the fact you signed your soul away?" He peels off part of the label before glancing up. "Or maybe you found out this club belongs to the Four Horsemen and your friend has just signed a contract with them?"

"I *knew* you knew about that," I snap. "Is she in danger?"

He shrugs and continues peeling the bottle. He only looks up when I grab his wrist.

"Relax. It's not the end of the world." The corner of his lip tugs up. "Yet."

I squeeze, nails digging into his skin.

"Seriously, relax, little Demon. They're good lads. And when the Apocalypse comes, it's not a bad idea to be on good terms with the Horsemen. Your friend is in a good position."

"So you think the Apocalypse is coming too?" I say.

"I've heard rumors. It's why your friend's contract with this club interested me. They've never had reason to recruit extra staff before. And you . . ." He licks his lips, and my eyes flit down to his mouth before I can control them. "You interest me even more, little Demon. So is that all you wanted to talk to me about?"

I release his wrist but don't move away. "No." I take a deep breath. "I'm here to talk about my brother, Jonathon Mortimer."

Intrigue flashes in his eyes. "I was wondering what relation he was to you."

I swallow, my mouth suddenly feeling dry. "You know him?"

A smile broadens on Crow's face. "Oh, aye, I know him."

Chapter Seventeen

The club around me is a blur, the fast pulse of music competing with the thudding of my heart.

"How do you know Jonathon?" I ask, suddenly worried. Crow's a Bad Omen. How could they have crossed paths?

Crow says nothing for a moment. Then he shifts as though he's getting up.

"I'm hungry. Let's go get some food."

Reflexively, I reach for the collar of his shirt, ready to demand he talk to me *now*. This time, though, he grabs my wrist and pulls. It's only by gripping the table that I stop myself from face-planting.

He brings his mouth to my ear. "There are eyes on us here, little Demon," he says, his gravelly whisper sending a shiver down my spine. "Three o'clock."

I look to my right and see William, the dark-haired bartender, watching us as he wipes down the surface of the bar. When I turn back to Crow, his face is close enough to mine that our noses almost touch.

"Let's go and get some food," he says.

I scan the crowded dance floor. Josie and Lucas have joined a group of Josie's Wicca friends, which is reassuring. There's safety in numbers at least.

"You'll tell me what I want to know?" I whisper.

"Aye." He inclines his head. "I'm as curious as you are to know what he has to do with all of this."

He lets go of my wrist, and I pull back, smoothing down my black dress.

He gestures to the stall opening. "Ladies first."

"So you *do* have *some* manners," I say, sliding past him.

"Some? I'm a perfect gentleman."

I turn to raise an eyebrow at him, and in the process, I catch him staring at my ass. "Seriously?"

"What?"

I shake my head and push across the crowded floor without looking back.

"I think you sat in something is all!" he shouts over the music.

Heat creeps up to my face. As I surreptitiously brush at the back of my dress, I bump into girl in a white dress, causing her to spill her red cocktail down her front.

Crow swoops in to shuffle me out as she yells.

"Just messing with you," he says. "I was checking out your arse. But that was fun to watch."

I grit my teeth as we leave the dance floor and head up the stairs. "I'm so glad you were entertained," I say, voice loud now the music is muffled. I'm annoyed at myself; I don't normally let people get under my skin. But I need to keep it together—at least until he tells me what's going on with Jonathon.

He nods at the woman on the door, and she smiles. It seems he's less unpopular here than he is at Devils Inc. and Halo Corp.

There's a long line beneath the buzzing Apocalypse sign, and the window of Evie's is filled with students. People walk to the bus stop, chat in doorways as they wait for Ubers, and vape beneath the tall palm trees that line the road.

If he wants to talk in private, we're out of luck here.

"How do you know Jon—?" I start.

"Patience is a virtue, little Demon," he says in a singsong voice, then he points down the road. "This way."

He leads me past the old bookshop and a clothes store. Ahead is the bus stop to campus, and at the end of the street, shrouded in shadow, the Trinity Falls church. Given it's shut at night, I wonder if the churchyard is his great idea. We definitely won't be overheard there, but the gates will be locked.

To my surprise, he steers me toward Diablos.

Crow leans against the counter. "I'll have the Diablos special, mate," he says to the gangly guy in the black apron. "And for the lady . . ." He stops at my look. "What? I told you I was hungry. Now, what do you want?"

"I want to know how you know my brother!" I hiss under my breath.

He raises a dark eyebrow. "You sure? You'll be hungry later."

I say nothing, jaw set.

"Suit yourself," he says, reaching over the counter to take a hot dog loaded with cheese and chili. "Don't be moaning to me later though."

The sweet scent of fried onions hits my nose as he pays. After drowning it in mustard, he takes his first bite.

"Mmm," he says, a bit of sauce dribbling out of the corner of his mouth.

I look to the aproned guy behind the counter. "I'll have the same, please," I mutter, ignoring Crow's grin. "And you've got food on your face."

When I'm handed my hot dog, I cover it with mustard too, then pull my card out of my pocket to pay.

"'S okay. I've got this," he says, nudging me away. After wiping his face with the back of his hand, he hands over the cash.

His attempt to be nice gets under my skin just as much as his active attempts to annoy me. I don't want to owe this guy anything. Even if it's only a few dollars.

"You didn't have to do that," I say as he steers me away, toward the church.

He shrugs, taking another big bite. "Force of habit. In my day, men always bought dinner. Plus, I have some spare cash lying around." He throws me a sideways glance. "You may not be aware of this, but I completed a couple of jobs this past twenty-four hours."

"Well, that's true," I say, taking a bite. "A hot dog is the least you can do."

He chuckles as we reach the church's tall, black iron gate. It's chained shut, held in place by a heavy padlock. I was right: this was his great idea.

"So, genius, how exactly—?"

Crow whistles, and a crow flies out of one of the surrounding palm trees, almost giving me a heart attack.

"Jesus Christ!"

The bird lands on Crow's arm and drops a small rusty key into his open palm. Crow gifts the bird with a bit of hot dog before it caws and flies off into the darkness.

Acting as though nothing strange has happened, Crow unlocks the padlock. The gate screeches against the concrete as he pulls it open.

"After you," he says.

I eye him warily as we head down the wide path that cuts through the gravestones toward the church. The moonlight reflects off the white stone walls and the cross sitting atop the spire.

"What the hell was that?" I finally ask.

"What?"

"Erm, the freaky bird thing?"

He laughs. "I'm an Omen, little Demon. Perk of the job."

We reach the steps that lead to the chapel's arched oak door. Crow sits down on one, legs spread. I sit beside him, making sure there's a few feet between us. I feel his body heat all the same.

"So are you finally going to tell me how you know Jonathon?"

Crow takes another bite of his hot dog, chews deliberately, then swallows.

"Everyone knows Jonathon, little Demon," he says. "He's the founder of Afterlife."

Chapter Eighteen

The world around us goes still. The tombstones jut out of the lawn like they always have, the shadows cluster under the palm trees undisturbed, and the church building behind us lies deathly silent. But my mind is in overdrive. I have so many thoughts and questions that I don't know what to say first.

"I thought so," I say at last.

"Aye?" says Crow, arching an eyebrow. "Because of your feather tattoo?"

"Yeah." I take a deep breath. "How do I find him?"

Crow stares out at the churchyard. He takes the last bite of his hot dog, then he scrunches the wrapper and drops it on the concrete step.

"I don't know, little Demon. He disappeared around a year ago."

"What?" I get that god-awful feeling in my stomach that feels like I'm falling. "What does that mean?"

"He was a big name after he created the app. A real celebrity. What's that show all you girls like? Kardashian. We're talking

Kardashian-level here. Anyway, he was always contactable through the app. Had a pin on that map just like everyone else. Then, one day, he just disappeared from it."

"That doesn't mean something bad happened to him, right?" I say. "If he created the app, then he could have taken himself off it."

He looks back out at the graveyard. He's playing it cool, but I sense a tension.

"That's what I always thought. That perhaps he got fed up of it all," he says. "I mean, if I were him, I couldn't be arsed with the stiffs over at Halo Corp. and the dickheads from Devils Inc. But now—"

"What?"

"Well, no offence, but you're not exactly the Devils Inc. type."

"I don't want to be their type."

"They usually recruit, you know, *good* lawyers," he continues, ignoring me. "Ideally, ones who have been involved in dirty-dealing."

"Is there a point you're trying to get at?"

"Well, it's strange that Jonathon's sister is recruited after he goes missing, isn't it? And by someone anonymous . . ." He gives me a pointed look.

"You think Jonathon recruited me—? No." I shake my head vehemently, gripping my uneaten hot dog so hard it squirts mustard onto my leg. "Shit." I put it down and wipe my bare thigh, sucking the mess off my thumb. "No," I repeat. "He wouldn't do that. He wouldn't make me sign my soul away to the Devil. Never."

"People change. You don't know—"

"I do know." We stare at each other, tension crackling in the few feet of space between us. "I do know."

Finally, Crow raises his hands in surrender. "Okay, little Demon. But I've been doing this Omen gig for long enough to not believe in coincidences. This is connected, one way or another. He goes missing, you get recruited, and now, we have an Apocalypse on our hands."

"So let's find him."

He gives a dark laugh. "People have tried. No one has managed it."

"Well, I haven't tried. If anyone can, it's me."

He looks thoughtful. "Aye. Perhaps."

Silence falls like a shroud over us. I pick up my hot dog, but it doesn't take long to realize my appetite is gone.

"How does it work anyway?" I say. "I thought when you die, you go up or down. That's what you said earlier."

"That's how it works usually." He absently twists at his ring finger, though there's no ring around it. "But sometimes, one side or the other makes an investment in a soul—exchanges a Miracle for a position at Halo Corp., or trades a Desire for a position at Devils Inc."

"So what happened with Jonathon?"

"He worked for Halo Corp. for a bit. Then he found a loophole in his contract and joined Omens Limited. After he created the app, he went freelance. Moved to LA."

I feel like I've been stabbed in the gut. I've mourned him for seven years, his loss like a hole I could never fill. For months after it happened, I was numb, invisible, barely making it to school every day. Meanwhile, Mom stared dead-eyed on the sofa between her nursing shifts at the care home, and Dad nearly lost his electronics store because he spent so much time barking on the phone to lawyers as he tried to find someone to blame.

Now, here, I discover Jonathon was living this whole other happy life.

Coldness spreads through my body. "Why did he never visit me?"

Crow gives me a look. "He was dead, little Demon."

"Yes. And apparently, his dead self created an app! So that doesn't really—?"

"Okay, keep your knickers on," he says.

"My what?"

Crow exhales. He rubs the back of his neck, fingers brushing a tattoo hidden by his collar. "Look, there are laws," he says. "Halo Corp. and Devils Inc. both have company policies. Any employee who joins them after death has to cut off ties with their life. Breaking the policy would result in immediate termination and the reversal of whatever Miracle or Desire was granted. Most do desk work until everyone who knew them died anyway." He pauses. "Omens Limited's policies are a little more lax, but even we have rules. We're not supposed to visit anyone who would recognize us."

"Oh," I say.

We fall into silence. He eyes my hot dog.

"You going to eat that?"

"Yes."

I take a defiant bite, but when it only makes my stomach churn, I hold it out to him. He takes it, stuffs it in his mouth, then lies down on the steps, folding his arms behind his head and looking up at the night sky. He has mustard in the corner of his mouth.

"You know, most people like to chew when they eat," I say.

He chuckles. "I'm not most people."

I roll my eyes, leaning back so I can stretch my legs too. "You said you knew him?" I say.

"Aye. I met him. Once. He liked me about as well as you do."

"Not very well then," I say.

"Aye." He turns his head, a glint in his eye. "Though I don't think he wanted to sleep with me as much."

I snort. "I don't want to sleep with you."

"I wouldn't annoy you so much if you didn't."

Irritation flares inside me. *Not* because he's right. No way. Although . . . Josie and Lucas might disagree. After reading some pop psychology book, Josie tried to convince me that I only date guys who are ultimately unattainable. Apparently, I'm protecting myself from the heartache. Meanwhile, Lucas thinks the adrenaline junkie in me—the one who enjoys boxing and horror movies and really wants to go skydiving—treats dating like an extreme sport.

I think they should both mind their business. I just suck at dating—as my lack of serious boyfriends attests. Other than an on-and-off relationship my senior year of high school and a few hook-ups after parties since being here, I've not had any luck in that department.

I glance at Crow, with his hard body and tattoo and undertone of darkness. If I *did* view dating as an extreme sport, taking on this guy would be like competing in the Olympics.

"I'm pretty sure you'd find a way," I say.

He laughs again. "You're not my type. Sorry, little Demon."

"Who is your type?" I ask. "Drunk blondes in clubs?"

"Jealous?"

"Do you want me to be jealous?"

He chuckles. "I can't say I have a type in terms of hair color. But I do prefer my women not to have damned souls."

"Then maybe you shouldn't take such an active part in helping women damn their souls," I say, failing to keep the bite out of my tone.

"Aye. Maybe not," he says softly, his gaze burning into mine.

I look away, focusing on the angel statue weeping over a tombstone by one of the tall palm trees that line the churchyard. "What about your soul?" I say. "Hate to break it to you, but you're hardly a model citizen."

"My soul doesn't belong to anybody," he says. "So my guess is, it works the same way as for a mortal. The big bosses aren't exactly forthcoming."

"Aren't you worried though?"

"Aye, about some things."

"Well, don't you think you could absolve some of that worry by not being a complete and utter dick?"

"And how do you suggest I do that?"

"You could start by not getting people to sign away their souls to the Devil."

"I didn't," he says, grinning. "That was all you. I warned you not to—"

"And you could maybe not terrorize the elderly at retirement homes," I say, recalling where he was when I looked him up on the app.

The smile on his lips dies. Before, he was soft and relaxed; now, he's all edges. The churchyard is dark, the only light coming from beyond the barred gate at the end of the path, and the shadows do their swirling thing as they gather around him.

Then he blinks, and he's back again. The transformation is so fast I could almost make myself believe I imagined it. It puts me on edge, as if all of this charm is masking something darker. Whatever he was up to this afternoon, he's not proud of it. I dread to think what someone like Crow would be ashamed of doing.

"You were stalking me, little Demon?" He clucks his tongue. "Don't you know, the Devil makes work for idle thumbs?" He sits upright. "Want to go back to the club?"

I hold his gaze, then I shake my head. "No. I'm just going to head back to campus."

"I'll give you a ride."

"No. It's okay. I—"

"I insist." He gets to his feet in one quick movement and hops down the steps to stand in front of me and hold out a hand.

Sighing, I let him pull me to my feet—something I regret when we're suddenly close enough for me to feel his body heat. He reaches over my shoulder and brushes the edge of my peacock feather tattoo with his fingertips.

I grab his wrist, throwing it away from me as I put some distance between us. I try to ignore the hot trail of energy his fingers leave on my skin.

"What are you doing?" I say.

"Why a peacock feather?" he asks. "What does it mean?"

I shake my head. "I've known you, like, five seconds," I say. "And for four-point-five of those seconds, you were being purposefully antagonistic. So let's save the childhood stories." As he chuckles, I look down at his hot dog wrappers still on the ground. "You going to pick those up? I hardly think littering on church grounds will win you any favors up there."

"I think it will take more than picking up litter to win me favors up there, little Demon," he says. His expression darkens, his irises a silvery gray in the faded moonlight. "Does that scare you?"

As we stare at one another, the night circles us like thick smoke, cool and suffocating, and my heartbeat quickens. The black shadows from the church building rush toward him, and whatever this is, I understand now that he's doing it on purpose.

I'm just not sure whether it's to impress or scare me.

Am I scared? The tightening of my chest feels something like fear. But the buzzing beneath my skin and the lick of heat in the pit of my stomach feel like something else entirely.

I keep my eyes on his and force my expression to remain impassive.

"No," I say, dismayed when it sounds more like a gasp.

A slow, satisfied smile broadens across his face. Then he bends down, grabs the wrappers, and stuffs them into his jeans pocket. As he does, the shadows retreat, and the lights from the surrounding streets come back.

I take a deep gulp of the musty churchyard air when he's not looking.

"There," he says, rising. "Happy?"

"Ecstatic." I'm pleased to hear my voice sounds normal again.

He laughs as we walk back to the iron gate. I remain silent, eyes fixed ahead, unsure whether to trust this man who seems to shift seamlessly from darkness to light. I can usually trust my gut about these situations, yet something about this guy has my mind reeling.

"What about the last half a second?" he says, interrupting my thoughts as we rejoin the world outside.

"Huh?"

"You said I intentionally annoyed you for four-point-five seconds. What about the last half a second?"

"You annoyed me by accident," I deadpan.

He laughs, and, surprisingly, one erupts from my lips too. Damn. I can't help it. As annoying and frustrating as he is, there's something magnetic about him. Like the shadows, I find myself attracted.

I study his full lips, the hard line of his stubble-covered jaw, and the edge of the mysterious tattoo brushing the back of his collar.

When he catches me looking, he gives me another wicked smile.

Ugh. No. What am I thinking? I start walking again, making a vow not to go there. He's not trustworthy, and he clearly knows how to manipulate women.

"What's your tattoo of?" I ask when he catches up, trying to make it seem like my gawking was a simple curiosity.

"You won't tell me about yours, but you want to know about mine?" He shakes his head. "Nah. Doesn't work that way, little Demon."

I shrug. "Okay. Fine."

We pass the growing line outside Apocalypse before we come to the side road where Crow's black Mini Cooper is parked.

111

"If you drove here, why didn't we just have our private conversation in the car?" I ask.

"I like churches. They give me a sense of peace."

"You're a complicated guy, aren't you?" I say.

He appears to consider what I'm saying. "Nah. Pretty simple, really. Like everyone else. You'll learn that in this line of business. There are only two things you need to know about a soul: what they want, and what they're willing to do to get it." He smiles, gray eyes glinting in the light of a nearby streetlight. "After that, everything else makes perfect sense."

"So what do you want?" I ask.

"That's for me to know, and you to figure out," he says, opening the driver's door. "Come on. Let's get you back to campus."

We don't talk much in the car. I message Josie and Lucas to tell them I've headed home, then I take stock of the situation. True, I am apparently an intern to the Devil, but I have a shot at finding Jonathon again. It seems almost too good to be true, but what choice do I have but to believe it?

Five minutes later, Crow pulls up to the road nearest my dorm building. Engine still running, he turns to me.

"You're really going to look for him then?" he says. He twists at his ring finger again.

"Jonathon? Yeah."

"Then you're going to need someone to protect you."

"I don't need protecting."

He chuckles. "You can handle yourself—I'll give you that. But you have no idea the danger you're in. You'll need help."

"I'm not paying you, if that's what you're after," I say, opening the door.

"No need. I'll do this one for free."

I raise an eyebrow. "Right. *You're* going to help me out of the goodness of your heart?"

"Well, I never said that."

I sigh. "What's in it for you?"

His eyes travel down my body, then up to my face again.

"I'm not sleeping with you," I say.

He grins. "Who said anything about that? Your brother is a powerful man. Way I see it, if I keep his little sister safe, maybe he'll do a little something for me."

I shake my head and get out of the car. "You're the worst."

"I know." Amusement glitters in his eyes. "Though, I prefer diabolical. You going to let me help then? Or no?"

I sigh. Given that I do need to find Jonathon, I suppose it wouldn't hurt to have someone who knows how to navigate this new terrain of Angels, Demons, and the afterlife. I place my hands on the top of the car and peer inside.

"Fine. You can help," I say. "But just so you know, I'm never going to sleep with you. So you need to stop"—I point my finger at him and move it in a circle—"this thing."

He raises his eyebrows in faux innocence. "I can't help my raw sex appeal."

"Fine. But we're not happening."

When he smirks, I realize I've made a critical error. I've essentially turned myself into a challenge for someone who has admitted to being perpetually bored.

"Right, well, thanks for the ride," I say, shutting the door only for him to roll down the windows.

"Anytime, little Demon," he says smoothly, and then he calls out as I start to walk up the sidewalk. "Oh. Rachel?"

"Yeah?" I say.

A wicked grin crosses his face. "I lied before. I don't mind my women having damned souls." He gives me a corny wink. "See you soon!"

Before I can retort, he's driven off.

Chapter Nineteen

On Saturday morning, I meet Josie and a seriously hungover Lucas in the food hall, where Josie chatters about the previous night while we sip coffee from paper cups. She danced all night at the club, Lucas kissed a guy from his Faustus play, and Chris will be training her on the bar at Apocalypse tonight.

I'm quiet through most of it, afraid to let something slip that will give me a one-way ticket to Hell. I don't say anything when we head to the library to catch up on assignments either. From the way Josie's eyes brim with concern, I know she can tell something is up.

I decide to spend my Sunday alone in the gym, pummeling a punching bag that's once again a stand-in for Crow's face. Both Josie and I have ended up signing weird contracts because of him. And yet, clearly, he thinks he can charm his way into my pants.

I don't hear from him or Gabriel all weekend.

I resist the urge to look them up on the Afterlife app, although I tap in Jonathon's name at every opportunity. *"User unavailable"* shows every time.

On Monday morning, I send the email to the college admin team letting them know I've secured an internship. I need the credit, but actually telling the university feels like fully accepting the truth. This is really happening. I signed my soul away to the Devil.

Before I know it, it's 7:00 p.m., and I'm stepping off the bus in front of the tall black building.

The street is fairly quiet apart from the odd person in a disheveled business suit. What kind of legal internship starts this late in the evening? Feeling eyes on me, I pull up the collar of my leather jacket. Somewhere in the warm twilight, a crow caws.

The atrium is mostly empty, and my footsteps echo off the obsidian tiles as I pass the eggy statue of Lucifer.

"You're late," drawls Adalind when I reach reception. Boots on the counter, she examines her bitten fingernails with those inhuman eyes.

"No, I'm not." I glance at one of the flashing monitors depicting the day's news—the time is in the bottom-left corner. "You said come in at seven. It's seven."

"It's two minutes past seven." Dropping her legs, she sits up. "Not that I care. Why do I always get stuck with the interns?" She trudges out from behind the high desk, white shirt collar unbuttoned to reveal the tail of her snake tattoo. "Come on then. Let's get this over with."

"Are *you* training me?" I ask as we step into the elevator. I instantly regret it when she looks at me like I'm a bug. A bug she's been ordered to teach how to file.

"Oh, poor you. I can see how *you've* got the bad end of the bargain." She shakes her head, silver piercings glinting, as the elevator lurches up. The doors ping open. "Millennials. So ungrateful. Back in my day, I would have . . ."

She heads out of the elevator, so I never hear about what undoubtedly horrible thing she would have done once upon a time.

"I'm Gen Z, actually," I mutter as I follow her out.

"You know, I used to be someone. Now, I'm stuck here babysitting petulant little—" She snaps her head to glare at me. "What did you say?"

"Nothing."

We're in another open office, although this one looks like a Demonic police station. It has a shiny black-tiled floor, big desks lit by sultry red lamps, blood-colored filing cabinets, and outer rooms marked with golden plaques.

Something catches my eye through the glass walls of the nearest one. A Devils Inc. employee with floppy black hair interviews Richard Livingstone, his flushed face and disheveled suit still covered in blood. There's a pile of paperwork between them. Above the door is a bronze plaque reading, *"GREED."*

I survey the rest of the plaques, all of which represent one of the seven deadly sins, one of the seven heavenly virtues, or one of the Ten Commandments.

Right in the center of the floor is a black podium showcasing a pair of silver scales.

"What is this place?" I ask.

"My God," drawls Adalind, glaring at me as she leans beneath a plaque reading, *"THOU SHALT NOT TAKE THE LORD'S NAME IN VAIN."* "What does it look like? It's the interrogation rooms. Part of the legal department."

"And that means?" I say, not bothering to hide my annoyance. It earns me a sharp look from a bearded employee flipping through a file—at least, until he sees the target of my sass.

Adalind exhales sharply out of her nostrils. "Chances are, if *up there* doesn't want a soul, neither do we. The Demons on this floor work in Soul Defense. If a soul has committed an Ethereal offence, they go through their paperwork and try to build a case for them to go elsewhere. Either by finding a loophole, calling the evidence into question, or by showing that their Virtues outweigh their Sins."

"And then what?"

"What do you think? Then there's a trial with our competitors. If we win, they take the soul."

I fold my arms across my chest, glancing at Richard Livingstone as he waves his arms aggressively. According to the news stories, this guy was a real piece of work.

"So you really want me to help send bad people to Heaven?"

She barks out a laugh. "You thought you'd be building cases for our clients on your first day?" She claps her hands, and the people in black blazers turn. "Got a new intern, guys. Anyone want anything from Starbucks?"

Chapter Twenty

Given I'm working at a company allegedly founded by Lucifer, the week that follows is surprisingly uneventful. Adalind mostly makes me run to a coffee shop in downtown Los Angeles to purchase obnoxiously complex coffees, complete with multiple shots, soy milk, extra whipped cream, and caramel syrup. Since there are perfectly functional coffee machines in the kitchenettes, I start to wonder whether this is an exercise intended to torture both me and the barista, who looks like she wants to kill me every time I walk in.

The silver lining, however, is that I get to visit all of the company's various departments. As I do, I keep an ear out for anything that might shed any light on Jonathon's disappearance and any information I could give to Gabriel about the Apocalypse.

Tuesday, I'm sent to the Soul Investments Department, which reminds me of a trading floor on Wall Street. People with slick hair and fancy suits run around yelling into headsets. An island of black screens in the center of the room shows spiking red and green lines.

"They depict the value of souls," says Adalind. She leans against a black pillar as I take the orders of any employee who runs up and shouts at me.

"How?"

She rolls her snakelike eyes. "Via their useful sins, virtues, or skills. How else?"

I dodge out of the way as a woman in a pantsuit powers past yelling about the lowered value of some soul due to an incident of sexual harassment, and how they need to "put a hold on recruitment."

"Recruitment?" I ask.

Adalind sighs as she studies her fingernails. "The Soul Investments Team identifies the souls that might be of use, then they send intel down to the Recruitment Team."

"Then what?"

She pushes off from the wall and walks toward the elevator, clicking her fingers. "Come on. I've got better things to be doing."

On Wednesday evening, I get to see the Soul Recruitment Department. With its desk arranged in pods, it's got more of a traditional office feel. Bleary-eyed workers scroll through spreadsheets and social media feeds. Framed posters say things such as, "Remember the core desires!" and every so often, there's a potted plant that no one seems to have watered.

As I'm taking coffee orders, two men by the water fountain grumble about how it isn't fair they do all the work while the field team gets all the credit.

"So what actually happens in here?" I ask Adalind when I'm done. She leans against the wall again, and I start to wonder if she even has the ability to stand up straight.

She looks like she's not going to answer, but eventually, she exhales. "This department identifies a person's Desire—the thing a person is willing to exchange for their soul. Then the field team goes out and presents them with the contract. Halo Corp. do the same, though they trade in Miracles instead of Desires. Bunch of stiffs."

On the far wall, there's a big whiteboard listing things such as, "Money," "Revenge," "Sloth," and, "To Prove Themselves." Each category has a series of tally marks.

I nod to it. "I never got offered a Desire."

"You got free Wi-Fi."

"But that sucks."

Adalind lets out a noise that almost sounds like a laugh. "I know." I give her a blank look, and she averts her eyes, though her pierced eyebrows knit together. "It's not the department's fault. Your case didn't come through here."

"Where did it come from?"

She shrugs, then pushes off from the wall. "I'm bored. Come on."

On Thursday, I get a glimpse of the Military Department. They're on one of the underground floors, and Adalind makes me wait by the door while she talks with the severe-looking man in charge. While she looks bored, he seems agitated.

Behind them, men and women run drills across the black mats, grunting and shouting. Red punching bags hang from the walls, and a display of weapons dominates one whole side of the room. The air smells unpleasant—like sweat and sulfur—even though the air-conditioning is down so low that my breath mists in front of my face. I shiver, pulling my new black blazer around my shoulders.

Minutes later, my grumpy babysitter shuffles me back upstairs.

Finally, Friday evening arrives. After studying during the day and working half the night, I'm ready for the weekend—especially as today, my assignment is to help the floppy-haired Demon working on Richard Livingstone's defense.

Under the light of a sultry red lamp, I'm left to sift through a huge pile of paperwork documenting the business tycoon's entire life and record every Sin or Virtue I find. If we can find more Virtues, we can make a case for Halo Corp. to take him.

It's insanely boring, so I'm almost happy when Adalind emerges after a few hours and demands I get the team coffee.

"The nearest coffee shop's closed for the night," she drawls, "so you'll have to go to the one near the mall."

Great. I get to torture another barista with all my specialty orders.

I'm halfway down the street from Devils Inc. when I hear a *Pssst* sound coming from the alley between two office blocks.

"Gabriel!" I say brightly.

"Shh!" He ushers me into the shadows, peering around the corner to check no one is watching. He misses the crow standing at the other end of the alley.

I've caught a few flashes of big black birds in the skyscraper windows all week, though the Omen himself has been absent.

I shoo it away before Gabriel spins back around.

"Any updates about the impending Apocalypse?" he asks.

"No," I say. "It's not as if someone's going around the office waving around the stolen scrolls. I think we need a better plan than this."

"I agree," says Gabriel. "I'd very much like to find out what the Horsemen know. I'm looking into ways we can bring Josie into this without breaching any Ethereal contracts. We'll meet again tomorrow to discuss."

Half an hour later, I'm heading out of the coffee shop when my phone buzzes in my jeans pocket. Thanks to a tray of thirteen fancy coffees, a bag full of overpriced cake slices, and a few bags of potato chips, it's too risky to check it.

As I walk through the darkening maze of skyscrapers, the hairs on the back of my neck start to prickle.

Someone is watching me.

"Crow, if that's you, cut it out," I mutter.

I scan the street for any big black birds. Not seeing any, I quicken my pace. Someone's low-fat caramel macchiato with soy milk and extra cream sloshes out of its paper container.

"Shit," I hiss, then I pause to adjust the tray.

As I do, a chilling laugh floats up behind me. I glance over my shoulder. A female figure in a red hooded sweater stands in the middle of the road.

"Double shit," I mutter.

I pick up my pace again, and from the echo of footsteps, I can tell she does as well.

Soon, I take a turn and find myself in the parking lot of a closed shopping center. There's an exit across the way, but two more red hooded figures block my path.

I spin around, more coffee sloshing, to find myself facing the girl behind me. She's close enough now that I can see a pair of red eyes gleaming beneath her hood.

If I can make it to the center of the lot, I'll have more room to fight. As I start to move, though, more hooded figures emerge from the shadows.

My heart thunders in my chest as they surround me.

"This the girl?" says one, looking at his phone, then back at me.

"That's her," confirms a huge guy who looks like he's spent way too much time at Muscle Beach. "Kill her together and split the proceeds?"

"Split?" says a raspy female voice. "I'll kill her and keep the proceeds myself."

"*Woooah,*" I say, spinning around as I try to determine the biggest threat. "Kill? Let's not be hasty."

The girl laughs as she pulls an ornate dagger from a belt holster. "Nothing personal, Rachel Mortimer. Although I will enjoy slitting you open."

Before I can say more, she lunges at me.

I drop the tray, sloshing hot coffee over the concrete, and strike her across the face.

"Bitch," she snarls.

"Me?" I say, grabbing her hand and snapping her wrist back. As soon as her blade drops to the floor, I elbow her face, then headbutt her backward, paper cups rolling at our feet.

And then the mob charges.

It happens in a blur. Hands grab at my jacket, something sharp nicks my cheek, and something heavy hits my head and makes me see red dots. Some of my attackers are fighting each other—wanting to kill me individually, apparently—but most are trained on me. I dodge a fist, hit something hard, then duck as a silver blade cuts through the shadows by my face.

Shit.

Shit. Shit. Shit.

The air thickens like it does before a storm. Adrenaline pounds through my body, making everything seem distant—as if all the violence is happening to someone else.

But it isn't. I need to get away. There are too many of them. They're armed. They're not human.

They want to kill me.

I slam my elbow into Muscle Beach's neck as he reaches for my arm. He wheezes, stumbling back, and I lurch at his chest to help him on his journey to the concrete. He falls, but he grabs my ankle, causing me to stumble in my escape.

It's then that I notice the air is dark. Too dark. It's cold too, chilling my blood. The hairs on my arms stand on end, and breath steams from my mouth. There's another threat here. Something even worse than my mob of attackers. My heart pounds in my chest as I hurtle toward the exit on the other side of the parking lot.

A strong wind picks up around me, and thunder rumbles across the sky. I'm almost at the last store when I catch my reflection in the mirrored wall of the shopping center. A crack snakes across it, cutting through the hooded girl approaching me from behind.

And then I fall to my knees, hands clutching my midriff, as she pulls the blade from my back.

What? How?

Spots distort my vision. My body feels numb. I feel life spilling out of me along with my blood. I feel pain. But it's dull. Faraway.

All I can hear is laughter.

"It's done," says the girl. "Log it."

I'm dying.

How can I be dying?

I don't want to die.

Is this how Jonathon felt?

I fall on my face.

And then darkness. Pure, crackling darkness. It's outside of me, and inside of me, and everywhere. Thick shadows twist around me. Cold. Like smoke. I think this is what infinity must feel like. And somehow, it's terrifying and comforting at the same time.

Then a female scream punctures the blackness. Seconds later, it's replaced by a chorus of male shrieks, and strong wings flapping, and groans, and the sound of tearing flesh.

Then silence.

No. Not silence

I can hear crows. Crows are cawing.

Heavy footsteps approach. There's a deep sigh.

"Why'd you have to go get yourself killed, little Demon?" says a gruff Scottish voice. "Ah, shit. I can't believe you're going to make me do this."

I smell leather and smoke and blood as strong arms scoop me up from the ground.

"We're going to need a Miracle," he mutters as I black out.

Chapter Twenty-One

Male voices cut into my dreamlike state. There's something warm and soft beneath me.

"Do you know the amount of paperwork I'll have to do to cover this up?" a familiar voice snaps and my eyes blink open to reveal an off-white ceiling. "An unauthorized Miracle! You think you can just call on me to fix your problems?!"

I groan, propping myself up on the pillow as I try to figure out where the hell I am if it's not actually Hell. The room I'm in is small, yet the bed is large. To my right, an old wardrobe spills creased shirts onto the exposed floorboards. Other than a single chair in the corner, which has my soiled black blazer hanging over the back, it's the only furniture. The blue and cream comforter beneath me smells of woodsmoke and sweat, but, weirdly, it's not a bad combination.

A humorless chuckle from the other room puts my thoughts on hold. "My problems? So she's not your mole, then? I thought you would have learned by now that your little schemes don't work, mate."

"Yes," Gabriel replies icily. "You'd think I would have."

I rub my lower back as memories of my death come crashing back. It not only doesn't hurt, there's no wound there.

What. The. Hell?

"For God's sake, you're leaving already?" says Crow.

"I can't be seen here. People are watching."

"Right, everyone's conspiring against you. You know, I've got some aluminum foil in the cupboard. Maybe you could fashion yourself a little hat." There's a pause then a rustle of fabric as someone sits down. "No one's watching you, mate. You're irrelevant."

"And whose fault is that?!"

Silence. Then agitated footsteps. Then a deep sigh.

"Gabe, wait. At least wait until she's woken up. What if something's gone wrong?"

"It hasn't."

"But what if it has. Please, mate. For old time's sake."

"For old time's sake?" Gabriel scoffs. "Half a century and you haven't changed a bit."

"Please."

"No."

"Pretty please."

"No."

"Pretty please with sugar on top?"

"Fine," snaps Gabriel. "I'll check on her. But once I've assessed that she's okay, I'm leaving. I don't want to set eyes on your nauseating face again."

Crow laughs. "If you say so."

Footsteps come closer. Someone puts a hand on the door handle. Then there's a pause.

"What's in it for you?" Gabriel says coldly.

"Huh?"

"Saving the girl. What's in it for you?"

"I can't save a girl because I like her?"

"No. You're incapable of any kind of affection."

Crow starts to say something but Gabriel cuts him off and opens the door, looking more Angelic than usual thanks to the backlighting from the living room. His pale face is drawn. He's wearing jeans and a checkered grey and black shirt.

"Oh. You're awake," he says, not bothering to warm his tone.

"Nice to see you too," I say.

"I should think so, seeing as I just saved your life."

He enters the room, wiping his hand on his jeans. He takes an exaggerated step over a pile of clothes before perching on the edge of the chair, nose turned up like he smells something terrible.

Seconds later, Crow appears in the doorway.

"Look who's awake," he says with a grin. Dressed in gray sweats and a long-sleeved black T-shirt, he looks like he's just gone for a run. "How do you feel?"

"Good, actually. Which is weird. Seeing as I was stabbed. How am I not dead?" Panic jolts through me. "Oh God, I'm not dead, am I?"

Crow chuckles. "No, little demon. Our Angelic friend over here—"

"I'm not your friend," snaps Gabriel before focusing on me. "I performed a Miracle to heal you. At great personal cost, I might add."

"Oh," I say. "Thank you."

"Yes, well . . ." He looks down and clasps his hands in his lap.

I turn to Crow. "Who were those people?"

"Demons," he says with a shrug. "Pretty low-grade. But it won't stay that way as the price goes up. You're in serious shit, little Demon."

"What do you mean? Why were they trying to kill me?"

He holds my gaze for a moment, then pulls his cell out of his pocket, unlocks it, and tosses it onto the bed. Afterlife is loaded, and in the center is a picture of my face. Below it is a number.

Five thousand dollars.

"What's this?"

"Someone's taken a hit out on you," says Crow.

I meet his eyes. "Why?!"

He glances almost imperceptibly at Gabriel, but the Angel is frowning at the clothes spilling out of the wardrobe. "Dunno."

He's hiding something,

"Really? You have no idea?" I say.

"Nope."

"None at all—"

Gabriel abruptly rises to his feet, wiping his hands on his shirt even though he hasn't touched anything. "I'm glad you're okay, Rachel. Perhaps we can reconvene later to discuss Apocalyptic issues in someplace more . . . pleasant. I wish there was a way to get the hit on you taken off." He sighs. "It would be easier if the founder hadn't gone missing."

As Gabriel heads for the door, I meet Crow's eyes. His half smile confirms he's thinking the same thing.

"Someone's trying to find him," I say, swinging my legs off the bed and jumping to my feet. "Someone's trying to find Jonathon. They're using me as—"

"Bait," says Crow. "Aye. I think so too."

While we've been talking, Gabriel has been awkwardly trying to shoulder past Crow, but now he halts. "What are you both talking about?"

Crow lazily pushes off the doorframe and disappears into the next room. I follow him and Gabriel into what turns out to be a messy living space. A worn leather couch draws my eye first, followed by the huge plasma TV, a tall shelf full of DVDs, a vinyl record player, and a kitchenette area behind a breakfast bar. The carpet beneath my feet is a shabby grey. I think we're in a basement flat; the only window is a horizontal slit above a sink piled with dirty plates.

"Your new mole has an interesting family connection," Crow explains to Gabriel, who is hovering by the couch.

"The Founder of Afterlife is my brother," I say.

Gabriel's eyes widen and then he snaps his head towards Crow. "You really haven't changed. I get it now, why you're involved. You think if you keep Rachel safe then Jonathon will grant you some kind of favor." He turns back to me. "He's playing with your feelings. You can't trust this crook. You have to know this."

"Oh, come on, mate," says Crow, unperturbed. "This is all connected. Rachel being recruited, Jonathon being her brother, the Four Horsemen taking on bar staff, the scroll being stolen. You know as well as I do that coincidence is bullshit. And if you want to stop the world from ending, you need me. Come on, it'll be like old times."

Crow's lips broaden into a wicked smile as Gabriel continues to glower.

"What do you say, mate? Want to join Team Apocalypse?"

Chapter Twenty-Two

"Absolutely, unequivocally not," Gabriel says, then he storms toward the door, knocking his hip on a coffee table as he goes. But he turns when his hand is on the knob, cheeks flaming and clashing with his red hair. "Join Team Apocalypse? *I am* Team Apocalypse. Rachel is helping me to stop this in exchange for her soul. And you . . . *you*. . . " He points a slender finger at Crow. "You have *no* part in this."

"There's no 'I' in team, mate," says Crow with a half-smirk.

"There's no 'U' either," retorts Gabriel. "In fact, Rachel, you should come with me now. Don't stay here with this good-for-nothing."

"Rachel stays with me."

As Crow steps in front of me, the bare bulb hanging above the coffee table flickers.

I rub my face and exhale. "Guys, can we please cool it for a minute and talk this through? What is it between you two anyway?" I try to shuffle between the two of them, but Crow puts his hand on the back of the sofa and bars my path. "Crow," I warn.

130

He looks lazily down at me, but the storm in his eyes belies his calm demeanor. "I said I'll protect you, little Demon. I can't do that if you go off with him, can I?"

"I'm not going off with him—"

"He's using you, Rachel," interjects Gabriel.

"Oh, and you're not?" Crow's eyes blaze into mine. "He can't protect you—"

"I just saved her life!" hisses Gabriel.

"Aye, you did, didn't you, mate?" Crow takes a step forward, and the shadows in the corners of the room swirl toward him. "One little Miracle. One *easy* little Miracle."

Gabriel's jaw clenches, but his eyes remain defiant.

"Guys, what's—?"

"Easy?" Gabriel spits. "You have no idea what I risked. You have no idea what is at stake. And you don't care." He steps forward, poking a finger into Crow's chest. "You don't care about anything. Or anyone."

"Oh, and you do?" Crow chuckles, but the darkness continues to slither toward him across the floor.

"Guys . . ."

"Stuffed up in your office all day long," continues Crow, ignoring me. "Isolated from everyone and everything, surrounded by your precious books, all in some misguided, desperate attempt to prove yourself to Daddy?"

There's a ripping sound, and then two large white-feathered wings erupt from Gabriel's back and scrape against the ceiling.

I stumble back and fall onto the sofa. "Jesus Christ!"

"I told you about my father in confidence!" snaps Gabriel. His checkered shirt is in ruins at his feet, his slender torso bare.

Both men breathe hard, still nose-to-nose.

Then Crow takes a step back and raises his hands. The shadows pooling at his feet dissipate.

"No need to get excited, mate. . ."

"As if you could ever excite me."

131

Gabriel's wings fold back into his shoulder blades so quickly that if it weren't for the tattered shirt on the ground, I could believe I imagined them. Then he bends down and picks it up haughtily, as if he's not half-naked in what seems to be his archnemesis's lair.

"I need to borrow a shirt," he says calmly.

Crow chuckles. "Aye, looks like you do."

"Give me one of yours," he says.

Crow retreats to lean against the wall, arms folding across his chest. "I could."

"Oh, for God's sake." I push off from the couch and stride into Crow's bedroom, scooping up the first shirt I see. It's black like the one he was wearing the night I met him. On second thought, it *is* the one he was wearing the first night I met him.

I go back into the living room, where the vibe has changed from anger to irritation.

"Here," I say, passing the shirt to Gabriel.

He takes it, sniffs it, then pulls a face. "It's dirty."

"Well, it's not as if I know where he keeps his fresh laundry," I say. "Come on, Gabriel, work with me here."

"I'm not wearing it. I don't want to smell *him* on me all the way home." He throws it to the floor at my feet.

Crow and I both exhale. Then Crow heads into his bedroom. There's the sound of a drawer opening. A minute later, he reemerges holding a black T-shirt. He throws it at Gabriel, who swipes it from the air then sniffs it. It seems to pass.

Then he pauses, his expression softening. "The Beatles. Good band," he murmurs. "Is this vintage?"

"Aye. Picked it up from one of their gigs myself."

Gabriel turns it over, inspecting the date: 1969. "I used to love them," he says.

"I know."

Gabriel neatly folds his tattered shirt on the arm of Crow's chair before slipping on the top, which shows the Beatles walking over a zebra crossing. Despite the two men's difference in size, it fits him perfectly—a fact Gabriel notices too. He frowns and looks at Crow.

Crow gives a half-shrug, back to leaning against the wall.

After a heavy silence, Gabriel nods sharply, brushing himself off. "Right. Well. I'll be going then." He opens the door. "Rachel, meet me for brunch tomorrow at Evie's. We'll discuss next steps."

"Am I invited?" asks Crow.

"No," says Gabriel, but then he pauses in the doorway, shoulder blades sharp against the black T-shirt. "But if you happened to be in Evie's at eleven a.m. tomorrow to make sure no one attacks Rachel while we speak, I suppose I wouldn't hold it against you."

He slams the door shut behind him.

I turn to Crow. "Are you going to tell me what *that* was all about?" I ask.

Chapter Twenty-Three

Crow holds my gaze for a moment, arms folded across his chest. Then he pushes off from the wall.

"Hungry?" he says.

"Hungry for answers."

"How about lasagna?" He heads to the kitchenette and pulls two microwave meals from the freezer. "Or . . ."—he studies the packet—"spinach and ricotta cannelloni?"

"Cannelloni," I say, going to stand on the other side of the breakfast bar.

While I can tell he's trying to distract me, I'm also famished. I feel light-headed too. I wonder whether it's due to the whole "getting stabbed to death" incident or the Miracle afterward.

I slide onto the leather barstool as Crow rummages through the dirty sink. There's a load of old mail piled up on the counter. I glance at one of the opened letters.

Thank you for your generous donation to Brain Trust Research. We—

I flinch as Crow violently forks the plastic on top of the meals.

"Did the lasagna do something to offend you?" I ask, turning my attention back to him.

He chuckles as he shoves the containers into the microwave and sets the timer.

"So what's with you and Gabriel?" I try again.

He leans across the breakfast bar. "He doesn't like me very much."

"Hmm." I raise an eyebrow. "Doesn't he?"

The corner of his full lip quirks up before he pulls back. "Beer?" he says.

"Sure. But stop trying to distract me."

His gray eyes glint. He turns to the fridge and opens the door, releasing an odor that smells like sour milk mixed with off cheese and old cabbage.

"Wow, that is . . . pungent," I say, nose wrinkling.

He produces a bottle of beer and slides it toward me. Then he turns back around to rummage for another one. "Aye . . . sorry about that. I don't have people over much."

"You do have a nose though."

He chuckles as he pulls out his bottle. "You're hardly Little Miss Princess Pristine," he says, flicking the lid off. "You forget that I was contracted to follow you for twenty-four hours. The things I saw—"

"For the love of God, shut the door!" I say, arm over my nostrils.

He laughs as he shuts it, and I find myself laughing too. I can't help myself. Why do I feel so oddly comfortable in this guy's presence when I know—I *know*—I should feel exactly the opposite?

"You have a nice laugh," he says.

I shake my head, lips still twitching. "Stop trying to change the subject. Or trying to poison me with the deadly biological warfare you're brewing in your fridge. What's the deal with you and—?"

The microwave interrupts me with a loud beep.

"Saved by the bell," he says.

"Crow!"

"Rachel!"

His low chuckle reverberates around the small kitchen as he pulls the meals out of the microwave and sets them on the breakfast bar. He washes some forks in the sink and hands one to me, and I go to wipe it on the bottom of my black T-shirt before realizing it's still crusted with my blood. Given I almost died earlier, a bit of dirt on a fork is hardly the worst of my problems. I dig into the cheesy pasta.

"I betrayed him," Crow says then. "He never forgave me. There's not much more to it."

Of course he would tell me when my mouth is full. I quickly swallow and ask, "In what way did you betray him?"

"It's a long story."

"I've got time."

"I don't like explaining stuff, little Demon," he says, starting to eat his own meal. "I already told you that."

I take a sip of the beer, then put it down on the counter, deciding on a different tactic. "Okay. So when we find my brother, you want him to pay you for 'protecting' me, right?"

Crow watches me, fork paused halfway to his mouth. "Aye," he says.

"Well, seems like your plan is pretty reliant on what I tell him."

"Oh, really?"

"I mean, the way I see it, I *could* tell him you helped me. Or I *could* tell him that some annoying, pain-in-the-ass Omen has been following me around for days after doing *nothing* to stop me from signing away my soul."

Crow takes another bite of his lasagna and chews. For a second, I think I've gone too far, but then he smiles.

"Well, look at you. Thinking like a Demon." He takes a swig of his beer. "Okay, so you want the juicy details."

I put down my fork and lean close enough to smell the beer on his breath. "Yes."

"Well, I moved to Los Angeles in the late thirties, not long before the Second World War. I was a boxer, trying to make a name for myself. You box too, right? We should spar sometime."

"Don't change the subject."

"Fine," he says, still amused. "I started getting into trouble—gambling, throwing games for money, that kind of thing. Couldn't get out of it even when I wanted to get clean." He shrugs. "Made me a perfect candidate for Devils Inc., so I signed my soul away. And not long after, I died in a car accident. Started working for them."

He takes another swig of beer.

"Anyway, at that time, our conspiracy-loving friend over at Halo Corp. had this theory that the Second World War was a sign the Apocalypse was nigh. And that the reason Devils Inc. had started to recruit so many soldier-like people was part of Lucifer's dastardly ploy."

"Ploy for what?"

"Well, the Book of Revelation states that when the Apocalypse is triggered, Lucifer's side will lose. Our friend Gabe thought Lucifer was trying to even the playing field by recruiting men, to give Hell a chance of winning in the Final War."

"So he asked you to spy for him?" I say, starting to understand. "Like he has with me?"

"Aye. He took a bit of a shine to me, I suppose. Took me under his wing. Said he could save my soul if I worked for him."

"And what? You told Devils Inc. about him? That's why he feels betrayed?"

"No. I did what he asked. And, to give him credit, it turned out he was right. Devils Inc. was planning for a War. I reported it all back to Gabe. And Gabe got me out of my contract with Devils Inc."

"So it's possible?" I say, momentarily distracted. "To get your soul back?"

"Aye. In some cases."

"How?"

A flicker of darkness crosses Crow's face. The light above blinks on and off.

"Well, in my case, Gabe found out the accident that killed me was no accident at all. Devils Inc. orchestrated the whole thing to get me into their ranks quicker."

"They murdered you?"

"Aye." He absently twists at his finger. "And that's against the rules."

"I'm sorry," I say.

"'S okay, little Demon. Not your fault."

There's a heavy silence, and I shift in my seat.

"And then what?" I ask, taking a sip of beer.

"I started working for Halo Corp."

"You worked at Halo Corp!"

He chuckles. "Aye. But it wasn't really my scene. Broke some rules, worked on some stuff behind Gabriel's back, did some stuff I shouldn't have. . ." He shrugs. "Hence the betrayal. When I was thrown out of Halo Corp., I took him down with me. The higher-ups blamed him for bringing someone like me in; for letting our friendship cloud his judgement."

He holds my gaze a little too steadily, his expression carefree. But his grip on the beer bottle tightens.

I shake my head. "There's more to it than that."

"Gabe takes his job pretty seriously, little Demon."

"I know. But he seemed . . . hurt."

Crow exhales. "Gabe took it personally. Said he stuck his neck out for me." He moves back a little. "I never meant to hurt the lad."

I frown, thinking back to the weird tension in the room. "Did anything ever . . . happen between you two?"

"Like what?"

"You know."

He holds my gaze then. "I know what you're asking. I never had feelings for Gabriel, little Demon," he says, putting his bottle on the counter. "I'm going for a piss. Help yourself to more beer."

He heads out of the kitchenette and into a door beside his bedroom. As it clicks shuts behind him, it occurs to me that he didn't exactly answer my question.

Nor did he say Gabriel never had feelings for him.

My Devils Inc. cell buzzes in my pocket.

"Shit," I mutter as I read the message from Adalind.

How long does it take to get a cup of coffee?

Chapter Twenty-Four

As I'm wondering how to respond, my phone starts to ring.

Adalind. She's actually calling me now. Shit.

The clock tells me it's eleven. I've been gone for hours, and I've no idea what to say to her.

I would have died if Gabriel hadn't done something against the rules. I don't want to go back to an office of Demons when Demons just tried to kill me. And Adalind hates me. Even if she believed me, I wouldn't expect any sympathy.

But if I don't get through this internship, I'm bound for Hell.

The bathroom door clicks open just as I make a decision.

"Hi, Adalind," I say.

"Where the Hell are you? I've been calling you for hours! How hard is it to pick up some coffees?"

"Yeah, about that . . . There was a slight problem—"

Crow swipes the cell out of my hand, leaning over me from behind.

"Adalind," he says. "So nice to hear your beautiful voice."

I hear an irate hissing on the other side of the line but am unable to distinguish anything but a few choice words describing Crow. I feel his chest vibrate against my back as he chuckles. The proximity of his body causes an unwelcome lick of heat in the pit of my stomach.

"You want to know where Rachel is?" he says. "Bad news, Adalind. She's dead."

I twist to better frown up at him. *What the hell are you doing?* I mouth.

He raises his eyebrows at me but ignores the question. I hear another round of hissing from Adalind.

"Aye," he says. "Terrible business. Dead. Dead as a doornail. Croaked it. Sleeping with the fishes and all that. You didn't see the hit on Afterlife?"

There's more chattering.

"Aye. They must have forgotten to log the kill. But she's dead, all right. Saw it with my own eyes." Pause. "Aye. Bringing her in to Devils Inc. to be processed would be the proper thing to do."

Adalind's voice raises.

"Wow. Sounds like there'll be a lot of paperwork to do when she gets there to reassign her from Live to Dead." He studies the microwave on the other side of the kitchen. "I guess you'll be stuck with that. I don't envy you that—not one little bit, Adalind. Not one bit . . . Although . . ." He looks down and winks at me, his chin momentarily brushing against my forehead. "I suppose I could keep her out of your hair for a little while. Give you the weekend to yourself at least."

There's silence on the other end of the line. Then a slightly less aggressive muttering.

"Aye. Aye, I'll keep her safe. No . . . no, I won't kill her again for the money." The corner of his lip quirks up. "Aye . . . I know that would cause you more paperwork . . . Aye, I'll bring her in on Monday. Okay, Adalind. Always a pleasure!"

He hangs up midway through her stream of cursing.

"There, sorted," he says. "She'll be pretty pissed when she finds out you're not actually dead, but she's pretty pissed-off most of the time, so what's the damage?"

I look up at him, still feeling a little buzzy from having his chest against my back. "What actually happens? When we, you know, die?"

"Well. Anyone who has a contract in place with either of the organizations essentially gets one free pass at death. But if we suffer a mortal injury on the job, we're shipped upstairs or downstairs for the rest of eternity. It's a law intended to stop us from fighting each other."

"So I can die once?"

"Aye. In theory. Although you'd have to give up everything from your mortal life. And then, if you died again . . ." He pulls a face and points to the floor.

I know I should be thinking about how close I came to having to cut off all ties with my friends and family, but enveloped within his body heat, the smell of him surrounding me, I'm thinking more about what it would feel like to run my hands over his annoyingly well-sculpted chest.

"Looks like you're stuck with me for the night, little Demon."

As I process his words, I hear my own accelerating heartbeat. He stands too close, yet somehow not close enough. I don't know what the Hell is wrong with me.

A slow smile spreads across his face as his gaze drops to my lips. "So . . . what shall we do now?"

The warmth in the pit of my stomach licks through my entire body.

"You're in my personal space," I say, tearing my gaze away.

"Not moving, though, are you, little Demon?" he says, dipping his head to whisper in my ear.

Slowly, he runs his hands down my arms, leaving a trail of prickling energy in his wake. My pulse thrums.

And it's madness. This feeling. This desire. It has to be the aftermath of the fight; adrenaline needing to be released. I don't want Crow. I don't want to rip off his top and bite his bottom lip and force my tongue against his. I don't want him to lift me up onto the counter and take me roughly while I dig my fingers into the muscles of his back.

But if I did want that . . . it would be so easy to take it from him.

Oh, God.

Something clenches in the pit of my stomach as he slides his hands over mine. His chest rises and falls against my back—and I feel his mirrored desire for something violent; for some kind of release.

I steady my breathing.

I'm wound up. Frustrated. Because I lost the fight.

Not because Crow's breath is tickling the skin behind my ear.

"So?" he whispers. "What do you want to do?"

What do I want to do?

I want to exorcise this pent-up frustration. I want to take it out on the guy who got me into this mess in the first place. I want to use him like he is using me. I want to put my hands on his body and pound into him and make him cry out.

I want a release.

"You said you used to be a boxer?" I say, forcing the breathlessness out of my voice.

He doesn't say anything for a moment. Then he chuckles, his chest vibrating against my back.

"Aye," he says, his tone one of understanding. "It wouldn't be a fair fight, little Demon. But I'll happily throw you around the gym for a bit."

"I wouldn't be so sure about that."

"I would. You're no match for me." He circles his rough thumb across the skin of my hand, and it's hard not to let it distract me. "Not until you learn to use your Demonic powers, anyway."

I frown. "Demonic powers?"

"Aye. Part of the compensation for working for Devils Inc. It's all in the contract you signed." There's amusement in his tone. "You're going to make a shit lawyer, you know?"

A laugh escapes my lips, breaking some of the tension. "Yeah, I know."

The admission might have stung a few months ago, but I'm finding the impending Apocalypse puts things into perspective. Plus, I hate to admit it, but I'm kind of enjoying the danger that comes with this new world of Angels, Demons, and Omens.

Pulling my hands from his, I swivel around to face him. He moves back so I can fit within his arms, but not so much that I don't have to spread my legs to make us fit. From the mischievous glint in his eyes, I know that's intentional.

"So you're saying I have access to some freaky superpowers?" I say. "Like yours?"

"Not like mine, no," he replies. "But similar."

Smiling, I lean forward until our lips are only inches apart. "Teach me."

Chapter Twenty-Five

Half an hour later, Crow and I are standing barefoot on the black mats of the Trinity Falls Gym.

It's deathly quiet. The gym closed over an hour ago, and Crow picked the lock so we could get inside. Now, he stands in front of me, shrouded in the shadows he seems to wear like a cloak. The ones from the tree branches outside stretch toward him.

His eyes are bright and watchful, though never moving from mine.

He's still wearing his gray sweats and black top, but I've changed out of my bloodstained clothes into some borrowed ones: a plain white T-shirt and a pair of navy-blue sports shorts, the cord of which I've had to tie around my waist to stop them from falling to my ankles. I can smell him on me: smoke, and outdoors, and a trace of sweat. It agitates me. Which is good, I guess.

Seeing as I'm planning on kicking his ass.

His lips quirk as if he knows what I'm thinking. I can't wait to wipe the smirk off his face.

145

"So?" I say. "How do I use my powers?"

"Try and hit me first, little Demon." His grin widens. "I want to see how good you are."

Neither of us move for a moment. Then I run at him.

I throw a right hook at his face, which he blocks and counters with a jab to my stomach. After narrowly avoiding it, I go on the full offensive, throwing a series of jabs. He blocks them all but doesn't manage to get a hit on me either as we dance a violent circle around the mats.

He's good. His moves are effortless. So why can't he hit me?

"You're going easy on me," I say between punches, a strand of hair from my messy ponytail sticking to my lip.

"Aye," he says with a grin.

He's a little breathless, but not enough. I want him on the floor, gasping. His eyes glint as if he knows it.

"Don't," I say.

He raises his eyebrows. "Okay."

This time, when he goes on the offensive, I'm driven backward as I block blow after blow, my bare feet sliding across the mat. I cry out, almost stumbling, at a particularly hard swing. He grunts as I duck, shoulder-barge him, and attempt to left hook his nose.

His block is clumsy. Too clumsy. I throw my right fist at his unprotected face.

"Stop going easy on—"

The words die in my throat as the shadow of the tree erupts up from the mat, surrounding my body with cold, black energy. My fist swings at nothing just as a muscular arm hooks around my waist.

Crow pulls me back into his body, the cotton of his top damp with sweat. My breath hitches, my heart pounding so hard I think he must be able to feel it.

"What were you saying?" he murmurs into my ear, amused.

Darkness tickles my face like smoke—a cold contrast to the heat emanating from the male body behind me.

"Show me," I say, breathless. "Show me how to do it."

The shadows fade, but Crow doesn't release his grip.

"An Angel's power can be drawn from Virtue," he says. "And a Demon's . . . well. . . I think you can guess."

"Sin," I say softly, dread and excitement twisting inside my gut. "What does that mean?"

"Raise your left hand," he says, and when I do, he traces the skin on the underside of my forearm until he's gently holding my palm. "There are seven documented. Sloth, Pride, Envy, Gluttony, Greed," he says. "All a little hard to access. But Wrath . . . well, that's a little easier."

"You want me to get angry?" I say, trying to ignore the way his breath tickles the skin behind my ear. "Shouldn't be too hard."

He chuckles. "We could do it that way. That's how Demons usually access their power. Or . . ." He tugs at my damp shirt, pulling it out of the waistband of my shorts.

I tighten my grip on his wrist. "What are you doing?" My voice comes out as a whisper.

He slips his hand beneath my top, his rough thumb brushing against the bare skin of my stomach. My breathing quickens.

"You're forgetting the other Sin," he says.

I swallow hard, trying to ignore the fire his touch ignites. "You're telling me Demons can get their powers from . . . what? Horniness. That's ridicul—"

The words die in my throat as his lips brush my neck. Instinctively, I press my body closer to his.

I try again. "You're just saying that to . . ."

Slowly, he trails his fingers down to linger at the waistband of my shorts. Energy swarms inside me. It takes everything I have not to push his hand further down.

"Think about what you want," he says. "Think about the power building up inside you. Focus. Think about how good it would feel to get it out . . ."

He gently slides his hand further down, but not far enough. My whole body burns from the inside out. Something electric pulsates through me, racing through my veins. I feel strange. Buzzing. Aching. I lean back, tilting my head, desperate for his mouth on mine; desperate to ease this . . . *fire*.

When he leans in closer, I think he's going to kiss me.

Then he moves his head to look past me. I follow his gaze to my left hand, still held upright by his gentle grip.

My eyes widen. "Holy shit!"

A ball of blue flame crackles in my palm.

Twisting out of his grasp, I spin around and hurl it at him. As he instinctively raises his arms, the shadows in the room rise to protect him.

When the darkness subsides, smoke curls around his imposing frame. His muscles are taut, straining the cotton of his black top as his chest rises and falls. His jaw clenches, lips absent their usual smile.

Then he crosses the space between us, forcing me back against the wall, his hands cupping the sides of my face.

And then his mouth is on mine.

I grab his shirt, pulling him closer as the crackle of blue-flame energy runs through me. Then I push.

He goes flying, landing on the mats with a hard thud. I can tell he's truly stunned and busy catching his breath. He chuckles, eyes still on the ceiling.

"Not bad, little Demon," he says.

He makes a movement with his fingers, and the shadows on the mat elongate, curling up and around my legs and arms.

Oh, shit.

I try to access my newfound Demonic power, but I'm yanked forward. Soon, I'm on top of Crow, my hands flat on the mat on either side of his face. Our noses almost touch, and I breathe hard, mouth hovering above his.

"But not good enough," he says with a wicked smile.

Slowly, he sits up, forcing me upright. I grip his top, material balled in my fists as his hands slide up my back. His nose brushes against mine, and I move my mouth toward his, desperate to ease this heat. But when my lips brush against his, he doesn't respond. So I dig my teeth into his bottom lip.

He flips me onto my back, pinning me to the mats with his body, his mouth hovering above mine. I cry out, then draw on this new energy building inside. A weak flicker of blue flame crackles in my outstretched hands.

I grab his shoulder, then roll us over again so I'm on top. The fabric of his shirt hisses as it burns. He grunts, his breathing labored, as his eyes hold mine.

Then he moves his fingers.

Darkness rises around us, thick and alive. It pulls me to my feet like a shadowy tornado, and when it clears, Crow stands in front of me. There's a charred hole at the top of his sleeve, and his face is flushed.

I must look even more disheveled. Sweat rolls down my skin, and escaped strands of hair hang in front of my face.

We stare at each other.

Slowly, a smile spreads across his face. I smile back.

Then he grabs me and throws me over his shoulder.

"What are you doing?" I yelp, failing to keep the giggle out of my voice. "This is very undignified."

"Things are going to get much more undignified in a minute, little Demon."

My arms dangle down his muscular back as he walks us across the room.

"Where are you taking me?" I yell.

"Bed."

Both of us laughing, he carries me through the door.

Chapter Twenty-Six

The sun creeping through the gap in my blinds is what wakes me the next morning. I'm warm. Relaxed. In fact, I feel more relaxed than I have in a long time.

I've felt so pent-up lately—from college, and the pressure of not disappointing my parents, and the questions about what I want to be doing with my future. Last night, I was finally able to let some of that go.

I yawn, shifting beneath my black-and-red duvet. The heavy arm curled around my waist pulls me closer.

"Morning, little Demon," says Crow, voice gruff with sleep. He nuzzles the back of my neck.

I roll onto my back to look at him. As he props himself up, the comforter slips down, exposing his ridiculously muscular chest. His eyelids are heavy with sleep, but they don't hide the mischief.

"Morning," I say with a groan.

"So . . . last night was . . ." The corner of his lip tugs up. "Fun."

I put my hands over my face. He laughs, pulling one of them away and looping his fingers through mine before pinning it to the pillow.

"No use getting embarrassed now, little Demon. We have no secrets anymore."

"Mmm." Untangling my fingers from his, I trace the pillow mark on his temple. "I'm sure that's not true."

He turns his head to bite my wrist, then he leans down to brush his lips against mine. I tilt my head away.

"What's wrong?" he says.

"I haven't brushed my teeth."

"I don't care about that."

"Well, I do."

His face lingers above mine. "Okay, a closed-mouth kiss then."

"A closed-mouth kiss! What the hell is wrong with you?"

I laugh, and he laughs too, the corners of his eyes crinkling.

"You're weird," I say.

"How am I weird?"

"I don't know. You're just. . ." I struggle for what I'm trying to say. "You're more affectionate than I expected."

"Aye? Well, you're more violent than *I* expected." He puts on a face of mock shock. "Jesus Christ! Last night was terrifying!"

"Oh, shut up!" I say.

After brushing his lips against my forehead, he rolls onto his back. As he does, I note the red burn mark on his left shoulder where I grabbed him with my weird blue-flame hand.

"Sorry about that," I murmur, propping myself up on my elbow to touch it.

"You should be. You're an absolute monster," he says, turning his head to meet my eyes. "I think you need to make it up to me."

"Oh, you do, do you?" I say.

"Aye. It really hurts."

"Liar."

"It's the truth! I swear on my soul!"

"I'm not sure that means much coming from you."

"It does." He takes my hand, kisses the underside of my wrist, then puts my palm on his chest. "I need something to distract me. From the pain."

"And what exactly would distract you?" I ask.

He slides my hand down beneath the covers. "I read in an article once that orgasms are excellent painkillers."

I burst out laughing as he feigns innocence.

"It's not me!" he says. "It's science, little Demon."

"Well, I suppose I can't argue with science," I say, bending down to kiss him just as a knock interrupts us. I glance across my room to the door by my broken mirror.

"Ignore it," whispers Crow.

The knocking persists. When I start to climb over Crow, he pushes me back.

"'S okay. I'll get it. You reserve your energy," he says, kissing my forehead as someone knocks again. "You'll need it in a minute."

As he slides out of bed—completely butt-naked—I can't help but be entranced by his ridiculously good physique. My eyes trace the muscles of his back, the scratch marks I left on his skin, and the tattoo on his left shoulder blade: a lily surrounded by black feathers.

Then, when he makes no move to cover himself, I snap out of my trance.

"Crow!"

He looks over his shoulder. "What? I'm just going to peek through the door."

"I don't care! Put some pants on!"

I scoop his sweats off the floor and throw them. As he turns to catch them, my eyes flick down. He smirks, pulling them over his hips.

"Just get back in bed and cover yourself up," I say, shuffling out of the covers.

Crow laughs and does as he's told.

I'm not all that better-dressed than Crow given I'm wearing nothing but his T-shirt and my underwear, so I only open the door enough to peek outside. It's Josie, bright-eyed and annoyingly awake. Her Afro is styled to perfection, and she's in skinny jeans, boots, and a black leather jacket.

"You still sleeping, babe? It's almost eleven." She starts to push past me. "Anyway, I—" She closes her mouth when she spots Crow on my bed, the duvet tucked around his waist.

"Oh. *Hello,*" she says, but then her brow furrows. "Wait. Do I know you?"

"Aye. You threw a packet of salt into my eye."

"No shit! I knew I recognized you. Sorry about that, babe."

"'S all right," he says, then he twists a little to show off his back. "I'm getting used to you Trinity Falls girls having violent tendencies. You should see what Rachel—"

"Okaaay, that's enough from you," I say, shuffling Josie into the hallway and shutting the door behind us. "What's up?" I ask casually—or, as casually as possible when one is pulling at a white T-shirt in the desperate hope it covers her thighs. My hair is tangled, and I can smell both mine and Crow's sweat on my skin.

She just smiles at me, saying nothing.

"What? I *am* allowed to have a man in my bed from time to time," I say.

She raises her hands. "Hey, no judgement from me, babe. Although . . ." Her smile slips a little. "Isn't he the guy we saw making out with some blonde the other night?"

"Yeah, I know. Look, it just . . . happened. It's not like I'm going to marry him."

After a beat, she shrugs. "Well, whether he's marriage material or not, he's pretty hot! Exceptionally hot, in fact. Did you. . ."—she dramatically arches an eyebrow—"do the *deed?*"

153

I laugh. "Do the deed? How old are you?"

"You did, didn't you! Was it good? I bet it was."

"Is there a reason you're here so early on a Saturday?" I ask, trying to fight my smile.

She laughs. "Early? It's almost midday! Although, I guess I can forgive you for being a bit tired," she says, smirking at my door.

"How was your first shift at Apocalypse?" I ask, changing the subject.

"Yeah, good. For the most part anyway. It's actually why I stopped by."

I frown. Crow said the Horsemen would protect her, but he also said he'd protect me, and I just got stabbed.

"Did something happen?"

"Kind of. A group came in about midnight. They knew we were friends, and they said they were looking for you. Only . . . I've never seen them hanging out with you."

I tense. The Demons must be still after the bounty on me.

"What did you tell them?"

"Nothing. Chris was training me on bar and told them where to go before I could answer. They got pretty aggressive after that, started yelling about how it wasn't time yet. Then Darius saw them out. Which was super-hot, but . . ." She gives me a stern look. "You're not in any trouble, are you, babe?"

Other than signing my soul away to the Devil . . .

"No," I say.

"You sure?"

"I think they were people from my law internship," I say, not untruthfully.

Josie studies my face, brow furrowed. She's my best friend, and as such, she knows when something's up. Surprisingly, however, she lets it go.

"Okay. Well, if you ever need to talk . . ."

"Yeah." I smile. "Yeah, I know. Everything's fine. I'm fine."

She holds my gaze for a moment longer. Then she returns my smile. "Okay, well, I was going to see if you wanted to come watch Lucas's *Faustus* rehearsal. But I can see you have more pressing matters to attend to." She wiggles her eyebrows. "I'll catch you later, okay? You can fill me in on all the juicy details."

I laugh, promising to call her tonight, then watch as she heads back down the hallway. The smile dies from my lips as she disappears from view.

When I go back into my room, Crow's sitting up against my scratched wooden headboard, a slither of sunlight shining across his face. When the door clicks shut, he gestures for me to join him.

I stay put.

"Josie said some people were looking for me at Apocalypse," I say. "They asked her where I was."

"Demons. Or Omens," says Crow, bringing his knees up and leaning forward. "Makes sense. You set yourself to offline on Afterlife. Makes you harder to trace, so they have to do some digging."

"How did they find me last night?" I ask with a frown.

"I dunno. Guessing someone from Devils Inc. recognized you from the job advert and tipped off some of their friends."

I shake my head. "I don't want Josie in danger," I say, angry. "I just hope Gabriel finds a way for me to tell her what's going on so she can protect herself. If he hasn't—" The words get stuck in my throat. "Oh, shit."

"What?"

I hurry to my nightstand, picking up my cell. "Oh, shit!" I say again.

"What!"

"It's eleven!"

"So?"

"We're supposed to meet Gabriel for brunch at Evie's at eleven, remember?"

"Oh, aye . . . he did say something about that, didn't he?" Crow pulls a face, then he chuckles. "He is *not* going to be happy with us."

Chapter Twenty-Seven

We're twenty-five minutes late to Evie's.

Gabriel is sitting at a high table in one of the front windows. Today, he's all Business Angel in a gray sweater with a stiff-collared blue shirt peeking out from the top.

He scowls at us as we walk by the glass. Then he looks away to take a pointed sip from his apple blossom teacup.

"That's one angry-looking Angel," Crow mutters as we head inside.

Evie's in the morning is a different scene than Evie's at night. Only a few of the dozen or so tables are occupied, and instead of pulsing club music, we're greeted by the mellow tones of piano jazz. The only lighting is that streaming through the front windows, and the blackboard behind the bar advertises half-price apple muffins and juice.

Gabriel watches us coolly as we approach. A white folder rests beneath his elbows.

"Hi, Gabriel," I say.

Beside me, Crow shifts from one foot to the other. If I didn't know any better, I'd think he was feeling awkward.

"Hey, mate."

Gabriel's obviously pissed we're late, and given the weird energy yesterday, I don't want him to realize the reason why. I suddenly regret how quickly I got dressed. My jeans and T-shirt are all right enough, but I didn't have time for a shower and had to scrape my long hair back into a ponytail.

Gabriel slides his gaze over to Crow, who's still in the gray sweats from last night.

He puts down his teacup and turns his attention back to me.

"You're late," he says.

"Sorry," I say. "We . . . lost track of time."

"Oh, well, not to worry," says Gabriel. "It's only the end of the world."

Crow blows out a puff of air, absently twisting at his ring finger. "I'll go get us some drinks, shall I?" He pauses. "Evie in today?"

"She doesn't work Saturday mornings," mutters Gabriel, eyes fixed on his tea.

"Probably for the best," says Crow.

"Yes. Probably," says Gabriel.

It takes me a moment to remember that she threw him out of the bar not so long ago. Like a lot of people, she doesn't seem to like him.

"So an Earl Gray for you, mate?" says Crow.

Gabriel doesn't meet his eye but inclines his head.

Crow touches my shoulder. "Want anything?"

"Coffee," I say.

Crow squeezes my arm, then turns and heads to the bar. When I look at Gabriel again, his eyes are lingering on the place Crow just touched. When he realizes I'm watching, he averts his gaze to the folder on the table.

"So," I say, sliding onto the stool, "what did you want to talk about?"

He picks up the white folder but pauses in opening it. "Did you . . .? Did you and *him*. . .?" He purses his lips. "No. It's none of my business."

I shift a little on the high stool and look out the window, hoping to God he won't pry. It's embarrassing enough as it is. I let my desires take over any semblance of common sense. And the worst part of it . . . I liked it.

Crow is not to be trusted. Everyone seems to dislike him. He betrayed Gabriel. And he's a blatant player—I mean, he was making out with some girl in a club just the other night, for God's sake.

And yet I *liked* it.

I liked the feel of his body on top of mine. I liked digging my fingernails into his skin, and biting his chest, and working out the frustration that's been building up inside of me for . . . well, for a long time. I liked the feel of his strong hands pinning my wrists to the mattress, and his stubble scraping my skin, and his tongue, so forceful against mine . . .

I blink to clear the unwanted flashbacks and better focus on what's going on outside. Students in red-and-black Trinity Falls Rams hoodies wander past Apocalypse. They're completely unaware that the actual Four Horsemen of the Apocalypse work there and the world might be ending.

That's where my focus needs to be. On the end of the world and finding Jonathon.

Not some bad, yet irritatingly charming Omen.

Gabriel awkwardly clears his throat, and I turn back to him.

"Anyway," he continues, "I've been looking for way to get your friend Josie on board so we can use her as a source and—" He stops, exhaling through his nose. "You've slept with him, haven't you? No, no, sorry," he says hurriedly, looking down at the table. "Don't answer that. It's none of my business. It's just . . ."

"What?"

"Be careful, Rachel. This . . . this is what he does." He glances to the bar, where Crow is still ordering drinks, then leans forward. "He gets his hook in you and reels you in, and then he casts you adrift like an old. . ." He pauses as though searching for a word. "Haddock," he concludes, sticking with the fishing metaphor. "He's learned that if he can make people *care,* if he can make people like him, then they'll give him what he wants."

"Gabriel, it's fine. I'm fine. Everything is under control," I say, folding my arms across my chest. "I'm not getting *reeled* in. I'm in control. I'm not a *haddock.*"

"You might not think you're a haddock," says Gabriel, looking back at his folder, "but you are a haddock."

"I'm not a haddock!" I insist.

"You are," he insists, but he clamps his mouth shut when Crow brushes past me to take an adjacent school.

"Are you talking about fish?" says Crow.

We're saved from responding by the blond bartender, who exchanges Gabriel's teapot with a new one, passes me my coffee, then leans over the table to hand Crow a red mug topped with whipped cream and marshmallows.

He flashes her a big smile. "Cheers, love."

"No problem, sweetheart," she replies before heading back to the bar.

Gabriel raises an eyebrow as if to say, "Told you so;" as if we just witnessed them fornicating on the table rather than engaging in a polite—if a bit friendly—interaction.

"You were saying something about Josie?" I say, taking a sip of coffee.

"Yes," says Gabriel. "I thought if we could get Josie involved, we could find out who delivered the first scroll to the Four Horsemen and track them down. If Rachel's brother is connected to all this, it's likely that whoever stole the scroll put the hit out on Rachel."

Gabriel opens his folder and flicks through the papers within.

"It's a breach of the Devils Inc. contract to tell a mortal soul about any of this," he continues. "So telling Josie outright will have severe consequence."

Crow takes a sip of his hot chocolate. When he puts it back down, there's whipped cream on his top lip, and I have a horrible urge to lick it off. As I watch, he deliberately rolls his tongue over it.

"However, if the mortal soul were to *see* something," continues Gabriel, not looking up from his papers. "If they were to happen upon our world by accident, that is a different case entirely. So I was thinking . . . "

"We cause an accident," says Crow.

"Yes. And while it would be dangerous, one option might be. . ." He glances at me.

"Aye," says Crow, his smirk disappearing. For once, they seem to be in perfect agreement.

"What?" I ask.

"We set your Afterlife status back to online," says Gabriel.

"Aye," says Crow. "And then we take you to Apocalypse and let the dickheads over at Devils Inc. and Omens Limited expose themselves when they come to kill you." He raises an eyebrow at Gabriel. "And here you were thinking you wouldn't need me, mate."

Gabriel scowls. "I don't need you."

"So you're going to act as Rachel's bodyguard? An Angel protecting a Demon?" He chuckles. "Don't think so. Aren't you barred from Apocalypse anyway?"

I wonder if that's why Gabriel was wearing his "disguise" when I saw him there last week.

"Yes. Well." Gabriel tilts his chin up. "You're barred from *this* place, yet here you are, lingering like a bad smell. Speaking of which,"—he looks Crow up and down—"have you ever heard of a shower?"

161

When Crow only laughs, Gabriel turns his attention to me.

"What do you think, Rachel?" he says. "It'll be dangerous. We'll only proceed if you're happy."

"I don't know," I say. "I don't want to put Josie in danger. A fight while she's working is still risky."

"They have security cameras," says Crow. "We stage the fight when she's not there, then find some excuse for her to look at the footage. She'd be safe."

"Okay. If it means I can stop lying to Josie, and we can stop the end of the world, then I'm for it," I say. Plus, I'm starting to feel pent-up again; I wouldn't mind beating up some Demons.

"Excellent," says Gabriel. "Well, we'll proceed with our plan on Monday night, just before the club closes."

"Great." I pause. "I get to be bait. Again."

Crow takes another sip of his hot chocolate and glances at me. "Aye. But at least you're not a haddock."

***

After the three of us finish our drinks, we awkwardly part ways, Gabriel giving Crow a dark look when the Omen says he has business to attend to.

I spend the rest of the day with Josie in the library, where I try to catch up on the contract law lecture I missed due to the appearance of the very dead Richard Livingstone.

By the time I'm back in my room, my bare feet on the desk as I watch music videos on YouTube, I've got a serious headache thanks to hours of legalese and Josie pestering me for details about Crow.

I'm dressed for bed when there's a knock at the door. Making sure my green shorts and white tank look decent enough, I answer it. It's Crow, dominating the doorframe, hands in the pockets of his dark jeans. He wears a blue shirt that makes his gray eyes seem darker.

"Hey," he says.

"Hi."

"Can I come in?"

I stare at him, waiting for my brain to kick in and override the stupid desire that's appeared just from the heat in his eyes.

"I said I'd look after you, little Demon," he says when I don't reply.

"Look, Crow, about last night . . ." I say finally. "I think it's best if it was just a one-time thing."

He presses forward and closes the door behind him, eyes fixed on mine. "Uh-huh."

"I mean, there's a lot going on," I say, my hand moving to his chest to find the gap between two of his buttons. I slip my finger inside, feeling the soft hair.

"Aye."

"And me and you . . ." I say, heartbeat quickening. "We don't work."

"Probably not." He slides a hand around the back of my neck, brushing my cheek with his thumb.

"It would be a disaster."

"Aye."

The small space between our bodies crackles with energy. The moment stretches, seeming to last an eternity.

Then it snaps.

Our mouths collide, hot and needy. I force my tongue against his, wrapping my hands around his neck as he grabs the bottom of my thighs and picks me up.

But after a few steps toward the bed, he stops, pulling his mouth away. His bitable bottom lip is plump and swollen.

"Too bad it was just a one-time thing, huh, little Demon?"

When he makes to put me down again, I cling to him.

"Fine," I groan. "A two-time thing."

He chuckles, hoisting me back up. "I think we can do better than that, little Demon."

I put my hands on his cheeks and raise an eyebrow. "Yeah?"

"Oh, aye. Two or three times tonight. At least."

I laugh, wrapping my legs around his waist as he carries me to bed.

Chapter Twenty-Eight

My room is dark, only a slither of moonlight creeping in through a gap in the curtains. Crow's arm rests heavily over my stomach as I look at the ceiling. Then he grabs my right hand and turns away, pulling me onto my side. My university mattress creaks and dips.

"Spoon me," he says.

I laugh. "How very masculine," I say, brushing my fingers against his warm chest.

He chuckles, wriggling his butt against my pelvis. "Masculinity is a social construct, little Demon. And everyone likes to be little spoon. Only, I never get to be on account of my *large size.*"

I hear the innuendo and choose to ignore it. "Must be tough for you."

"Aye. It is."

I run my fingers up and down his arm, feeling the hard muscles. He makes a low, contented sound as I pause on his shoulder, circling his lily tattoo. I study it for a moment, intricate and beautiful. Then I brush my lips over it.

He tenses, then he rolls over and roughly maneuvers me so that our positions are reversed.

"I thought you wanted to be little spoon," I say.

"Aye. But you were right. I felt very emasculated," he says in my ear.

"Mmm. What's the meaning behind your tattoo?"

"Well," he says, stroking my belly, "I got the feathers after I became an Omen. Crows are kind of my specialty, if you hadn't guessed."

"And the flower?"

"Liked the look of it when I was in the tattoo shop," he says.

"Liar," I say.

He doesn't say anything for a minute.

"Fine," he says. "I got it for my mum. It was her favorite flower."

He paused before the word *mum*. I'm not sure if it's because he's not used to being open with people or whether he's not being truthful. But then, why would he lie about something like that?

I put my hand over his and squeeze. "I like it," I say.

He brushes my hair off my shoulder so he can study my tattoo.

"What about you, little Demon?" he says. "Why a peacock feather?"

"I really like peacocks," I say.

"Liar." He kisses my neck, his stubble rough against my skin.

"I don't like talking about stuff," I say.

"I noticed."

"I barely know you."

"I dunno." He kisses the back of my neck again. "I think we've gotten to know each other pretty well over the past couple of days . . ."

"It's not the same."

"Aye. I know," he says with sincerity. He brings his hand back around to my stomach and pulls me closer. "It's something to do with your brother, right?"

"Yeah." I exhale and put my hand over his, lacing our fingers together. "You really want to know?"

"Only if you want to tell me."

I pause, searching for the words. "Growing up, my parents put a lot of academic pressure on us. They never did the whole college thing, and they wanted us to have opportunities they never felt they had. Lucky for them, Jonathon was a prodigy. He was ten years older than me, and so it always felt like I grew up in his shadow. I was always 'Jonathon's little sister.' It didn't help that I was a shit student, nothing like him at all. I couldn't focus. As soon as people realized that, it was like they gave up on me; like I was invisible."

"Sounds rubbish."

"Yeah. I never held it against him though. I idolized him. He was my cool big brother. He always stood up for me with my parents, and he'd help me with my homework and let me hang out with his friends—at least, until he went to college. He graduated early, then went and did a PhD in computer science while working for a tech company over in San Francisco. I didn't have anyone to take the pressure off me anymore. And I always felt like being myself wasn't good enough somehow. When I was thirteen—"

I stop, my whole body tensing at the memory.

"What happened?" Crow asks gently.

"I was going through a hard time," I say. "It was like a shadow swallowed me. And it's not because of Jonathon," I add quickly, feeling the need to say it. "But I started acting out. Doing stupid stuff. Getting into trouble, hanging out with older kids. One time, they dared me to swim in the River Hudson."

I sink my teeth into my bottom lip, a heaviness settling on my chest.

"It was winter, and I . . . I nearly drowned," I say. "Jonathon was back visiting at the time. When I didn't come home, he came to find me and saw me in the water. Saved my life. Pulled me out himself and got me to hospital. But I got pneumonia. The doctors thought I was going to die, but I somehow managed to pull through."

I take a deep breath. The next words catch in my throat, thick and heavy and wrong. This is not something I talk about.

Crow strokes my stomach, his breathing a steady rise and fall against my back. It's calming enough that I can continue.

"After that, Jonathon decided to stay home. He pretended it wasn't because of me, but I knew it was. He made me go to therapy, to share my feelings instead of acting out. He took me to the sessions. It helped a lot. And after each session, he'd take me to the Bronx Zoo, and we'd get an ice cream and talk. And I started to feel better, like myself again.

"Anyway, we found this peacock there. He used to slink around the cafe with his feathers all tucked up and trailing behind him on the floor. We saw him every time. It was stupid, really, but we became obsessed with seeing him fan them out."

I take a deep breath, steeling myself for what's coming.

"Then, on my last day of therapy, he finally did it. He finally fanned them out right in front of us—all these beautiful colors. It felt like a sign from Heaven or something; a sign that everything was going to be okay. And I felt happy. Really happy. Hopeful, even. As he was strutting around the place, one of his feathers fell out, and Jonathon picked it up. He gave it to me. Told me to hold onto it, and to remember to hold onto hope. And I would have. I would have held onto the feather. Only, Jonathon left to go back to San Francisco a few days later. And on the way. . ."

The words clog up in my throat. My eyes start to burn.

"On the way to the airport, he was hit by a car." I squeeze my eyes shut to stop the tears. "He died instantly. And, stupidly, I dropped the feather onto his coffin when we buried him. And so

168

that's why I got the tattoo. Because I got rid of the feather he told me to keep. And because I miss him. And because . . . *it was all my fault."*

Despite everything, tears spill down my cheeks. Tears I've been holding in for so long. It's as if a dam has broken, and all the emotion I've been trying to bury along with Jonathon floods in.

"No." Crow turns me around and pulls me to him, pushing my head to his chest. "No. It wasn't your fault, little Demon," he says into my hair. "It wasn't your fault."

My body shakes against his chest. One hand cradles the back of my head; the other strokes my back. All the while, he makes soft, soothing noises.

I don't know how long we lie like this until my breathing steadies. Finally, though, I give a muffled half-laugh.

"I bet you wish you never asked," I say, voice thick.

"No. I'm glad you told me," he says, serious. He pulls back a little so he can tilt my chin up with his finger.

I avert my gaze, embarrassed. My eyelids are swollen, my face wet.

"Look at me, little Demon."

When I do, his expression is serious.

"We're going to find your brother," he says, and his stormy gray eyes hold such ferocity that I can't help but believe him. "And he can tell you himself that it wasn't your fault."

I sniff, giving him a weak smile. "Yeah," I say. "Yeah. We'll find him."

"Come here." He rolls onto his back and pulls my head into the little nook between his shoulder and his neck. I lay my arm across his chest and hook one leg over his.

"Is that why you decided to do the whole law thing?" asks Crow after a while. He rubs circles into my skin with his thumb.

"I guess," I say. "I just wanted to make my parents proud. And after Jonathon died, they talked to a lot of lawyers, but the guy driving the car basically got away with it. I think maybe that

169

rubbed off on me; made me want to be someone who could fight for what's right and win. And law seemed suitably academic. But it only took a few semesters for my opinions to change. It's like you said before you took me into Devils Inc.—good and bad can be pretty arbitrary."

"I said that?"

I nod. "I started to wonder whether right and wrong were quite so clear-cut. And I started to see that bad people got away with stuff all the time, and good people sometimes went down for small things. That Richard Livingstone case Adalind's making me work on proves it. The guy's a shit, but it looks like he's going to Heaven because he's such a shit Hell doesn't want him. I'm not sure justice is entirely fair."

"The rules are rigged," says Crow, and I'm surprised to see his expression darken. When he sees me looking, though, he smiles. "So you don't actually want to do law, just find a way to prove yourself. How do you know your parents wouldn't be proud of you if you did something you were, y'know, good at?"

I kick his calf, and he yelps.

"Hey! Just saying!"

I sigh. "I guess I don't."

"What would you do? If you felt like you could choose?"

"I don't really know. That's the problem. Lucas thinks I should be studying film. I like movies. But what the hell could I do with a film major?"

"Maybe if you let go of your core desire—proving yourself—then you'd be free to do whatever you want to do. To be happy." He stares at the ceiling, but his focus seems faraway. For a moment, I wonder whether he's talking to me or himself. "You should talk to them."

"Hmm. Maybe." I change the subject. "You said you met him once. Jonathon."

"Aye."

"And that he didn't like you."

Crow chuckles. "No. He didn't."

I tilt my head to look at him, my forehead brushing against his chin. "Why?"

"I came across him a few years back," he says, trailing his fingers down my arm. "I was monitoring some of the senior Angels over at Halo Corp, hoping to catch them doing something naughty." He raises an eyebrow at me, lips twitching. "I reckoned I could blackmail them into giving me a Miracle."

"You wanted to blackmail an Angel?" I roll my eyes. "You really are a shit, you know?"

"Aye, I know. But Miracles fetch a lot of money on the black market."

"Stop looking so pleased with yourself," I say, suppressing my own smile. "It's not something to be proud of."

"Okay, sorry." He forces his face into a serious expression, though his eyes still have that glint. "Anyway, I noticed a few of them would disappear off the map for hours at a time. I reckoned that meant they were doing something they shouldn't be, so when your brother was in Los Angeles on business, I managed to get a meeting with him. Asked him to give me privileges to track users when they were offline." He pauses. "And when I say asked, I mean, tried to blackmail . . ."

I give him a hard look. "You tried to blackmail my brother?"

"Aye. I told him that not sharing meant he was covering up whatever these senior Angels were doing, and that I would cause a scandal. In return, he told me where to go."

I laugh. "You're the worst."

He has the nerve to look offended. "I told you before, I prefer diabolical."

"But it didn't work?" I say.

"Nah. But you can't blame a man for trying."

"You definitely *can* blame a man when the man is trying to do something *diabolical.*"

He laughs—a low, gruff sound that fills my small room.

"Is that what you want from him when we find him?" I say, tucking my head back against his chest. "To get those privileges on Afterlife?"

"Maybe that. Maybe money. I dunno, little Demon. I'm opportunistic. I'll take what I can get."

"What if he still doesn't give you anything?" I trace a circle on his torso. "I doubt he'll be very happy if he finds out what you've been doing to his little sister."

Crow chuckles. "Aye. I suppose not." He stares up at the ceiling. "If I can't get anything from him, I suppose I'll just move on to my next dastardly plan," he says. "Got to kill time somehow."

"'Cause you're bored," I say.

"Aye." He brushes his lips against my forehead and smiles. "Although, not so much lately."

Chapter Twenty-Nine

"You're not dead," Adalind says when I skip class on Monday morning to come in early.

She's peeling an apple with a small blade, boots up on the desk. The green skin curls down in one long, twisting strand before falling onto a pile of memos beside her legs. The top one's subject line says, *"Re: Purgatory Vaults."*

"Surprise!" says Crow, leaning over the desk.

Though the sun beams brightly outside, the Demonic color scheme gives the atrium a gloominess that mirrors my feelings about being here. The air smells even eggier today too. I'm unsure if it's just the brimstone statue of Lucifer, or the stream of Demons walking to the elevators carrying breakfast sandwiches. Either way, it's unpleasant.

Adalind assesses Crow with her snakelike eyes before sliding her gaze to me. Then she sinks her teeth into the white flesh of her apple and chews.

173

"We need to get you a new blazer," she says, noticing the tattered one hanging over my arm. "You can't go around wearing that."

"Okay?" I reply, surprised. I expected a shitstorm. "You're not . . . mad?"

"Mad? I'm ecstatic you're okay," she says flatly. "Do you know how much paperwork your death would have required?"

"Oh. Right," I say.

She sighs. "Although, the value of the hit on you has increased. And, of course, I'm the one who has to babysit."

"What?" I hurriedly pull out my company cell.

"Yep." She tosses the half-eaten apple onto her desk, flicks the blade of the penknife back into its holster, then swings down her legs and gets up. "I'm not paid enough for this shit."

The image of me in my latex Demon outfit materializes on my screen. I really need to change that profile picture. Sure enough, the price on my head has increased—and drastically. It's now at fifty thousand dollars. Whoever is trying to draw out Jonathon is getting desperate.

"At least that's less insulting," I mutter.

"Aye," Crow says, leaning intimately over my shoulder. "Looks like they updated it this morning."

Adalind studies us, nose wrinkled. "What the Hell is this? Are you two—? Ugh."

For a brief moment, something seems to pass between her and my Omen, though I can't for the life of me figure out what it is. It's like they're sizing each other up.

Or something.

Surely, he hasn't slept with her too.

"Intern, come with me," Adalind says after an awkward beat. "Omen, pick her up at one. I'll keep her safe until then." She walks to the elevators, not bothering to see if I follow.

"I thought I was just coming in this morning to show you I'm not dead," I protest. "My shift doesn't start until this evening."

"I know," says Adalind. "I'm guessing the Demons who attacked you know that too. So you can get yourself murdered, or you can make yourself useful. You coming?"

I sigh.

"Looks like I'll resume my babysitting duties later, little Demon," says Crow.

"I don't need babysitting," I say, folding my arms across my chest. "I don't know if you remember, but I have super awesome powers now."

"Aye. And just how did you channel those powers?" he says with a wink. "I seem to recall giving you a little helping hand."

"You know nobody winks anymore, right?" I say. "I mean, it might have been all the rage in the Forties, but flirting has evolved."

His laugh causes a few of the disheveled souls waiting for appointments to look up in distress. "Aye? I'll make a note."

"Stop that. Both of you," snaps Adalind from the bank of elevators. "You're going to make me barf. And guess who would have to clean that up? Me. Get out of my reception, Omen."

Crow raises his hands in surrender. But not before shooting me another wink.

When I make it to the elevator, I turn to watch him go, only to find he's paused at the statue to watch us. His smile is gone, and his forehead is creased. Adalind's expression mirrors his, her posture stiff and alert for once.

Then the doors slide shut, and the elevator starts to move down.

There's something going on here, but Adalind's hostile face keeps me from asking. I have a better chance of finding out what the deal is from Crow—although, if it's some sordid history, I'm not sure I want to.

A few seconds later, the doors slide back open, and I know immediately that something isn't right. Shrouded in darkness, the air is deathly still. Clenching my hands into fists, I remember what

175

Crow taught me about Sin as I try to build up enough anger to protect myself.

Which isn't hard, seeing as Adalind is clearly leading me into a trap.

Heat shoots through my veins, and I feel the telltale crackle at my fingertips. But when I turn to ask her what the Hell she thinks she's doing, her inhuman eyes are wide and trained on my fists.

If I didn't know any better, I'd think she was afraid.

She quickly trains her expression back to disdain. "Oh, relax," she says, stomping out onto the floor. As lights flick on automatically, I see we're in a windowless space lined with rows of towering shelves. "Why would I kill you? What use would you be to me then? Come on."

Rubbing my palms against my jeans to cool them, I follow. More lights flick on as we walk.

"What is this place?" I ask.

"Legal archives," she says as she unlocks a room whose door bears a plaque reading, *"GENESIS."* She flicks on a light.

The small room looks like the victim of a tornado. It's messier than my bedroom pre-Gabriel. Although shelves line the wall, cardboard file boxes are scattered across the floor, their parchments strewn everywhere. I spot a box labeled, *"CAIN: GUILTY,"* and another one, empty, reading, *"EVE: NON-DISCLOSURE."*

"Why have you brought me here?" I ask, fearing the reason may be even worse than murder.

"Some moron messed the place up a year or so back." She leans against the doorframe and studies her bitten fingernails. "It needs sorting. Match the papers with their folders. They're labelled. Then organize them chronologically." When I grimace, she gives me a hard look. "What do you expect? I have to keep you out of the way. This place is crawling with Demons, in case you haven't noticed. Can't trust a single one of them. And seeing as you proved incapable of collecting a few coffees—"

"I was attacked," I snap.

She rolls her eyes. "Whatever. Just do this and stay safe, okay? I can't be assed with the paperwork if you get kidnapped and it all goes to shit."

"Your concern is touching," I say in a monotone.

In response, she stomps out, muttering how much she hates interns.

Staring at the mess around my feet, I sigh. A morning of this, then a contract law lecture this afternoon makes the prospect of fighting for my life at Apocalypse tonight seem like a step up. As I pick up the nearest folder, my work cell buzzes in my pocket.

It's a text featuring an emoticon of a bird, a Demon, a winky face, and an eggplant. The phone vibrates again as Crow's next message pops up.

Modern flirt. Did I do it right?

I shake my head, biting back a laugh. Then I stuff the phone back into my pocket and get to work.

***

By midnight, the three of us are sitting at one of the window tables at Evie's. Being a Monday, it's fairly quiet, but there are still a couple of students milling around the apple trees.

Crow's black leather jacket has made its reappearance. Paired with his day-old stubble and the dangerous look in his eye, he's really channeling the Bad Omen vibe.

Gabriel, on the other hand, has gone the other way with his wardrobe, wearing a fuzzy pastel-pink sweater that clashes horribly with his red hair. It's oversized enough to expose his collarbone, and there's a canvas bag at his feet reading, *"Save the Planet."* As he absently takes a slurp of his appletini, Crow asks the question for both of us.

"What are you wearing, mate?" he says. "We're off to fight some Demons, not go to a pajama party."

Gabriel's cheeks turn a new color that manages to clash with both sweater and hair. "I thought I'd better wear something I don't mind damaging. In case I have to provide you with backup or happen to get . . . emotional." He juts out his chin. "I don't want to ruin another perfectly good shirt, thank you very much."

"Fair enough." Crow chuckles and takes a sip of his beer. "Wings," he adds for my benefit, as if anyone could forget the last time Gabriel last lost his temper.

"Aren't you coming in with us?" I ask the Angel.

"They don't like me in there," he replies, looking out of the window. "They say I stick my nose in where it's not wanted."

"Can't imagine why," says Crow.

"Is that why you were in disguise last time?" I ask, remembering his inappropriate club attire last time I saw him there. "You know, my friend Lucas is a theater major. I could have got you a fake moustache from the costume department."

Gabriel's eyes brighten. "Really?"

"She's joking, Gabe," says Crow, playfully nudging me.

"Anyway, no, I thought I'd keep a look out from here," continues Gabriel. "I need to catch Evie anyway. At first, I assumed her Wi-Fi had been hacked, but I've heard rumors she's been more open to black market dealings since Adam left her. I'll find what she knows."

Crow nods once. "Aye. Good idea, mate."

Gabriel tries not to look pleased with himself as he stirs his appletini with the paper umbrella he requested for his drink. Apparently, it makes it taste better.

"I am prone to them on occasion," he mutters.

"Holy shit!" I say suddenly, feeling profoundly idiotic. "Evie . . . Eve!"

"Aye," Crow says slowly. "That's her name, little Demon."

I glance at Gabriel's drink and the bar's apple theme. "She's *the* Eve? As in, Adam and Eve? As in, the first woman Eve?"

Crow chuckles and leans back against the window, giving a slow clap. Even Gabriel smirks a little, although he tries to hide it.

"Give me a break," I say. "I'm new to all this. So is she an Angel or something?"

"No," says Gabriel.

"But she's immortal?" I ask.

"To an extent," says Crow.

"They call people like her Ethereals," says Gabriel, taking a sip of his drink. "There are a few others like her—our Horseman brothers, for example—who have been granted immortality for one reason or another. Eve and her ex-husband were the first man and woman on Earth, so their life forces are linked to all of mankind. They can't die of old age and can only be killed by someone with Greater-level powers, such as a Greater-level Demon or—"

"An Archangel," says Crow.

"Yes, well. . ." Gabriel goes back to fiddling with his umbrella. "Those with such power are constrained to Heaven or Hell. There are very few who can pass between, and even those who can only do so on certain occasions. Lucifer, for example, can only set foot on earth in the event of the Apocalypse."

"Speaking of which. . ." Crow tilts his head toward the club in question. "Must be almost closing time."

Gabriel nods sharply, then he looks at me. "Are you ready, Rachel?"

My work phone is already on the table, the Afterlife app open to my profile.

"Yeah," I say. I glance at Crow. "Good to go?"

"Aye."

I suck in a deep breath, then change my status from offline to online. My red pinpoint instantly pops up on the map of Trinity

Falls, conveying my exact location to every Demon and Omen looking to kill me.

Crow rises to his feet and grins. "Let's go fight some Demons, shall we?"

Chapter Thirty

When we enter Apocalypse's main room, Josie is wiping down the middle bar, while a redheaded guy stocks the towering shelf of liquors behind her. They're both in uniform: an off-white flannel shirt with black suspenders tucked into black riding-style leathers.

My stomach sinks. Josie should have left by now.

"Don't worry. I've got a plan," says Crow, detecting my unease.

Josie beams as we approach. "What you doing here, babe?" she says. "We're just closing."

"We thought we'd drop in and say hi," I say as Crow and I slide onto the barstools.

The tall guy stocking bottles turns. He's as good-looking as the other two brothers I've met but more disheveled, complete with stubble and tufty hair that looks like he's been carelessly running his fingers through it. His greenish-blue eyes are amplified by the neon lighting.

181

"Felix, mate, how you doing?" says Crow, leaning over the bar to shake his hand.

Felix. *Famine?*

As Felix meets Crow's firm grip, I notice tattooed scales inked on his forearm.

"Crow! How's it going? Saw you in here the other week with a busty blonde." His eyes glitter. "Was going to say hi, but you seemed . . . preoccupied."

I try to hide my irritation, but Josie catches it. She flashes them both a disapproving look before focusing on me.

"Want some drinks, babe? I need to finish closing up, but I'll join you after."

"Oh, no, thanks," I say, wanting to hasten her exit out of here. "Why don't you—?"

"I'll go for a beer, if you're offering," says Crow, ignoring my glare.

As she nods and turns to the fridge to pick up a couple of bottles, he turns to Felix. "Chris around, mate?"

Felix's smile holds, but it's gone cold. "Not at the moment. Why?"

"Just weird," says Crow. "What about William?"

I throw Crow a sideways glance as Josie returns with our drinks. He needs to stop needling this guy about things we're not supposed to know about and help me get Josie out of here.

"They're both a little preoccupied right now," says Felix.

"Oh, aye? That's unusual," says Crow. "Doing what?"

The smile disappears completely from Felix's face. "What's it to you?"

I squeeze Crow's thigh, digging my nails into the dark denim. His leg muscles harden, but his expression doesn't change.

"Played some cards with them a month or so back. They owe me some money," he says.

"I'll let them know when I see them," Felix says tersely.

"No need. I'll catch them another time."

"Right. Well, I best get back to work," he says. "Josie, I'm off to the cellar. You okay to wipe down the booths?"

"No problem," she says.

Once Felix is out of earshot, Crow leans forward to rest his elbows on the bar. "Oh, Josie, I almost forgot. I bumped into Darius on the stairwell. He wants to see you in his office."

Her eyes brighten.

After she exits the room, Crow spreads his hands. "Ta-da."

I turn my whole body to glare at him.

He chuckles. "What?"

"Well, first, you could have said that as soon as we sat down. And second, you just couldn't help yourself, could you? You had to antagonize one of the Four Horsemen of the freaking Apocalypse?"

He takes a sip of beer and shrugs. "Now we know Conquest and War both have their scrolls. Puts a bit more urgency on the whole thing, doesn't it?"

"Oh, right, you did it for information. Not just to be a dick."

He laughs. "Well, he brought up the blonde first. Dick move. He's been hanging out with his brother too much."

I take a sip of my Coke, then ask, nonchalant, "So does the busty blonde have a name?"

"Jealous?"

"No."

I stare at the wall of liquor in front of me, focusing on the little symbols carved into the glass shelves. But thanks to the mirror behind the bottles, I know Crow's eyes are on me.

"You wish I was jealous," I add.

"Aye. I do a bit." When I turn to him, surprised, his eyes glint. "I like it when you're all wound-up, little Demon."

"Well, I'm not. Have all the busty fun you want." I take another sip of my Coke. "It's no business of mine. Unless, of course, she's your girlfriend or something. In which case, it would only be a courtesy to let me know."

He grins. "Nah. Nothing like that."

"Wait—is this the same blonde I saw you making out with the other night?"

"Nah. Different one."

"You like blondes then?"

He shrugs. "I like you. But aye, I usually go for blondes."

He's clearly angling for some sort of reaction—which I'm not going to give. Although, I do think back to the weird moment between him and Adalind, my non-blonde Demon friend. I hesitate. Do I really want to know the answer to this?

"What about Adalind?" I ask.

"What about her?"

"Have you slept with her?"

He gives an exaggerated shudder. "Definitely not."

I search for signs of the lie, but I can't find any. "Really?"

"Aye, really. I'm not sure she even likes men." He takes another sip of his beer. "Not sure she likes women either, for that matter. Not sure she likes anyone." His forehead creases. "Why would you think something happened between us?"

I shrug. "There was a weird moment between you. I thought maybe it was a sex thing."

"Oh, right . . . that," he says.

I raise my eyebrows, relieved I didn't imagine the moment between them—because that would imply I care about Crow's sexual history.

And I definitely don't.

"So what was it then?" I say before he can interrupt. "And don't say you don't like explaining things. Remember, you want to remain in my good graces."

He raises his hands as if to say, "You're the boss," and then he sighs. "She thinks I'm up to something. One of my diabolical plans. And that made me think perhaps *she* is up to something."

I frown. "What do you mean?"

"She knows what I am, little Demon. A Bad Omen who doesn't do things unless they benefit me. But if I was going to kill you for the money, I'd have done it already. So I reckon she thinks I'm up to something even more diabolical."

"Well, she's not wrong. You are trying to get a favor off my brother."

"Aye. But she doesn't know that, does she? She shouldn't even know about the impending Apocalypse. The theft of the scrolls has been kept pretty hush-hush. Gabe's the only one who thinks there's anything wrong."

"So you're saying she must know something to know you're up to something?"

"Aye. Otherwise, why wouldn't she just think we were hooking up?" He rolls his eyes to mine and smiles. "Because, let's face it, I *am* a little bit slutty."

The corner of my lip twitches. "You said it."

He finishes his beer.

"I saw a memo on her desk about the Purgatory Vaults," I blurt, thinking back to this morning.

Crow raises an eyebrow. "Aye? Well, that's suspicious, isn't it? Maybe someone at Devils Inc. is making enquiries about the missing scrolls too."

"Wait a minute," I say, head snapping to Crow. "You thought Adalind, a super scary-ass Demon, might be somehow involved in the Apocalypse, and yet you were perfectly happy to let her lead me down into the depths of Devils Inc.? Thanks a bunch."

He chuckles. "Well, I didn't reckon she'd try anything at work. Plus, you'd win in a fight, hands down."

"Yeah, in a fair fight, maybe. But I'm guessing she's been a Demon a lot longer than me."

"True. But it wouldn't have been a fair fight."

"That's what I'm saying."

"No—you misunderstand me. I meant fair for Adalind. I don't know what the hell she did to piss off the higher-ups, but in addition to demoting her to reception, they took her powers. She's pretty much harmless."

My mind flashes back to the moment in the elevator when she'd looked almost scared of me.

"Maybe that's why she's so awful all the time," I muse. "Overcompensating."

"Aye. Probably." He pulls his cell out of his pocket and glances at the screen. His face darkens. "Gabe—"

"What are you two lovebirds talking about?" Josie says, balancing a tray of empty glasses as she slips back behind the bar.

A jolt of alarm surges through me. "I thought Darius wanted to see you."

"I went down to his office, but he wasn't there."

"I'm pretty sure it's important," says Crow. "Maybe you should go and wait."

She shrugs. "He knows where to find me."

The lighting of Apocalypse flickers, answering my question of what Gabriel was messaging about. My eyes dart to the entrance.

Josie sets down the tray. "You know the owners, I take it?"

The lights flicker again, and the temperature in the room seems to drop a few degrees. Josie glances up at the ceiling but doesn't seem concerned.

"Old friends," says Crow.

"So you work for the company Rachel is interning for?"

"In a way," says Crow. "I'm a consultant."

A low cracking sound starts as a river of black begins to snake over the mirror.

"Oh, shit," says Josie, touching the silver crucifix hanging around her neck. "Bad omen."

"Aye," agrees Crow, jaw set.

Shadows start to seep in under the door behind us. Crow's eyes meet mine in the mirror.

Then the whole warehouse plunges into darkness.

They're here.

Chapter Thirty-One

When the neon-blue lights of Apocalypse flash back on, our attackers are behind us. A dozen Omens and Demons, fanned across the back of the club.

Then the lights flash off again.

Josie yelps and there's the sound of smashing bottles. Heart pounding, I search for the anger that'll help me fight; the power that will help me protect Josie. It wasn't supposed to happen this way.

When blue light washes over the dance floor again, the Omens and Demons are closer. Josie rises to her feet behind the bar, eyes wide, gripping the small knife used to cut limes.

Then darkness again.

Anger builds in the pit of my stomach. Anger that these Omens have come for my life. Anger that they had the audacity to come here before we had a chance to get Josie to safety. Anger that someone is trying to draw out my brother.

Anger that my brother never came for me.

When the lights flash on again, there's a blond man right behind me, blade raised.

Cold air whooshes by as Crow blocks the hand about to slit my throat. Thrusting my head back, I break the Demon's nose with a crunch, then jump to my feet. As Crow spins him around, I thrust my crackling blue hand against his back. He goes flying across the room, skidding along the sticky dance floor.

"Rachel! What the hell!" says Josie, lurching over the bar to grab my wrist. "We need to get out of here!" She jerks her head toward the door marked "NO ENTRY." "There's a room back there. Come on."

That's when I see the ball of blue flame hurtling toward us in the mirror. Jumping over the bar, I push Josie down just as more bottles break, releasing the pungent scent of mixed alcohol. With a rush of heat, it ignites. Blue flames lick the floor near Josie's feet.

"Shit!" yells Josie as I scream for Crow.

He's still in front of the bar, drawing shadows from the room's corners until they surround him like a shroud. He sends them to us. There's a sizzling sound as the flames are swamped by darkness.

Josie's eyes are wide. "Rachel, what's—?"

I grab her face and make her look at me. "Stay down. When you get a chance, run to that door and get out of here. It's going to be all right."

She tries to hold me next to her, but I pull away and reenter the fight. I feel the crackle of power building up from my belly.

Beside me, Crow's fingers move almost imperceptibly, controlling the shadows until they form a barrier between us and our attackers. A brunette by the door hurls another ball of flame, but the wall of darkness rises to swallow it. When it simmers back down, no one moves.

My eyes do a sweep of the room. Eight of the intruders have shadows pooling at their feet. The rest have blue flames winding up their bare arms, and eyes that flash.

Heat burns through my body. I want to release it. I want to unleash Hell. But my gut tells me it's not time yet.

"Crow," caws a girl standing in the center. She wears black skinny jeans tucked into heavy-duty work boots, and her curly black hair is pulled back in a neat ponytail. Black pawprints trail from her left arm to her collarbone, and catlike shadows wind around her ankles. She grins. "Fancy seeing you here."

"Hey, KittyKat," says Crow. "It's been a while."

"That it has." She takes a step closer to Crow's barrier. "When I saw your name next to the target's on the map, I feared we were too late. Yet here she is. Alive."

"Aye. Here she is."

She grins. "Give her to me."

"Can't do that, KittyKat."

"And why's that?"

"Well, she's mine."

She laughs. "Come on, Crow. We'll do it together. Share the money. We've shared jobs before. It'll be like old times."

Crow only shakes his head. She watches him for a moment, then she touches his shadow barrier. A wisp of it curls around her fingers.

"You're not *protecting* her, are you?" she asks, seeming shocked. "You *are,* aren't you? Now, why would you be doing a thing like that?"

"Perhaps I know something you don't," he says.

"Katherine, can we just get on with this?" grumbles a dark-haired Omen at the back. "We—"

She raises her hand, and he shuts up.

"I don't want to fight you, Crow," she says.

"I don't want to fight you either, KittyKat."

She smiles, and the darkness at her feet begins to twine up her body. "There's going to be a fight though. All these people. And just the two of you. I don't fancy your chances."

"I think our chances are just fine."

Frowning, she studies the ball of shadow that has collected in her palm with an air of deliberation.

"Okay," she says. "You've convinced me. I want in on whatever deal you've spun to keep her alive."

Crow chuckles. "If I let you fight with me, you'll sink a knife into her back the moment I'm not looking."

She sighs. "Fine. If that's really the way you want to play this."

In a vicious movement, she hurls the ball of shadow at him. His barrier of darkness rises like a tidal wave to catch it, then crashes down on all of them.

There's a yell and the sound of bodies thudding to the floor, but Kat's hand rises from the writhing darkness. With a simple flicking movement, she shatters the mirror behind the bar completely.

Josie screams, and I have to duck, arms over my head, as shards of glass fly toward me and Crow.

As the darkness ebbs, the Omens and Demons start to rise. The blue lights flash on and off.

And then, chaos.

Katherine lunges, but Crow catches her and pins her to the bar with one arm. A blade flies at my face, and I stumble to the side, glass crunching beneath my feet. Three Omens run toward me, shadows rippling behind them like cloaks.

This time, I don't hesitate. Sweat rolling down my face, I scream and hurl a ball of flame.

The lights go off, and the air fills with grunts and shrieks. To my side, Crow whistles, loud and piercing.

Footsteps race toward me.

When the lights come back on, I'm ready. I land a right hook across the bloody face of the blond guy with a blade, and his dagger clatters to the floor. The next time, he comes at me with flames, but before I can react, I'm dragged by shadows toward the impatient dark-haired Omen. He wants the kill for himself.

Crow releases Kat and spins around. A wall of shadow sends both men reeling backward but stops when Kat pounces onto his back.

The lights flash off. Heart pounding against my ribs, I will a new set of flames to my fingers and hurl my next missile blindly. It hits a bearded Demon who was seconds from being at my throat, knocking him back to the wall. The neon-blue trumpet sign crashes to the ground.

I feel someone behind me. Heart in my throat, I spin, fist raised.

"Steady, little Demon," Crow says, catching my wrist.

Suddenly, we're cocooned by a protective tornado of darkness. Everything is muffled. I can smell him: sweat, leather, and darkness.

Both of us breathe hard.

"I don't think Josie's escaped," I say. "We should have made sure she wasn't working! And how are we supposed to kill them all?"

"We aren't," he says. "We just have to stay alive for a bit longer. Couple more minutes, I reckon."

Our shadow barrier jolts as someone tries to punch through. Crow winces, his face flushed.

"What happens in a couple of minutes?" I say.

"You'll see," he says, jerking back when flames surge up from my hands.

"What do you mean, 'You'll see'?" I demand.

He chuckles, though the sound is strained. "That's right. Get angry. You need it." He grunts as the tornado shudders again. "Can't hold it much longer."

The flames grow in my hand. *"Me neither."*

"Ready?" he asks.

I nod, jaw clenched.

He lets go of my wrist, and we both spin around, our backs touching. I throw my growing ball of fire at the same time Crow sends his tornado hurtling forward. Mine knocks the blond Demon into the wall, while Crow's causes Kat to dive out of the way and a few Omens to scatter.

Back-to-back, we fight, hurling shadow and flame. My heart pumps fire through my veins, and adrenaline makes my body buzz.

There's a smashing sound, and I notice a new stream of liquid snaking over the floor. I throw a fireball at it, and blue flames whoosh up around the club, engulfing a couple of Omens.

"Not sure that was the best idea, little Demon," singsongs Crow as the flames get closer.

"Yeah. I'm having second thoughts too," I say as heat licks my foot.

Then, suddenly, the flames disappear, and the whole club plunges into darkness. The temperature drops, and the hairs on my arms stand on end. A terrible feeling overcomes me, worse than anything I've ever felt—even in the dark times before and after Jonathon's death. Horror and emptiness. Nothingness.

Crow's back tenses against mine. He feels it too.

There's a murmur of confusion. The Omens and Demons pause their attack.

Then the scraping sound of a metal blade being dragged along the floor fills my ears.

"Enough."

The low voice seems to come from everywhere and nowhere at once.

The club lights flicker on, painting the scene of destruction in a cool blue glow.

A man stands in the center of the dance floor. He has black hair, short at the sides and curly at the top, and he holds a scythe upside down, his big fist curled around the ornate black handle. There are symbols inked onto his knuckles.

The air around us is cold enough that my ragged breath puffs in front of my face.

The man's dark eyes survey the room, sliding over the smashed bottles and damage to the walls and booths. Tension hangs like a shroud over us all.

"Are you all lost?" he says calmly as he rights his scythe and drags one finger over the blade. "Do you forget yourselves? Do you forget who owns this club?"

Death.

Kat stands nearest to him, and when she doesn't lower her gaze, he brings the scythe to her throat, stopping just before it cuts her skin. Her eyes widen. Crow jerks as if to help her, then stops himself.

"Perhaps you forget that my scythe can bring about a fate even worse than the Hell you are all headed for," he says. "Perhaps I should remind you."

"Darius, mate . . ." Crow starts.

Darius holds Kat's eyes for a moment longer, then he pulls his scythe away.

"Everybody out," he says. "Last orders were over an hour ago."

Our attackers can't get out of the club fast enough, fighting to be the first out of the wooden door and up the stairs. The last one out is Kat, who pauses in the doorway and looks over her shoulder, eyes lingering on Crow for a moment before she too disappears.

Twirling the scythe, Darius looks at Crow. "I might have known you'd be involved in this, my old friend. I'm very interested to know why you brought this *mess* into my club."

When Crow doesn't answer, Darius's eyes slide to me. Something clenches in my chest when I meet his gaze. It's like looking into an abyss.

"And who have we here?" He puts the blade of the scythe beneath my chin, tilting my head upward when I try to avert my gaze.

"Darius, mate," Crow says again, placing a protective arm in front of me.

The humor leaves Darius's eyes.

"Don't assume such familiarity with me, boy." He pulls away the scythe and holds it to Crow's neck instead. *"I know exactly what you're all about. I know the damnation of your soul. You bring this horde of fools to my place and expect me to sort out your mess. I am he who will bring doom and salvation upon this world. And you dare—"*

"Darius?" says a high female voice.

Darius swiftly pulls away his weapon.

Josie stands behind the bar, her black hair wild and glittering with small specks of glass from the broken mirror. Her flannel shirt is splattered with alcohol, and there's a small cut on her cheek. She's still holding the small knife used to cut limes.

"Is someone going to tell me what the *hell* is going on?" she demands.

A muscle twitches in Darius's jaw. "Josie, darling," he says. "I think it's about time we had a little chat."

She folds her arms across her chest. "Yes, babe. I think it is."

Chapter Thirty-Two

Darius takes a step away from Crow and me. "Josie, darling, this may be hard for you to believe. But I am—"

"Death. One of the Four Horsemen of the Apocalypse," says Josie, eyes blazing. "Yeah, I gathered that much."

Darius's shoulders sag a little. It could be my imagination, but he seems disappointed his big identity reveal is ruined. "Oh. Since when?"

Josie ducks under the bar, shaking her head.

"There's been some weird stuff going on since I started working here, babe," she says. "But the final clue was *that* monstrosity." She glares at the scythe, causing Darius's fist to clench around it. Then her eyes flick to me, and the sudden hurt behind them makes my chest feel heavy. "That doesn't explain why my best friend is involved in all this though. Or why the guy she's hooking up with is shooting shadows out of his hands." She looks at Darius. "Or why *you just threatened her.*"

Josie prods Death in the chest. Despite him being a head taller, several degrees more muscular, and a scythe-wielding harbinger of doom, he looks a little scared.

"Josie, darling," he says, attempting a reassuring smile. "I can see you're upset—"

"Don't you start acting like I don't have a damn good reason to be upset," she says, waving at the scythe. "And you can put that thing away when you're talking to me too."

Darius starts to glower, but when that only makes Josie's chin tilt higher, he turns it on Crow and me. Once again, I'm awash with the feeling of emptiness.

"You two had better be gone when I get back," he says, his voice like ice. "I need to have a conversation with my employee."

Then he strides across the dance floor, glass crunching beneath his shoes, and exits through the *"NO ENTRY"* door at the back.

Crow squeezes my shoulder. "I'm going to check on Gabe. Tell him we're okay. I'll wait for you outside. Be quick."

With that, he leaves me alone with my best friend.

We stare at each other, tension thick. Josie said she'd been noticing weird things ever since she started working here. I wonder if we both have been keeping secrets.

Then something breaks, and she throws her arms around me.

"What's going on, Rach?" she asks when she pulls back.

"I accepted a contract I shouldn't have," I blurt "The internship I got. It's for a company run by the Devil. I signed away my soul."

A strangled cry escapes her lips. "Why didn't you tell me?"

"I wanted to. I couldn't."

The sound of footsteps causes Josie to glance over her shoulder at the "NO ENTRY" door. She puts a hand on my arm.

"You should go."

"You're going to be okay?"

"Darius won't hurt me."

"Are you sure?"

"Positive."

Feeling numb, I let her pull me into one more quick hug. As the door opens, she nudges me toward the exit.

Crow waits for me outside. He stares at the dark front of Evie's over the road, though his thoughts seem to be elsewhere. There's an uncharacteristic frown playing on his lips. He starts when I touch his arm.

"You okay?" I ask him.

He forces a smile. "Aye. Fine. Make sure you set your Afterlife status back to offline."

As we walk through the door of Crow's apartment ten minutes later, I realize I'm still anxious. Even though Darius seemed pretty in awe of Josie, I'm having my doubts we should have left her alone.

"Well, that was fun." Crow was uncharacteristically quiet on the way home, so his voice startles me.

He tosses his keys onto a side table and turns on a dim table lamp while I pull out my cell. I slid my status to offline as soon as Crow told me to, but now I find myself compulsively checking. When I look up, he's staring at me.

"Your friend'll be fine," he says. "She's one of them now. He'll look after her."

"You don't know that."

"I do know that."

Heat surges through my body. "How can you possibly know? We left her with someone who calls himself *Death!* I don't know if you noticed, but he had a freaking scythe and everything." *And if something happens to her, it'll be my fault. Just like what happened to Jonathon was my fault.*

"I noticed, little Demon. But Darius doesn't lie. Ever."

Shadows flicker across his face, highlighting the faint line across his throat where Darius held the scythe to his neck. For all his reassurances, he's tense as well. Something has bothered him. Just as I'm bothered.

When he puts a hand on my shoulder, I feel his heat through the sleeve of my leather jacket. Closing the door behind me, he steers me up against it, then he puts his leg between mine, holding me there.

"You're upset," I accuse.

"So are you," he says, his palms now on either side of me, making a cage.

I place my hand on his chest, looking up into his eyes as he rests his forehead against mine. My breathing quickens.

"Shall we talk about it?" he says.

I glare up at him. "No."

"Good."

I pull him forward at the same time he claims my mouth with his.

Somewhere in the back of my mind, a voice tells me this isn't a healthy way to deal with everything going on—but then Crow bites my earlobe, and I cry out. His low grunt vibrates through my body as I slide my hands beneath his shirt to scratch at his back.

It's a relief to let my mind shut down.

***

Later, we lie in a tangle of covers, our clothes now part of the mess spilling out of the wardrobe.

"We should talk," I say as he strokes my shoulder absently.

"Aye? About what?"

We need to figure out what the hell is going on between us, but I don't want to. If I try to rationalize this, it has to stop, because I still don't trust him. Yet a horrible part of me likes being around him.

"A lot of things, probably," I say.

He tilts his head down to meet my eyes. "Go on then."

199

"You were upset when we got back from Apocalypse."

"So were you."

"You know why I was upset. I'm worried about Josie," I say. "But what about you?"

He doesn't reply.

"It's something to do with that girl, isn't it?"

He frowns. "Girl?"

"Yeah. The Omen from the club. You almost went to her rescue when Darius threatened her. What was her name? Kat or something?"

His eyebrows lift in genuine surprise. "It's nothing to do with her. It was what Darius said about my soul. He said he knew the damnation of my soul. And like I said, he doesn't lie." Crow meets my eye. "I mean, I always presumed my soul was damned, but it stings a bit to have it confirmed."

"Oh." I stroke his chest. "You *could* always try to be a better man. Get sent to the other place."

"Aye." He doesn't sound convinced. "Or I could be so terrible that Hell doesn't want me and makes a case to keep me out."

"Hmm . . . Maybe let's start with my plan first."

He chuckles, brushing his lips against my forehead. "Maybe. You're forgetting something though. If I *do* redeem my soul, little Demon, it means I won't be able to hang out with you come Judgement Day."

"You're forgetting something too," I say.

"What's that?"

"Gabriel's helping me get my soul back." I prop myself up on my elbow. "Do you think he'll actually manage it?"

"He's always come through for me," says Crow. "Oh. Speaking of which, I had a chat with him while you were still with Josie."

"He get any information from Evie?"

"She wouldn't say much, apparently. But she *did* say, 'It starts with an apple.' Whatever that means. It was enough for Gabe to head off to 'investigate' the forbidden fruit in the Purgatory Vaults."

My mouth twitches. I imagine him dressed as Sherlock Holmes, heading over to the Purgatory Vaults with a giant magnifying glass.

"That's weird," I say. "What would an apple have to do with anything?"

"No idea. Could be nothing." He pulls me back into his arms, and I stifle a yawn. It must be the early hours of the morning by now.

"So who is she then?" I ask. "A friend? An ex?"

"An old friend," says Crow.

"*You* have a friend?"

He chuckles. "I know. Surprising, isn't it?"

After he pulls up the covers, I turn on my side, and he spoons me.

"How did that happen?" I ask sleepily.

"Well, although I thought she was hot, she didn't seem interested in me at all. Which, of course, drove me mad."

I pinch his hand at my waist. "What's wrong with you?"

"So many things, little Demon." He laughs, his breath warm against the back of my neck. "Anyway, finally understood why when I saw her with some girl outside Apocalypse. Turns out she likes women as much as I do. By that point, though, I'd spent so much time getting to know her that I ended up liking her. And I didn't want all my efforts to be for nothing, did I? So we stayed friends." He pauses. "In an Omen way, of course. Don't trust her in the slightest." There's a note of respect in his tone when he says it.

"What a beautiful story," I say. "She said she hadn't seen you for a while?"

"Nah. Not been doing many jobs for Omens Limited of late. Other things taking up my attention."

"Like Apocalypses," I say.

"Aye." He grins, pulling me closer. "Apocalypses. And little Demons."

***

When I wake, it's with a start and the realization something's wrong. I reach for Crow, but the space beside me is empty, nothing there but a dip in the mattress.

A clatter comes from the living room.

"Mate! You've got it wrong!" Crow's voice says, followed by a thud and a grunt.

I jump out of bed and pull on a black T-shirt and sweats I find on the floor, anger and adrenaline surging through my veins. With it comes the crackle of energy I've not quite gotten used to yet.

There's another clash as something topples over.

"You piece of shit!" a male voice cries. "If you've hurt her—"

Flinging open the door, I raise my hand in preparation to strike.

And then I freeze. The room sways, and my heart pounds so hard in my ears that I can't hear what's going on.

Crow is on his knees, naked except for black sweats he must have pulled on to go investigate our intruder. There's a cut across his eyebrow, and his skin is flushed. Old mail is scattered across the carpet, and the breakfast stool has been knocked on its side. His muscular arm is raised protectively over his face. While his attacker is no physical match for him, Crow makes no attempt to fight back.

The intruder wears neat dark jeans and a red San Francisco 49ers hoodie that I know from personal experience smells like the takeout food he used to subsist on. His soft mouth is turned down at the corners, and his light brown hair is wild.

He doesn't look a day over twenty-three.

The age he was when I last saw him.

The age he was when he died.

"Jonathon?" I croak.

They both turn their heads toward me.

As Jonathon's eyes meet mine, a mixture of emotion crosses his face. Still on the floor, Crow twists his fingers, and my shadow curls up from the ground to snuff the ball of flame.

"Jonathon?" I say again.

His fist drops to his side.

He gives me a weak smile.

"Hey, sis," he replies.

Chapter Thirty-Three

Jonathon looks exactly the same as I remember, only less fuzzy around the edges; more *real.* My eyes flit from his round brown eyes, to his neat eyebrows, to the scuffs on the toes of his sneakers. I must look so different to him now. I was a child when he died.

For the first few moments, we do nothing but stare at one another. And then something snaps.

Rushing forward in tandem, we collide in a hug so hard the air is knocked from my lungs. As Jonathon pulls me close, I bury my face in his shoulder and take big shuddering sobs, breathing in the familiar smell of his old red sweatshirt.

"I've missed you so much," he says, the words muffled against my hair. I mumble something incoherent about thinking I'd never see him again.

When I pull back, his eyes are watery and bloodshot.

He smiles. I smile back.

And then I punch him in the shoulder.

"Um. Ow?" he says, rubbing his arm.

"Seven years!" I say, stepping back. "Seven years, I've grieved for you. Where the hell have you been?"

"Rach," he says, voice pained. "I couldn't. You know that."

"Don't give me that shit. You couldn't risk checking in on me *once*? Do you have any idea what it's been like?" I take a shuddering breath. "Do you have any idea what it's like to lose someone you love?"

"I do. I've missed you so much." He tries to put a hand on my arm, but I jerk away. "God, I've missed you every single day, Rach. It's been so hard—"

I fling my arms up. "Then why didn't you visit me?"

He runs a hand over his mouth, pinching his bottom lip the way he always did when we were kids and he was hiding something from our parents. "I just couldn't, Rachel, okay? I just couldn't."

"Why? What possible reason—?"

"He didn't want his Miracle reversed," says Crow.

We both turn our heads to look at him. He's on his feet now, leaning against the breakfast bar as he studies his fingernails. A trickle of blood runs down the side of his face from the cut where Jonathon hit him.

"You stay out of it," snaps my brother. "You're not part of this conversation."

Crow looks up at Jonathon slowly. "Not wrong though, am I, mate?"

My brother is suddenly fascinated by his old sneakers.

"You exchanged a Miracle for your soul?" I ask quietly. I was so fixated on the desire to see him again that I didn't think things through properly. For him to have been an employee at Halo Corp., he must have entered into a legal agreement with an Angel.

He touches his mouth again. "Yeah," he says. "Yeah. I did."

"What could you possibly have wanted?" I say, my voice rising again. "What could possibly be more important than letting me know you were okay?"

He sighs. "It doesn't matter, Rach. I'm here now."

"It. Matters." A building anger buzzes beneath the surface of my skin. "If you can't say why, you may as well leave," I snap.

"Rach—"

"Go on! Get out!" I don't mean it. I don't know why I'm saying it. If he leaves, it'll wrench my heart back out, and I don't know if I'll be able to put it back in again. And yet . . . "Just go!"

He raises his hands. "Fine. If that's what you want. I'll go."

He turns and strides to the door, shoulders stiff. Tears cloud my vision, and blue flames lick at my hands. I can't get rid of them. They burn.

Jonathon opens the door.

Is he seriously going to go?

But instead of leaving, he just stands there.

The shadow from the couch twists up my arm and puts out the flames. I feel relief—at the cooling sensation, and the fact Jonathon is still here.

"You going to tell her, mate, or am I?" says Crow. "We all know you're not really going to leave. And she's not going to calm down until you tell her. Which means I'm stuck with a domestic going on in my flat when I'd much rather be in bed."

Jonathon turns and shuts the door, jaw clenched. "I'm protecting her," he says.

"Aye? And look how that's worked out. She's sold her soul to the Devil, and people are trying to kill her. Because they're looking for you. Maybe if she knew from the start what you'd done—"

"I couldn't risk it."

"Risk what? What the hell's going on!" I cry, wiping my eyes.

"She can handle it," says Crow. "Just tell her, mate, and be done with it."

Jonathon sighs and runs a hand over his mouth. Then he walks toward me to gently take me by both arms.

"Okay," he says. "Okay. Look. Do you remember that time when you . . . you went in the river, and I took you to hospital? It

206

was pretty touch-and-go for a while. The doctors said . . . they said that you weren't going to make it."

"When I came around, they said my recovery was miraculous," I murmur, my voice barely carrying in the small space between us.

"Yeah," says Jonathon softly. "Yeah, they did."

I swallow, my throat feeling thick and wrong.

"In the darkest hour, I prayed," says Jonathon. "I'd never prayed before in my life—never believed in gods or angels or prayers. I believed in science." He lets out a short laugh that doesn't quite meet his red-rimmed eyes. "But the whole point of science is testing things, isn't it? Adjusting your methods. Trying everything until something sticks. And it seemed we were out of options. So I got on my knees, and I prayed you'd pull through. Told whoever might be listening that I'd do anything if they'd help bring you back.

"Not long after, a guy came in wearing blue doctors' scrubs. Told me he was an Angel and he'd come to answer my prayer. Said his organization had been keeping an eye on me for a while and that they wanted to make an investment in my soul. He presented me with paperwork. A Miracle for a soul." Jonathon shrugs. "I was skeptical, but I signed it. Seemed worth a try." He smiles a watery smile. "And then he touched your forehead, and you woke up."

He lets go of my arms and takes a small step back. "So that's why I didn't come find you after I died. I was scared they would reverse the Miracle. Even when I got out of the Halo Corp. contract and started working for myself, I was still terrified they'd take away that gift. I couldn't risk your life."

My chest feels heavy. "Then it was my fault," I say. "It's my fault you died. All of this is because of me."

No. I died because some asshole was texting while driving. It had nothing to do with any of this, and certainly nothing to do with you. Signing away your soul to Angels is hardly a terrible thing anyway."

Something eases inside of me a little. "I guess." I turn on Crow, still leaning on the counter. "You knew I was his Miracle?"

He gives a half-shrug. "I guessed when you told me about your tattoo."

"Why didn't you tell *me?*"

"Wasn't my story to tell," he says simply, then he turns to my brother. "If you don't mind me asking, how did you get out of your contract with Halo Corp.?"

Jonathon's mouth tightens. "Redemption Clause."

Crow nods as though that makes perfect sense. "Because you sacrificed your soul in exchange for Rachel's."

"You?" Jonathon asks.

"Devils Inc. murdered me."

Jonathon nods as though that too makes perfect sense. Then Crow pushes off from the counter.

"So did you come here to check I wasn't murdering your sister?" he asks. "Or do you have some information to share that will shed some light on who's looking for you and what it has to do with the Apocalypse?"

"Both," says Jonathon.

A smile spreads across Crow's face. "Excellent. I'll just go put a shirt on—"

"Please do," says Jonathon.

"Then we can have a nice little chat. Rachel, there are some beers in the fridge. Jonathon, make yourself comfortable."

As he disappears into the bedroom, I note how he didn't call me "little Demon" in front of my brother. I look at Jonathon, suddenly feeling awkward. This is the first time I've seen him in years, and he's just caught me in bed with a decidedly older, morally dubious Omen.

"Want a beer?" I ask him.

"Yeah. Yeah, please." He gives me a weak smile. "I think we're all going to need it."

Chapter Thirty-Four

What are you supposed to say when you reunite with the genius big brother who died seven years ago?

Even though I take my time getting the beers, holding my nose against the smell, I still haven't figured it out by the time I hand one over the breakfast bar. Judging by his terse smile, Jonathon's having trouble figuring out where to start as well.

I take a sip of mine. He takes a sip of his.

Jonathon's smile warms. He opens his mouth then shuts it again.

"What?" I say.

"Never thought I'd get to share a beer with my little sister," he says.

I smile back, then take another sip, not sure what to do with my hands.

"So," says Jonathon. "What you been up to?"

"Well, I'm studying law now, which it turns out I suck at because I accidentally signed my soul away to the Devil in exchange for free Wi-Fi. And a load of people are trying to kill me. You?"

"Well, I died, created an app that can track any Ethereal being in the world, and went on the run for a year in an attempt to save the world."

I shake my head, lips twitching. "You always had to one-up me, didn't you?"

He laughs, and I can tell it surprises him, as if he hasn't found anything funny in a while. Then a heavy silence falls once more.

"How are Mom and Dad?" he says.

"They lost their son."

He sighs and bows his head. "I know."

"You didn't check up on them either," I say.

"I wanted to. It was too hard." He lifts his gaze from the granite counter. "I did check up on you though. From time to time. How do you think you managed to get a private dorm room?"

"Are you serious?" I say. "Josie did always say that was a miracle."

He lets out a half-laugh. "Not a miracle. But I *have* developed some pretty good hacking skills. I was surprised you went into the law program though."

"Right, because I'm not smart enough—"

"Shut up, Rach. You're hella smart. I just didn't think it would hold your interest. I hope you're not doing it just to impress Mom and Dad."

Irritation flares inside me. "You don't get to come here and just start telling me how to live my life. You have no idea what it's been like since you've been gone—"

"I know, I know. I'm sorry." He raises his hands. "I just mean . . . I know they can pile on the pressure. But they're not bad people. They only do it because they want to help. They've always been proud of you, you know?"

My throat feels thick as the bedroom door opens and Crow strolls out wearing a navy-blue hoodie zipped to his collar. There's a smudge of blood on his cuff from where he wiped at his eyebrow.

"Well, this is awkward," he says, starting to pick up a few of the letters scattered across the carpet. When he drops them on the counter in front of me, I notice they have charity logos stamped in the headers. I also notice Crow is standing way too close. I nudge away from him and go sit on the other breakfast stool beside Jonathon, not wanting it to look as if Crow and I are a couple.

"Sorry about that," Jonathon says, his eyes on Crow's cut. Not that he sounds particularly sorry.

"No problem, mate. I probably deserved it." Crow leans in the corner of his kitchenette, one hand by the sink, the other holding a beer he's just grabbed from the fridge. "Floor's all yours."

Jonathon turns to me. "I'm sorry about the Wi-Fi situation. I should have seen something like this coming."

"So we were right," I say. "Someone recruited me to try and find you?"

"Yeah." He runs a hand over his mouth. "I shouldn't have come here now. Only, I saw on the map you were with *him*." He nods his head in Crow's direction while pointedly keeping his eyes on me. "Thought he must be trying to kill you. Got here as soon as I could."

As he shakes his head, his hair ruffles with the movement. He always let himself get a bit disheveled whenever he was studying, too busy with all his projects to do something as trivial as getting a haircut.

"Even now, I can't stay long," he says.

My heart starts to beat like a panicked bird against my rib cage. "You're not leaving me again," I say.

"I have to, Rach."

"Why? Because of the Miracle? I've already almost died in the past week. And I work for Devils Inc. now anyway. Do you really think Halo Corp. are going to get involved?"

He fiddles with his bottle, thumb running up and down the soggy label and curling back the paper. "It's not just that. I can't risk being found. Otherwise, we'll have an Apocalypse on our hands."

"We already do, mate," says Crow.

"Because of the scrolls?" says Jonathon.

"Aye. That's right. They were stolen." He pauses. "You know about that?"

"Yeah, you could say that. It's supposed to be a distraction," says Jonathon. "They don't want to trigger the *official* Apocalypse because Heaven would win the War, and Lucifer would be *pissed*. Rumors are, he's still working on a way to win. Call him early, and there'll be Hell to pay. So, yeah, it's a red herring. To keep everyone looking in one direction while something else goes down."

"And that is . . .?" I prompt.

"Because I created the Afterlife app, I always know where someone is. Specifically, I know where Adam is." He exhales. "I suppose it all starts with the apple."

Crow and I share a look at the unintentional echo of Gabriel's discovery.

"Do you know anything about it?" Jonathon asks, interpreting our glance.

"Our friend said it was brought into the Purgatory Vaults about a year ago." I pause, frowning. "Isn't that when you went missing?"

Jonathon inclines his head. "Do you know what the apple does? Either of you?"

Crow shrugs. "At a guess, I'd say it gives whoever bites it a taste of knowledge. That's what happened in the Garden of Eden, right? When Eve was a naughty girl and took a bite?"

"Yeah. Pretty much. When the Purgatory Vaults team brought in the apple, Adam swapped it with a fake, grabbed some of the paperwork, then came to me, begging me to remove him from Afterlife so no one could track him." Jonathon shoots Crow a pointed look. "I wasn't going to do it. I don't get involved in black market dealings."

The corner of Crow's lip tugs up. He clearly remembers his own attempt. "So what makes Adam so special then?"

"He said the continued existence of humanity was on the line. And he showed me the legal documents he stole. They were nondisclosure agreements. Three of them. Dated back to Eden."

Something clicks. "He's the one who ransacked the room at Devils Inc.! I saw an empty folder in the Legal Archives when I was filing. It was supposed to have a nondisclosure agreement signed by Eve inside."

Crow runs a hand over the stubble on his jaw. "So something happened in Eden that they don't want made public. And a bite of the apple could get around the nondisclosures and reveal knowledge otherwise concealed."

Jonathon nods. Then he shakes his hand, his sleeve now peppered with crumbs from Crow's unclean countertop.

"So who's trying to track *you* down?"

"Everyone knows the story from Eden," says Jonathon. "The Serpent tempts Eve into biting the forbidden fruit, she gets Adam to have a bite too, and they all get punished. Only, one party gets a worse punishment for their sin."

"Eve, right? Pain in childbirth, exile, blamed for the sins of all humankind," I say.

"No. The Serpent," says Crow, his voice low.

"The Serpent," Jonathon agrees, a dark look on his face.

I'm about to argue, but Crow cuts over me. "The Serpent's a Greater Demon, mate. If they're looking for the apple, then who cares? They're bound to Hell. Can't set foot on earth."

Jonathon looks troubled. "Not quite. You remember the punishments they all received? Adam and Eve were banished from the Garden, but the Serpent . . ."

"*Because you have done this, Cursed are you more than all cattle,*" says Crow in a low voice. "*And more than every beast of the field; On your belly you will go. And dust you will eat. All the days of your life.*"

"Yeah," says Jonathon. "The Serpent had its Greater Demon status revoked. No longer able to take their true form, they were forced into a body they detested. And Lucifer didn't intervene."

"So the Serpent is trying to get their Greater Demon powers back?" Crow puts his bottle down and absently drums a thumb on the edge of the counter. "And they need you to track down Adam and the apple to do that. Aye. Makes sense."

"Does it?" I say. "Newbie here, remember?"

"They want to force a retrial for what happened in Eden," says Jonathon. "And a bite from the apple might give the jury enough hidden knowledge to call the official story into doubt."

"Like what?" I say. "What is being hidden?"

"Adam couldn't outright tell me. From what I deduced, there's no question the Serpent was in the Garden to tempt them. But Eve was always a free-spirited, curious soul." He pauses and takes a sip of beer. "I think she was always going to take the apple, with or without the Serpent's encouragement."

"Hmm. So if the apple shows the jury that Eve was spending too much time beneath the forbidden tree, or maybe reaching to pluck it from its branches before the Serpent showed up . . ."

"Exactly." Jonathon looks pleased Crow is following his chain of thought. "I mean, it wouldn't give away anything conclusive, but it could call 'beyond all reasonable doubt' into question. And if the Serpent can use the apple to create that doubt . . . then things are going to get pretty bad. Their powers will be restored."

"And that would be a bad thing because . . .?" I ask.

"Well, I'm guessing they'd want revenge, little D—" Crow starts, but he closes his mouth when he remembers Jonathon. "I'm guessing they'll use their power to kill Adam and Eve. Only a Greater Demon can do it. Remember what Gabe told you? As the first man and woman, their life forces are linked to all of humanity. And if they die . . ."

When he raises an eyebrow pointedly, the cut across it reopens. Crow rubs the blood with a thumb then sucks it off. Jonathon eyes him with distaste, but Crow's eyes remain on me.

"If they die, everyone dies," I say quietly.

"Aye."

My stomach clenches. Jonathon's right: he has to disappear. And what will this Serpent do to him if he refuses to tell them what he knows? I take a sip of my beer to force down the panic.

"Shit. So I guess we need to—what, track down the Serpent?"

"Aye," says Crow. "I'll message Gabe and—"

"Track her down?" says Jonathon. "You've already met her."

Both Crow and I stare at my brother.

"What?" says Crow.

"Yeah. You'll have met her, I'm sure of it. Bitter. Powerless. Demoted from her position of Greatness. And what's more of a demotion than—?"

When I snap my gaze to Crow's, I can tell he's already figured it out too.

"Adalind," I say.

Chapter Thirty-Five

"So that's why Adalind's such an arse," Crow says with a low whistle. "I knew she was bitter, but I always presumed she was demoted from mid-management or something. Jesus. The actual Serpent."

He looks almost impressed. Then his expression darkens, jaw clenching as he glances at me, then back to my brother.

"Jonathon, mate, you need to get going," he says.

"Yeah." Jonathon sighs and stands up. "Probably."

I grab his arm. "Wait. Not yet."

"Adalind knows I know about your brother," says Crow. "Remember in the office when she looked at me funny?"

My stomach drops. "You think she's watching you?"

"I can't imagine Adalind lurking on a street corner wearing shades and a fake moustache," says Crow, "but best not risk it, eh?"

"Okay." I exhale and get up, scraping back my stool. "But you're not disappearing again." I glare at Jonathon. "We'll find somewhere safe to meet once we're sure Adalind's not watching. Okay?"

The corner of Jonathon's mouth quirks up. "Okay, sis."

We stare at each other, the small distance between us somehow just as excruciating as when I believed him dead. I don't want him to leave again.

"I've missed you," he says, pulling me into a hug.

"Me too," I mumble once we pull back.

Jonathon clears his throat, and I rub my eyes.

"So where is Adam anyway?" Crow asks.

Jonathon pulls the hood of his sweatshirt over his head. "Better that you don't know. If it came to light you did, she'd have it tortured out of you."

"Your concern is touching," says Crow.

"I don't give a shit what happens to you," Jonathon says easily, but then he leans over the counter to extend a hand. "Still, while I'd rather she was in better company, thanks for looking out for her while I've been away."

As they shake, Crow does a terrible job at concealing the smile tugging on his lips. He's proud at having semi-charmed my brother.

I roll my eyes.

He's such a shit.

"Anytime, mate. It's not been an easy job, but—"

The door to Crow's apartment bursts open. Crow is flung back against the sink, the hilt of a dagger protruding from his chest. As his hands flail backward, they bring the pile of dishes clattering down on top of him.

Adalind stands in the doorway, her snake tattoo just visible above the stiff collar of her black tailored suit. Behind her stands Kat, the Omen from the club, and a girl with red hair dressed in black leggings and armed with shadows dancing at her fingertips.

For a moment, I'm too stunned to do anything. Then anger flares in my gut, and the fireball comes to my fingers uncalled. I hurl it at the doorway.

Kat waves her arm, and a cloud of darkness rises to swallow it. With a twist of her fingers, Jonathon's shadow slips between my legs, rises from the floor, and grabs me from behind, its arms of smoke pinning my hands to my sides.

I cry out, thrashing against it, curses tumbling out of my mouth in an incoherent torrent.

Jonathon steps between me and the others. "Let her go," he says.

Adalind exhales heavily, her inhuman eyes sliding between the two of us.

"I had hoped we could do this the easy way," she drawls. "It's why I've been standing outside for the past forty minutes like some kind of idiot. But do you mention Adam's location? No." She sighs again, flicking the wing of hair over her eye back. "Looks like we'll be doing it the hard way."

She has the audacity to look put out.

A dark movement at my feet catches my eye. A black cat runs through the shadows toward Crow. Smashed crockery dusts his black hair, and a red stain seeps through his blue hoodie. Eyes closed, his hand on the floor is slick with blood.

"Crow!" I yell, but the shadow holding me clamps a hand around my mouth. I taste smoke and copper on my tongue.

The cat stands in front of him and hisses, its fur on end.

Jonathon takes a step forward, hands raised, and I swing my attention back to him.

"Stay back," says Adalind. "Adam's location, or I have Rachel killed." When he says nothing, she turns to Kat. "How easy would it be to kill Rachel?" she asks.

Kat smiles, flashing a pair of dimples. "As easy as . . ." She clenches a fist.

DEVILS INC.

I scream. The shadow squeezes me so tightly I swear my bones are about to break.

"Okay! Okay!" yells Jonathon as blood rushes to my face and pounds in my ears. He raises his arms. "OKAY! STOP!"

Through the spots dancing before my eyes, I see Kat uncurl her fingers. The crushing sensation ceases. As the shadow lets go of my mouth, I gulp in big breaths of air, tasting the metal of blood.

"He said you were his friend," I wheeze, trying to focus on Kat's face. Her expression is blank. "Look . . . at . . . him."

I wrench my head to Crow's body on the floor unmoving, the dagger sticking out from his chest. The cat has gone, but bloody pawprints stretch across the floor from the growing pool of Crow's blood.

"He should have let me in on his deal when he had the chance," Kat says, shrugging. "I was forced to find alternate means of payment."

Anger sends fire to my fingertips, but because my hands are still pinned at my sides, I only succeed in scorching my own thighs. Adalind watches lazily, then she slips a cell phone out of her pocket and places it on the back of the sofa.

"Give me privileges," says Adalind. "Admin-level, so I can track him down."

As Jonathon studies the phone, I desperately try to think of something—anything—we can do, but my senses feel dulled. I can smell Kat's shadow monster as wisps of it curl up my nose: heavy, bitter, and suffocating.

"Um, now!" Adalind says.

Jonathon doesn't move. For the first time in our lives, he seems uncertain.

He seems young.

It terrifies me. Jonathon's my genius big brother. He always knows what to do. He always has the answers.

219

But in this moment, he's just a normal guy. A normal, helpless guy.

Adalind sighs, checking her stubby fingernails. Then she looks at Kat, who raises her hand and starts to curl her fingers again. I close my eyes, waiting for the inevitable pain.

"Okay, okay," spits Jonathon. "Fine! But promise me you won't harm her."

"I have no reason to if you do as you're told," says Adalind.

"I need a verbal agreement, Adalind," says Jonathon sternly. "You won't harm my sister."

Adalind makes a tutting sound, then she exhales. "Fine. I agree not to harm Rachel if you give me what I want." She pauses. "Amendment. I agree not to harm her directly. Once I find Adam . . . well, my later plans may have an adverse effect on Rachel as well as the rest of humanity."

"Deal," says Jonathon, voice cold.

As he goes to the phone and starts to fiddle with it, Adalind slides her gaze to me, face devoid of any emotion. "It's not personal. Besides, she's just an intern."

The anger from that trivial barb gives me something to focus on. "Just an intern? Do you have any idea how long it took me to sort your stupid filing cupboard!" I snarl, feeling myself begin to burn.

"I thought that might make you a little more sympathetic to my cause. Adam left that mess for me to clean up, you know? The bastard."

"You're seriously messed up."

"I just want what is mine, little intern. Is that so wrong?"

"If you're going to kill everyone, yeah," I bite back.

She rolls her eyes. "Please. I only want to kill two people. As if I could be assed to kill everyone."

The anger in my stomach grows, but I've no place to release it. I'm burning. If it wasn't for Kat's shadow holding me, cold and thick, I think I'd burst into flames.

"You done yet, Jonathon?" Adalind drawls. "I don't want to be here any longer than necessary." Her eyes flit around Crow's messy apartment. "This place is a shithole."

Jonathon holds up the phone.

"Good," Adalind says. "Now, give it to me. And don't follow me. Or I'll kill her."

He hesitates. "How do I know that once you have this, you won't kill us both anyway?" says Jonathon.

She looks at him like he's an idiot. "Because who do you think would be stuck with the paperwork?"

She has a point.

When Jonathon tosses her the phone, she snatches it from the air. She lets out a small sigh as she looks down at the screen, running a loving finger over its surface.

"Adam, my sweet, there you are. I'll see you very soon." She flits her gaze back to us, and her lips twist into an unnatural smile. "And I suppose I'll be seeing you at the retrial."

She nods to Kat and the other Omen, and the shadow around me dissolves.

I hurl the ball of blue flames growing in my palm in their direction. It hits the wall across from my door, and cracks spread snakelike through the plaster. There's an explosion of dust and tattered wallpaper.

Then it clears.

Adalind is gone.

Jonathon grabs my arm before I can run after them. "No, Rach."

I don't have time to argue because Gabriel skids into the apartment, pink sweater ripped and half-hanging off his chest as his wings disappear into his shoulder blades. There's a black cat with bloody paws in his arms.

The color drains from his face when he catches sight of Crow. "Ewan! What on earth is going on?"

PART THREE
JUDGEMENT DAY

LAUREN PALPHREYMAN

APPEAL NOTICE AGAINST DISCIPLINARY ACTION:

In line with rules and regulations set out across all Ethereal organizations, I am writing to formally appeal the disciplinary action taken against myself following the incident that took place in the Garden of Eden during the Genesis period. New evidence has come to light that must be presented to a judicial party posthaste.

Yours Devilishly,
Adalind Gardiner

Chapter Thirty-Six

Gabriel drops the cat and strides past us to fall beside Crow's body. I feel frozen in place, unable to move closer for fear of knowing one way or the other.

"Ewan? Ewan. Wake up. Wake up, you intolerable, good-for-nothing—"

Crow wheezes, eyes slowly opening, and Gabriel's stiff shoulders slump with relief. As I release the breath I was holding, Jonathon puts an arm around my shoulders, pulling me close.

Crow's eyes are glazed, but he manages to give Gabriel a clumsy pat on the cheek, leaving a smear of blood across the Angel's pale skin. "Gabe . . . mate . . . you're here."

Gabriel shifts, hurriedly pulling his hand from Crow's face and wiping it on his jeans, his ragged sweater still hanging in shreds around his shoulders. He glances at the dagger in Crow's chest and makes a *tsk* sound.

"You're lucky you're not dead. This is *not* going to be easy to heal. I can't fake the paperwork for a Miracle again."

Crow mumbles something, eyelids drifting shut. In a swift movement, Gabriel grabs the hilt of the dagger and wrenches the weapon out. Crow's body jerks upward, eyes jolting open.

"MOTHER FUC—"

"Calm down," says Gabriel over Crow's cursing, dropping the dagger with a loud clang. More blood seeps through the front of Crow's hoodie, and Crow slams his hand against it as if to somehow staunch it, but Gabriel grasps his wrist and pins it to his side.

Crow grunts. "Get off me!"

"No." Gabriel unzips Crow's hoodie with one hand, then peels the sticky material from the wound. "Stop being a baby."

Crow continues to mumble atrocities, but the Angel pays him no regard. When he deems it safe to release Crow's wrist, he puts both his slender hands on Crow's chest before his lips start to move. I can't hear what he's saying over the Omen's continued stream of cussing.

"Will you be quiet?" Gabriel snaps. "I can't do this if I'm stressed."

"If *you're* stressed?" Crow says through gritted teeth, his bare chest moving up and down quickly with ragged breaths. "I'm the one who's just had a big bastard dagger wrenched out of my heart!"

"It didn't touch your heart. Now, shut up."

"Aye. I'll shut up. If you—"

"Do you want to die and get sent down to Hell?" Gabriel says testily. "Because there's a very high possibility that's where you're headed, Ewan. Especially after the stunt at Halo Corp."

Crow looks furious, but he shuts his mouth. After one final glare, Gabriel inclines his head and closes his eyes, looking for all the world like he's praying. Soon, a white light flows from his hands, and Crow's torn skin starts to knit back together. The tension leaves his face, and he sighs, eyes shutting.

Gabriel looks at him for a second, something unreadable crossing his face. Then he jerks back, removing his bloody hands.

"Is he okay?" I say.

"Yes. Though, he probably still has a concussion," he says. "He'll need keeping an eye on."

The black cat struts past, tail curling around my leg before it climbs onto Crow's stomach and curls up on his torso as if it's taken on that job.

Crow absently pats it on the head with a big hand. "Thanks, buddy."

"Oh, that's right, thank the cat. It's not like I was the one who just saved your life," mutters Gabriel, prompting a smile from Crow.

"I can look after him," I say, going to sit on one of the breakfast stools.

"Aye. You can give me a sponge bath, little Demon," Crow mumbles, smile widening.

Gabriel narrows his eyes. As does Jonathon.

Before I can figure out the best way to change the subject, Gabriel rises in a fluid motion. Blood soaks the knees of his jeans. His feet crunch over the broken plates as he moves to the sink to wash his hands.

"So are you going to tell me what on earth happened here?" he says over the sound of running water. "It's lucky I was already halfway here when his friend's cat came to get me. The alert has finally gone out that the scrolls are missing. Halo Corp. and Devils Inc. are in chaos."

"So Kat *didn't* betray Crow then?" I say, studying the purring cat on Crow's stomach.

"Who knows with Omens," says Gabriel.

Crow opens his eyes at that. "*I* know. Kat's with Adalind now. She follows the money. But that doesn't mean she wanted me dead."

"Just *everyone else* dead," I bite back.

Gabriel seems to want to ask more questions, but Jonathon taps me on the shoulder.

"Rach, I need to go now," he says.

"What? No!" I say. "We need to figure this out together. The damage is done now."

Jonathon looks at his sneakers, shame flickering across his tanned face. "I know," he says. "That's why I need to go. I need to get to Adam before Adalind does. Warn him she's coming. Hide the apple."

Gabriel whips around at that, spraying water from the tap onto the cat on Crow's chest. It hisses then resettles, tail swishing.

"It's a long story," I say. "But Adalind is looking for Adam, and if she finds him, it'll mean the end of the world."

Gabriel opens his mouth.

"You have blood on your cheek," I say to prevent an "I told you so" speech.

He spins back to the sink and starts vigorously scrubbing his face.

"Can't you just message him or something?" I ask Jonathon.

"He's been off the grid all year. No phone. No Afterlife. I have to go find him. It's the only way."

"Aye," says Crow, wincing as he pushes himself up to his elbows. The cat hisses again and this time jumps off his exposed chest. "He's right. We need to warn Adam. Jonathon's our best shot."

I curse under my breath. "You know how to find him?"

Jonathon nods, putting his hood back up. "He's currently hiding out in Cambodia. I think it'll take me a couple of days to track him, but I can get a private plane from LAX in the next hour. Adalind won't be able to get there much faster."

"I should come. She has two Omens with her. And you—"

"Don't have any powers. Yeah, I know. But. . ." He produces his cell phone and waves it in front of me. "Founder of Afterlife, remember?"

228

DEVILS INC.

"Show-off," I grumble.

"I can get a couple of Good Omens to accompany me with a few clicks of a button. Speaking of which . . ." He taps at his screen. "There. The hit on you has been removed."

"You couldn't have done that before?" says Gabriel, who's scrubbed his cheeks enough that they are rosy.

"I haven't logged in much this year," admits Jonathon. "But even if I saw it sooner, it wouldn't have been safe to take it down. Adalind would have known I'd seen it. She might have escalated. Sorry, sis."

"I don't care about that. But I want to come—"

"You're more use here." He puts his hands on my shoulders. "If I fail, Adalind will be coming back. And we need a plan B."

I sigh. "Fine." I punch his arm softly. "But you better come back."

"As soon as I can." He kisses me on the forehead, turns, then heads out into the wrecked hallway. With one last sad smile, he closes the door.

I swallow the tightness in my throat, blink a couple of times, then turn to Gabriel. I can't wallow in self-pity when so much is at stake.

"Well?" he says, blue eyes sharp. "What's going on?"

"Can I get some help?" Crow says, still on the ground.

Eyes on me, Gabriel offers a hand. Then, seemingly realizing he's helped Crow twice in the past ten minutes, he pulls his arm away. Crow simply looks amused. He touches the bloody scrap of ugly pink material still hanging like a sash across Gabriel's shoulders.

"At least some good has come out of all this," he says cheerfully. "You'll finally have to throw away this god-awful sweater."

Gabriel jerks away, stepping over a cracked plate to put some distance between them. Then he leans against the breakfast

229

bar, folding his arms. Crow leans against the other corner, making a show of mimicking the posture.

"Remember what Eve said to you about the apple?" I say, trying to distract Gabriel from the regret he obviously feels about saving Crow's life.

With some effort, Gabriel turns his attention back to me, and I tell him everything Jonathon told us. Meanwhile, Crow potters around the messy kitchen, grabbing a bottle of questionable milk from the fridge and pouring it into a dish for the cat. Then he heads into his bedroom, reappearing with one of his white T-shirts, which he tosses at Gabriel as I finish the story.

Gabriel's face is pale as he snatches the shirt from the air, then he pulls the scrap of bloody pink material over his head and folds it neatly on the breakfast bar. "While Jonathon is tracking down Adam, I'll take Evie into protective custody at Halo Corp. I'll do it now."

"Then what?" I say.

"If Adalind gets back to LA with the apple, she'll need to file for a retrial at Halo Corp. Once she does that, by Ethereal law, it can't be refused. But if I can intercept it. . ." He pulls Crow's top over his head. It's way too big for him.

Crow watches him, unusually serious. "Don't get caught, mate."

"I won't. In the meantime, you two might want to start thinking about what an earth we're going to do if the Serpent gets its powers back."

He heads for the door, but Crow calls him back.

"Thanks," says Crow. "For saving me. You didn't have to."

Gabriel glances over his shoulder, revealing a glimmer of raw emotion in his eyes. "You don't get it, do you? Still, after all this time?" He takes a deep breath. "Yes. I did."

Crow's eyes linger on door long after Gabriel leaves. When he realizes I'm watching him, he gives me a sad half-smile, which

I return. There's no need to say it out loud: Gabriel has feelings for Crow that aren't reciprocated.

Slowly, Crow walks over to stand in front of my stool, resting his hands on my thighs.

"You okay, little Demon?" he says.

"Yeah," I say with a sigh.

"Seeing your brother again must have been weird," he coaxes.

I stiffen, not really wanting to address the jumble of emotions writhing inside me right now.

"So . . . Ewan?" I say, deflecting away from the personal stuff. Or, at least, my personal stuff. "That's your real name?"

He smiles, but it's tight-lipped and doesn't reach his eyes. "Aye. It's been a while since anyone called me that."

"Why did you change it?"

He shrugs. "That's not me anymore."

"Hmm." I put my hands on his cheeks, forcing his eyes to meet mine. "You okay?"

He exhales. "Aye."

"Liar."

I look at his chest, covered in dried blood, and run my fingers over where the dagger protruded not even an hour ago. His breathing deepens at my touch, his heart thumping beneath my fingertips.

"I said I'd look after you," I say.

"Aye. You did, didn't you, little Demon?"

As he looks at my hand, a slow, wicked smile spreads across his face—genuine this time. My lips twitch at how simple it was to cheer him up.

"I think it's time for my bath," he says.

Chapter Thirty-Seven

A little while later, Crow sits in the tub while I kneel on the slightly damp black bath mat beside it. Halfway up his chest, the water has a rusty tint from all the blood, and there are a few stray bubbles leftover from my attempts to make a bubble bath using his Walmart-brand shower gel. As far as I can tell, the scent is called "Masculine."

The bathroom is small—only big enough for the tub, a toilet, a sink, and a towel rack with a single ragged pink towel that looks neither clean nor like something Crow would actively choose. I wonder if it was left by the previous owner. I wonder if he's ever washed it.

The mirror above the sink is cracked—an Omen casualty, I imagine—and the only light comes from the still-wrecked living room outside.

"I thought this was going to be a sponge bath, little Demon," Crow says. "So where's the sponge?"

"Oh, I'm sorry," I say, patting down my sweatpants. "Let me just pull out my personal loofa."

Crow laughs. "Well, if you're not going to rub me down, at least get in with me," he says. "Why have you still got clothes on?"

"I'm *not* getting in that tub," I say. "I can't believe you're in it. Have you ever even washed it?"

"You don't need to clean a bath, little Demon." He rolls his eyes. "It gets washed every time I use the shower."

I laugh, but really. "Seriously, don't you ever clean this place?"

"You know, back in my day, cleaning was left to the women."

I know him well enough by now to sense he's trying to provoke a reaction, so I just pat his cheek. "Well, it's not your day anymore, is it, sweetie?"

He chuckles, then slowly slides back and locks his hands behind his head, water sloshing over his torso. Despite the fact he's an ass and his bath is gross, I have a strong urge to run my hands all over him.

"Don't I know it," he says, looking up at the ceiling. "I told you before, I don't have people over, so I don't care if it's a mess."

"You never have *anyone* over?" I ask, skeptical given his apparent fondness for anyone with a vagina.

"No," he replies simply. "Never."

There's an awkward half-beat of silence as we both process what he's just said: that despite his apparent discomfort at people being in his apartment, here I am.

"Do you think your brother likes me?" he asks.

I trail my fingers over the hard ridges of his torso. "I think you were doing okay until you mentioned the sponge bath."

He grins. "Aye, it just slipped out. It's not my fault! I was under duress. I can't be held accountable for my actions."

I wonder how often he thinks that.

"You still going to ask him for a favor?" I ask, bringing my hand back to grip the side of the bath.

"Aye."

"Can I ask you a question?"

"You just did, little Demon."

"You said you wanted my brother's help to blackmail Angels or to get some money off him. And you're always going on about doing jobs for money. But what do you want the money for?" I look around the dingy bathroom. "What are you spending it on?"

He acts offended. "You don't like my place?"

"It's not that I don't like it. It's bigger than the space I have, and you're living on your own, which I'd love to be able to afford. But given how money-obsessed you seemed when we first met, this place isn't what I expected. I thought you'd live in a big mansion or something."

"Maybe I'm saving up for something."

"I saw some letters from a charity on your counter."

"Aye. I'm a charitable man."

I scrunch up my face, wondering if he's part of some kind of money laundering scheme or something. "Are you though?"

"I'm hurt, little Demon. I'd say I'm pretty generous." He winks at me. "In certain respects."

"Seriously though," I say. "Are you in some kind of debt?"

He doesn't respond, only looks back up at the ceiling. "In a way."

His full lips are wet and hard with tension. The water ripples a little as he breathes, obscuring his thick thighs.

"In what way?" I ask.

"Doesn't matter, little Demon."

I stare at him a moment longer. I have to admit, I'm curious about him—more curious than I'd like to be, given that this is just a casual thing. But I hate it when people push me to talk about stuff I'd rather avoid. So I shrug.

"Okay."

The tension in his face relaxes.

"So," he says. "If we haven't got a sponge, I guess you'll just have to use your hands."

"Yeah?"

"Uh-huh." He nods down to his body. "Go on then. I'm ready."

Holding his gaze, I dip my hand into the water by his waist. He closes his eyes, a smile spreading across his lips.

Then I splash him in the face.

His knee jerks up, sloshing water over both of us.

"You're the worst," he says.

"I prefer diabolical," I tell him.

Then we both start to laugh.

"You learned from the master, little Demon."

The smile lingers in his eyes even after the laughter fades, but there's something else there too. Vulnerability? Sadness? Pain, maybe?

"What?" I say.

"Nothing. I just . . . I like spending time with you, little Demon," he says.

***

After Crow's bath, we haphazardly tidy the kitchen, wiping the blood from the laminate floor and sweeping the broken plates into a trash bag. Then Crow insists the next step in his self-care plan is watching a movie together because I don't have class until the afternoon. I'm pretty sure he doesn't need looking after, but I'm having fun, so I go along with it.

Like me, it turns out Crow is a fan of movies. He has a huge collection of DVDs and even some VHS. Apparently, when you're a perpetually bored immortal, watching movies is a favored pastime.

"So what's your favorite movie, then?" says Crow, getting ready to select one from his tall tower.

"What have you got?"

We have similar tastes. Both of us like superheroes and old cheesy slasher movies. But he hates the paranormal horror stuff I love, saying it reminds him too much of work, and likes James Bond movies, which I think are terrible. Privately, I think it's because he views himself as something of a James Bond. He also loves monster movies, reacting in horror when I reveal I haven't seen many. This prompts him to produce the original black-and-white *Godzilla* made in the fifties.

After he slips the DVD into the player, we snuggle up on the leather couch. Crow's all warm and smelling like shower gel, with one arm around me, the other absently stroking the black cat curled up on his lap.

The movie is super cheesy, and the effects are shit, but it's fun all the same. It takes my mind off Jonathon and where he might be in the race to find Adam too. It's not until the end, when Crow suggests we move on to *King Kong*, that I realize the time with a groan.

"It's almost eleven," I say, rubbing my eyes. "I have a lecture this afternoon. Plus, I want to go check in with Josie, make sure she's okay with the Horsemen situation, and tell her what's going on."

Crow looks a little disappointed. "Okay," he says. He yawns dramatically and stretches, causing the cat on his lap to give him a disgruntled look. "I should probably check in with Gabe anyway—see if Adalind's submitted the document yet to call for the retrial. Want a ride to campus?"

"Nah, it's okay," I say. "It's not far, and I need a walk. It's been a weird twenty-four hours. Kind of need to clear my head."

"Okay."

I detach my limbs from his and head into his bedroom, reluctantly swapping his big, comfy sweatpants for my crumpled skinny jeans and slipping on my boots. When I come back into the living room, I go over to the couch and brush my lips against his without thinking.

When I pull back abruptly, there's an awkward pause as we both realize we've spent the whole morning together—snuggling on the couch and watching movies, joking, talking, and sharing personal things—all with no sex involved. And now I've just kissed him goodbye like that's a completely normal thing.

Like he's my boyfriend.

Oh, God.

I rock back on my feet. "See you later, I guess."

"Aye," says Crow, nodding a little too forcefully. "Have a nice day, little Demon."

"Right. Well . . . here I go."

Cringing, I head to the door. It's only Crow's low chuckle as I put my hand on the door handle that makes me pause.

"Little Demon?"

I don't turn around—my face feels too hot. "Yeah?"

"Come over again tonight after class. I can let you know if Gabe's found anything, and you can tell me about Josie. With any luck, maybe you'll have heard from Jonathon by then."

"Yeah. Okay. Cool. We can talk, um, business." I glance over my shoulder, meeting his eye. "And maybe we can come up with a plan B for if Adalind gets her powers back."

"Aye," says Crow with a smile. Then he presses the play button on his remote control and yawns again, slumping back into the couch. "I'll pencil you into my very busy schedule."

I laugh, rolling my eyes. "See you tonight."

His block of apartments isn't too far from Trinity Falls' main street, and when I pass Apocalypse, I notice an abundance of brightly-colored posters pasted around the door. *'PARTY LIKE IT'S THE END OF THE WORLD BECAUSE IT JUST MIGHT BE!'*

My worries flood back then. Worry about Jonathon and the Serpent; worry about Josie and the Horsemen; worry for Gabriel searching for confidential documents over at Halo Corp.; worry for the potential end of humanity . . .

. . . And worry about whatever the hell is going on with me and Crow.

Chapter Thirty-Eight

I spend the rest of the day checking my phone every five minutes, hoping for a message from Jonathon even though I know he's probably on a plane to Cambodia.

After an excruciating hour learning about negotiations, I meet Josie for lunch. Because Lucas tags along, we can't talk until he's strutted off to the drama studio to hang out with people he claims aren't weirdos.

As soon as he does, Josie leans over the table, not caring that her floaty chiffon top is dragging through a splatter of ketchup.

"Babe," she says in a lowered tone. "What the hell?"

"I know," I say. "God, I'm so glad I can talk to you about this. Are you okay? What happened after I left?"

"I'm fine. I mean, as fine as I can be." She shakes her head, causing her beaded earrings to jingle. "The Four Horsemen of the Apocalypse? I always said they were weirdly committed to their aesthetic, but this is something else! I would have thought they were messing with me, but I saw what happened in that club . . .

the mirror cracking, the fire, and, well . . . *you!*" Her brow furrows with concern. "Your soul, babe. Why didn't you tell me? "

"I know. I have someone trying to help me get it back," I say. "And I wanted to tell you. But they said if I told anyone, I'd end up in Hell." Josie makes a low, strangled sound that she tries to pass off as a cough. "That was why we decided to show you instead. It was a way around the contract I signed."

She pauses to worry her lower lip, rubbing off some of her red lipstick. "Babe, I'm not supposed to talk about this, but there's something you *really need to know.*"

"The Apocalypse," I say quietly.

Her eyes widen. "Oh, so you know. Darius told me my soul would be fine, but yours . . ." She puts a hand on my wrist and squeezes. "The third scroll was delivered not long after you left last night. Some girl with a snake tattoo gave it to Felix. One more scroll and Lucifer returns, there's a War between good and evil, and the world ends. We need to get you out of that contract before it does."

"We need to stop the end of the world," I say.

She bites her lip again, fingers automatically reaching for her silver crucifix. "We can't go against God's will, babe."

"This isn't . . ." I start. "Look, something else is going on."

I tell her about Adalind and the Apple of Knowledge, and how the scrolls being delivered are all part of a plan to distract everyone. She squeezes my wrist again as I tell her about Jonathon and his part in all this.

When I've finished, there's a beat of silence.

"So the fourth scroll isn't actually going to be delivered?" says Josie.

"No. The last thing Adalind would want is Lucifer returning," I say. "According to Jonathon, he'd be pissed to have been summoned when he knows he can't win the Revelation War."

Josie's eyes darken. "I don't think Darius will be happy when he finds out he and his brothers are being used." She pauses. "But enough of that. It must have been weird to see your brother. How are you feeling?"

"Good. Strange. Happy. Scared," I admit. "I wish we could have met under normal circumstances and spent some time together. But I guess nothing about this situation is normal. And I can't even tell my parents he's okay. It's messed up. I'm glad he's back though." I smile and turn her words back around on her. "But enough of that. What's going on between you and Darius?"

She leans back and takes a sip of her iced tea. "Oh, nothing, really. I thought there was something there, but I mean . . . he's *Death!*" She shakes her head. "I don't know if I want to go there. Although, is it weird I thought he was totally hot with his scythe?"

I laugh. "Crow said the Four Horsemen are good guys, if that helps."

"Crow said, did he?" She raises a dark eyebrow, and I avert my gaze. She takes another slurp of her tea, eyes bright. "It's time to tell me everything."

***

I walk Josie to work, where an excited line is already building outside Apocalypse. It's as though they can sense something big is coming. By contrast, Evie's Garden Bar is empty and dark, a sign taped against the glass front announcing its temporary closure. Gabriel must have her in custody already.

Jonathon hasn't messaged me yet.

When I get to Crow's, he's sitting on the sofa watching a boxing game, legs spread, cat on his lap. To my surprise, a couple of plates rest on the draining board, the trash bag full of broken dishware has vanished, and a hint of citrusy cleaning product wafts through the air. And that isn't the only scent. There's a horrible sickly-sweet cinnamon note as well. To my even greater surprise, it's coming from the cheap-looking red candle flickering on the coffee table. *"Christmas Spice,"* the label says, despite the fact it's March.

"It was on sale at the gas station," says Crow, taking in my alarmed expression. "Smells horrible, but I know you girls like this sort of thing. Thought I'd buy it for the romance."

I pull a face as I walk to the couch, dropping down beside Crow.

"What?" he says, grinning.

"Please don't try to romance me," I say.

He chuckles, then leans forward and blows out the candle, causing the cat to angrily jump off his lap and strut to the kitchenette.

"Glad you said that, little Demon," he says. "The smell was giving me a headache."

"That or you actually do have a concussion. Exhibit A— have you cleaned in here?"

He shrugs, leaning back on the couch. "Want to get a takeout? I'm starving."

"There's a good place around the corner if you like Chinese food."

"Aye," he says, pulling out his phone. "I know the one."

We spend the evening watching movies and eating sweet-and-sour chicken and egg fried rice. And we spend the night using each other's bodies to distract ourselves from the fact neither of us has had any news from Jonathon or Gabriel.

The next day passes in a similar fashion: lectures, lunch, Lucas getting moody because he knows we're not telling him something, hushed chatter about the Horsemen, no messages from Jonathon, then takeout with Crow at his apartment.

That night, in his bed, our time together feels more tender than usual—our movements slower, our kisses deeper, our eye contact more prolonged—until I cry out, and he grunts against my skin. Afterward, I wonder if the gentleness of it has disturbed him as much as me. We lie on our backs staring up at the ceiling.

Shit. Am I actually starting to develop feelings for him? Is this a good idea? Is he as bad and untrustworthy as I've made him out to be? Should I give this a chance? I glance at him out of the corner of my eye, noting his clenched jaw.

"You okay?" I ask.

At first, he doesn't say anything, looking troubled. Then he smiles, lightness flooding back in.

"Aye. Come here, little Demon."

Turning me around, he pulls my body into his, one hand flat on my stomach. After a tense moment, I relax. His breath is hot on the back of my neck as we drift off to sleep.

When I wake sometime later, I feel his absence instantly. I hear his voice, a low murmur, coming from the living room. I pull one of his big T-shirts over my head and slip out of bed, wondering if he's gotten some news from Gabriel.

When I open the bedroom door, he's fully dressed and facing away from me, phone pushed against his ear.

"Okay, sweetheart," he says, low voice gentle. "No. Calm down . . . Come on, Maddie, love. I'll come over now . . . Nothing important . . . I'm just home alone . . . Maddie, sweetheart?" He exhales. "Love you."

Afterward, he slips the phone into his pocket. Shadows swirl around him, but I can't tell if it's his powers or if it's how I'm seeing him now dread yawns in my stomach.

Then he turns and catches me standing in the doorway. His eyes widen before they harden.

"Who was that?" I say.

"Doesn't matter. I have to go." His tone lacks his usual warmth as he walks to wrench open the door.

"Crow," I say. "Who was that?"

He stops in the doorway, the darkness twisting around him, his shoulders tense.

"What do you want me to say, little Demon?" he says. "You caught me. I'm married."

I suck in a sharp breath, feeling like I've been punched in the gut. I expect to feel a lick of angry fire, but all that comes is ice—ice flooding my entire body.

"What?" I say.

"I have to go."

"Crow. Do not walk out of that door." As the ice in my veins starts to heat, I feel a telltale crackle at my fingertips. "Not without talking to me first."

"It was fun while it lasted," he says, looking at the doorjamb instead of me. "But it's probably best you're not here when I get back."

Then he walks out, closing the door softly behind him.

Blue flames dance in my palms. I'm burning from the inside out, and I can't control it. I need to let it out. With a cry, I hurl it against the wall. The plaster cracks, bits of white paint fluttering down to coat the stack of mail on the table. The cat on the couch startles, jumping down and hissing.

Then I hurry into his bedroom, pull on my clothes, and head out into the night, slamming the door behind me. My eyes burn as I head back to my dorm, but I refuse to cry. Not for him.

He's married—a fact he deliberately kept from me. But worst of all . . . he made me feel something for him. He made me open up to him. I *cried* in front of him. And for what? So he could get something from my brother?

I feel like screaming. I feel like an idiot.

Gabriel told me exactly who he was from the start. He said he was only trying to hook me so he could reel me in and get what he wanted. Gabriel knew what I was all along.

A fucking haddock.

I decide not to go back to my room. Instead, I break into the gym, remembering how Crow picked the lock last time. I want to pummel a punching bag. But when I arrive in the training room, the dark gym mats with their tree-shaped shadows only remind me of what happened last time I broke in here. With him. So I head back to my room and sleep restlessly.

I feel terrible the next day, like I'm hungover, but with no accompanying memory of fun from the night before. My head aches, I'm tired, and I can't focus. I sit at my desk in my scruffy shorts and a tank top, hair wild, trying to get assignments done, which—surprise, surprise—turns out to be a shitty form of distraction. I check my phone every five minutes.

Jonathon doesn't get in touch.

Neither does Crow.

Finally, I give up on studying. What's the point? The world might be ending soon anyway.

I decide to go for a jog. I debate leaving my phone behind—I *want* to leave my phone behind—but what if Jonathon needs me?

As it happens, I miss my brother's call anyway. I only see I have a message when I'm back in my dorm room, sweat running down my face.

It's Jonathon.

My heart skips as I check my message. Then I slump back against the wall. As if things weren't bad enough.

Rach, I failed. Adalind has Adam and the apple. I'm so sorry. J.

Chapter Thirty-Nine

"You shouldn't call me on this line," Gabriel snaps as soon as he picks up. "I've told—"

"Gabriel. Shut up," I snap back. "She has the apple."

Silence.

"Oh," he says. "Right."

There's another silence on the other end of the line as I lean against my bedroom wall and stare out the window. The sky is blue, barely a cloud in sight, yet there's a storm raging in my chest. And an Apocalypse coming.

"What do we do?" I say.

"I've been looking for a document from Adalind in our upcoming court cases, but I can't find an appeal letter. I thought she would have sent it here given the initial punishment was inflicted by Halo Corp. Perhaps I'm wrong. Perhaps she intends to file it at Devils Inc. But I can't get in there." He exhales. "Rachel, I hate to ask—"

"You want me to see if I can find something?" I say.

"If we can intercept it, we can at least give ourselves some more time." He pauses. "But you don't have to. If you—"

"It's fine. I can do it."

He pauses. "I'll get Crow to accompany—"

"No," I say a little too loudly, then I make myself take a deep breath. "No. It's fine. I can do it myself. No need to trouble him."

Gabriel doesn't say anything for a moment. "Is everything okay, Rachel?" he asks. "I mean, apart from the obvious."

"Yeah," I say a little too brightly. "All good. I'll go head to Devils Inc. now and see what I can dig up."

"Sure you don't want—?"

"Yep. Sure." I pause. "Just . . . well, you better be working on getting my soul back."

"Of course," he says. "Good luck, Rachel."

***

When I walk through the revolving glass doors of Devils Inc., I knock shoulders with a couple of scowling Demons ranting about the short notice of the Apocalypse. Looping on the nine monitors behind reception are the words *"THE END IS NIGH"* in bold red letters. The whole atrium is filled with chaos and confusion, people piling up at the elevators as they attempt to get to their departments.

I head over to Adalind's abandoned reception desk. No one notices as I slip behind it and sift through the piles of papers on her desk. There's a memo from Soul Defense noting they won Richard Livingstone's case, a request that the Soul Investments fridge be stocked with almond milk for lactose-intolerant Dave, and apparently, Frank from Soul Recruitment needs help rotating a PDF again. I scatter aside a bunch of birthday cards Adalind has clearly failed to pass on and switch on her computer screen.

I don't know her password, so after a few attempts, I log in to my account instead, wondering if she's saved anything on the server. As the desktop loads, I notice I have a couple of emails.

The first is a reminder from the PR department to engage with the #IdSellMySoulFor hashtag they're promoting on social media. As I click on the second, though, my heart sinks. It's a meeting invite for a court case. Sent by senior management a few minutes ago, it's gone out to all staff at both companies.

Attached is Adalind's appeal letter. Gabriel couldn't find it because she'd already sent it in.

Her retrial is tomorrow at noon.

"Shit."

I message Gabriel to meet me in the alley, then slip back out of the building.

Gabriel is already waiting when I get there, his white blazer a stark contrast to my black one. His face is grave.

"I know," he says before I can speak. "I've just seen the email."

"Do you think she can win?" I ask.

"I think we need to plan for it. We need to find a way to defeat a Greater Demon while making sure Adam and Eve are safe. I can work on that."

"And me?"

"Wait for Jonathon. Find out what happened. If the Omens have Adam, we can get Crow to strike a deal to get him back. Perhaps he'll prove useful after all."

I stiffen at the mention of him, and Gabriel notices. Before he can say anything, I make a show of smiling brightly. I really don't want to get into what happened right now. It shouldn't matter. It shouldn't be important. Especially not when the world might end.

"Okay, sure! I can do that! I'll let you know as soon as I speak to him!"

I cringe at my cheeriness, then I leave Gabriel looking perplexed in the alley.

Back on campus I sit at my desk, watching one YouTube music video after the next, trying to distract myself as I wait for my brother's return. I'm trying to distract myself from thinking of Crow. It's hard; my sheets smell of him, the mirror on my wall is still cracked, and *I can't believe I slept with a married man.*

It becomes even harder to do when the man himself appears, wearing the same jeans and blue shirt as last night.

He says nothing, only closes the door gently behind him, then drops a glossy piece of paper in my lap.

"What are you doing here?" I say as he takes a seat on the edge of my bed, expression serious.

He glances at the paper he dropped on my lap. Heart beating fast, I pick it up.

"Her name is Maddie," he says.

It's an old black-and-white photograph, creased down the center. Crow is in the center of the frame wearing a black suit. The curly-haired girl in his arms wears a floor-length wedding dress. They both stand outside a church, beaming. She clutches a bouquet of lilies.

I swallow, staring at it. "Why are you showing me this?"

"The contract I got into with Devils Inc. . . . I did it for her. Wanted to clean myself up. Get out of debt. Stop the gambling. Stop getting mixed up with bad people. We married the year before I died." He pauses. "The car accident that killed me . . . she was in the car."

I look up to find he's now staring at the threadbare carpet between his feet.

"She survived. But she suffered severe brain damage. Had to go into care because she couldn't function on her own anymore." He takes a shaky breath. "She couldn't even remember me."

My chest feels tight, and despite everything, I want to reach for him. To stop myself, I clutch the photograph tighter.

"When Gabriel took me under his wing, I saw an opportunity. I knew he liked me, and so I thought I could use that to get into Halo Corp., steal a Miracle, and use it to heal Maddie. I tried. But I got caught forging the paperwork. Gabe stuck his neck out for me. They agreed to have a hearing rather than just chucking me out. Only . . ."

He leans forward, resting his forearms on his thighs. He's still not looking at me.

"Only, I reckoned they were going to get rid of me. And in a last-ditch act of desperation, I ditched the hearing and went to her care home instead. I thought that . . . I thought that . . ." He runs a hand over his mouth. "I thought that if I killed her, it would free her soul, and I could tell her I was sorry."

Dread swells in the pit of my stomach.

"I don't know if I'd have gone through with it. Tell myself I wouldn't have, but, well. . . Never got the chance to find out anyway." His gruff voice is low. "Gabriel realized what I was going to do. He stopped me. He was furious. It went against everything he stands for. One of the Commandments. *Thou Shalt not Kill.* He couldn't allow me to stay after that, so this time when they decided to kick me out, he didn't argue. He was demoted for his faith in me."

Crow rubs his face with both hands.

"Since then, I've tried everything I can to get hold of a Miracle—trying to blackmail your brother to get dirt on an Angel being one of them. I started saving money, too, in case one came up on the black market. I just . . . it's all my fault. I know I'll never get her back. I can't turn back time. But if I could heal her mind . . . I just want to tell her I'm sorry." His voice breaks a little. "She's in a good care home for the elderly in LA now. I visit her when I can. She doesn't remember me, not from before, so it's not against the rules. Last night, the staff called to say she got herself worked up about something, so I went over to calm her down."

He takes another deep breath before finally meeting my gaze. "I'm sorry I hurt you," he says. "I didn't mean for it to get as far as it did. I just . . . liked spending time with you. It made me forget. But I don't have the room in my heart. It doesn't . . . it doesn't work properly." He shakes his head. "Not anymore."

I find I'm holding his wedding photograph so tightly my knuckles are white. I don't know what to say. I want to find the anger I felt earlier, but I can't. I just feel hollow and sad and confused. I want to pretend he hasn't hurt me, but at the same time, I want to yell at him that he has. I want to tell him that things will be okay even though they won't. I want to tell him it's not fair he's the one who messed up yet I'm left feeling the need to comfort *him*.

It's not fair. None of this is fair. Not what happened to him. Not what happened to his wife. Not what he did to Gabriel. Not what he did to me.

I hand him back the photograph. He takes it. Then he gets to his feet, slipping the photo in his back pocket as he crosses the room.

"I'm sorry," he says again.

And then I'm alone with the tornado raging in my chest.

The rest of the day passes by in a blur. Josie messages me to see if I want to hang out, but I can't face explaining what's happened. I sit at my desk listening to music and trying to push the feelings back inside me.

It's almost dark outside when a tapping at my window makes me jerk out of my numb state. Gabriel raps at the glass. Despite the fact I'm on the sixth floor.

I hurry to the window and open the latch. He climbs inside, topless, wings shuddering back into his shoulder blades as he straightens by my desk. He's holding his *"Save the Planet"* canvas bag.

"Jesus Christ, Gabriel," I snap. "What are you doing?"

He puts the bag on the bed, then pulls out a neatly folded flannel shirt.

"I heard about what happened with you and Crow," he says, slipping it on and quietly doing up the buttons. "And, well, I thought you might be upset, so I did some research about what to do with humans in this situation. I hope I got it right, but . . ."

With a deep breath, he pulls out a pint of Ben and Jerry's ice cream from his bag and offers it to me, his big blue eyes earnest. His gesture breaks the barrier I've been trying to keep up all day.

"Oh," I say. "That's really . . . That's really nice of you."

I burst into tears.

Chapter Forty

Gabriel's eyes widen with alarm, and he drops the ice cream next to my laptop as if it's suddenly scalding hot.

"Sorry. I'm okay. I'm just . . . It's fine." He's close enough that I can smell the citrusy scent of his bath products.

He frowns. "Did I get the wrong flavor?"

A laugh falls out of my mouth even as tears roll down my cheeks. "No! That's not . . . You're such a dork."

The corner of his lip quirks up. Then he tenses as though preparing for battle. "Should I hug you?"

"No. It's fine," I say, then I add, "I'm not really a hugger," when his coppery eyebrows knit together.

He visibly relaxes, though doesn't move out of my personal space. "Oh, good. Me neither. Although . . ." He pauses, biting his cheek. "I did read that hugs stimulate the production of oxytocin, which is supposed to help when someone feels sad."

I take a deep breath, my lip twitching. "Where did you read that?"

"Buzzfeed."

"What if we just have some ice cream?" I say.

His blue eyes brighten as he turns to pick up the tub of Ben and Jerry's again.

"Go and sit on the bed," I tell him, my voice still a little thick from crying. "There are spoons in the desk. I'm just going to go wash my face and change into some comfy clothes, okay?"

Five minutes later, I'm in my shorts and a T-shirt, and we're both sitting on my small bed, backs against the headboard. He holds himself like we're at boot camp, an inch between his stiff shoulder and mine. My knees are raised to better hold the ice cream pint against them. It's half-baked chocolate brownie flavor.

I don't really feel like eating, but he seems pretty invested in my enjoyment of it, so I have a spoonful. I offer it to him. For a moment, he seems to consider it, then he shakes his head.

"How did you know I was upset?" I ask him.

"I called Ewan—Crow—about the retrial. He seemed upset. Particularly when I mentioned you. And you were being strange earlier as well." He gives a stiff shrug, eyes focused on the wall planner hanging behind my desk. "So I asked him."

"You warned me about him."

"Yes."

"But you didn't tell me he was married."

Gabriel clasps his hands together in his lap. "I'm sorry for that. I didn't want to interfere in case my own feelings were clouding my judgement. I'd hoped he had moved on from the past. And when it comes to his wife . . ." He shakes his head. "I never told anyone what I stopped him from doing back then. I told myself I never would. Bringing her up again . . . it felt like opening old wounds. I hope you can forgive me."

My heart clenches at the sincerity in his plea. "There's nothing to forgive," I say softly, then I take another mouthful of ice cream, which seems to relax him. "Can I ask you something?"

"Yes."

"Did anything ever happen between you two?"

"Do you mean, physically?" he says, his eyes firmly trained ahead.

"Yeah." I take in the rigidness of his profile. "I mean, if you don't want to talk about it—"

"It's fine," he says. "No. We were more than friends, but nothing physical happened between us. Still, he made it very clear that it could if I wanted it to."

At that, he reaches for the second spoon, apparently forgetting his initial reluctance to share. He puts it in his mouth, swallows hard, then stares at it, turning it back and forth.

"But you didn't want to?"

"I was his mentor. It wouldn't have been right for me to take advantage. Back then, I thought *I* was the one in the position of power, if you can believe it." He pauses to sigh. "I don't think he's a bad person though. Not deep down."

"Just a shitty person?"

Gabriel gives a half-laugh. "Yes. He is a bit of a shit, isn't he?" he says before shaking his head. "He's on a path of self-destruction. Has been for years. It's like he's constantly trying to dig himself out of a hole without realizing he's digging the wrong way. If he'd just stop and make some peace with himself . . . I believe there could be salvation for him."

"It makes it harder," I say, leaning my head back against the headboard. "Feeling bad for him when I want to be angry."

"I know. But perhaps we can be both. His actions being understandable doesn't make them excusable."

"Yeah," I say, taking the pint back and eating another mouthful of ice cream. "I suppose."

We sit in silence for a moment, staring ahead. It's strange to be sitting here with Gabriel, an Angel, talking about a guy who screwed us both over—a guy who was in this bed just a few days ago. I try not to think about that, determined not to get upset again. And that's when something occurs to me.

"You said you did some research into what to do with humans when they're upset," I say.

"Yes."

"Weren't you a human once?"

"No," he says.

I wait for him to elaborate. He doesn't.

"How come?" I say.

He turns his head, seeming surprised by my confusion. "Oh. Well. Some souls are recruited for the organizations; some are born into them. I was born an Angel."

"How does that work?"

He shifts a little on the mattress. "Well, because my father is an Archangel," he says.

"Oh, my God," I say. "Your dad is *the* Angel Gabriel, isn't he?"

"No!" He shakes his head, muttering under his breath. "Why does everyone always think that?"

"Sorry! I just thought—"

"Well, you thought wrong. Although, my father could have been a bit more creative with the name."

I sense this may be a touchy subject from the way he's frowning at the spoon. If he clutches it any tighter, he'll bend it in half. "Who *is* your dad then?"

He pauses, and for a moment, I think he's going to stand up, take his *"Save the Planet"* bag, and storm out. But then he shrugs a slender shoulder.

"Michael," he says.

"The Archangel Michael," I say softly. "He's the Angel who's supposed to win against Lucifer in the final war, right?"

"Yes."

"What's he like?"

"I don't know. I've never met him. He's up in Heaven and, well, I assume he's very busy. I prayed to him a few times when I was younger, but I'm sure he has much more important things to be doing than having conversations with me. Preparing for the fight against evil."

"Oh," I say, remembering the snipe Crow made about this whole thing being another misguided attempt to prove himself to Daddy. And something about Gabriel suddenly makes sense.

"That must be a lot to live up to," I say gently. "Having a dad who is so powerful. Living in somebody else's shadow."

He inclines his head. "I suppose so. And unfortunately, I'm not doing a very good job of it."

"Why do you say that?"

"When I got Ewan to be my eyes and ears inside Devils Inc. all those years ago, it was because I thought Lucifer was trying to build an army to win the Revelation War against my father, and I wanted to help. But instead of acting like an Angel, I acted like a human, and moreover, like a foolish one. I got demoted, the World War ended without Lucifer making a move, and it was all for nothing. And now, this whole Adalind thing happened right under my nose." Gabriel's face is pinched. "I can't imagine he's particularly proud of me."

"I feel like that with my parents sometimes," I say.

Gabriel turns to me in surprise. "Really? Why would they not be proud of you?"

"Well, Jonathon was always the smart one—the one who could do nothing wrong," I say, taking another spoonful of ice cream. "It's no big deal. I'm used to it."

"Rachel, I think you're wrong. You might not be particularly . . . studious. And you're quite messy. And a little sarcastic—"

"Are you going somewhere with this?" I ask.

"Yes. You're kind, and strong, and assertive, and compassionate," says Gabriel. "You had one of the worst things imaginable happen to you when you lost your brother, and yet you kept trying and caring anyway. I think your parents should be very proud to have you as a daughter. I think they probably are."

I blink a few times, trying not to burst into tears again. Then I smile.

"I think you're wrong, too, you know?" I say. "I mean, sure, things didn't go to plan last time you worked to save the world, but here you are trying to do it all over again. And as for what happened with Crow . . . being human, having feelings—maybe that's not the worst thing. Maybe letting someone in, connecting with someone, is actually a good thing even if it didn't work out." I pause. "I think your dad is proud of you."

He gives me a half-smile, but his tone lacks conviction. "Perhaps."

I go quiet as I realize what I said could also apply to me— both about letting someone in, and about my parents. I've shut myself off since Jonathon. I've never let anyone get close; never let a relationship develop past anything casual; never wanted to let anyone help. I've even pushed my own parents away, worried that if they knew the real me—the adrenaline-junkie me who loves movies and hates law—they would be disappointed.

And yet Jonathon said they *were* proud of me.

Gabriel can't talk to his dad. But I still have a chance to speak to mine before the world potentially ends.

"So. Adalind's retrial is tomorrow?" I say after a while.

"Yes." Gabriel sighs. "I've brought Eve into the Halo Corp. offices and told Crow to get in touch with Kat. If we can get Adam before the trial, we might have a shot. I don't know what we're going to do in the long-term if Adalind gets her power back though. A Greater-Level Demon on Earth, unauthorized. I've never heard of it happening before. If she's intent on destruction, I'm not sure what any of us can do to fight her. None of us have that kind of power."

"So if she gets her power back, we're all pretty much screwed."

"Yes. Pretty much."

We settle into silence as the shadows in the room grow. When the ice cream has pretty much melted, Gabriel decides to head home. Despite my protests that he could just use the door, he takes off his top and heads for the window. As I watch him go, I realize I feel better than I did a few hours ago. So much so that when my mom messages again to ask whether I'm planning on coming home for Jonathon's anniversary, I pick up the phone and give her a call.

"Sweetie, it's so good to hear from you," she gushes after one ring. "How are your classes? Are you keeping well? Are you eating properly? Did you get your internship sorted? You've let the university know you got the internship, right? You don't want to do all that work only to not get the credit."

"Mom! It's fine," I interject, regretting my choice.

"Are you okay? We've heard so little from you lately. We've been worried."

"Yeah, I know. I'm sorry. I'm fine."

"How is the internship going?"

I take a deep breath. "To be honest, Mom . . . I'm not sure it's really me."

"No?" There's a pause. "Well, these big companies can have a way of grinding you down; sucking out your soul."

You have no idea.

"Maybe you should try for a smaller firm next time?" she continues.

I bite my lip. "It's not just that. It's . . . I don't know if law is for me. I mean, I'll finish the internship and my degree. But . . . I kind of want to explore other things too."

My heart thuds through her long pause.

"Oh. Well, okay. That sounds sensible."

My brow furrows. "You're not mad?"

"Of course not, honey. We only pushed because we thought it was what you wanted. We were always a little surprised you decided to go down the law path. I don't think anyone in our family is suited to the corporate lifestyle. I went into the nursing assistant role because I wanted to help people, your father opened his electronics store, and Jonathon . . ."—her voice wobbles—"I always thought he'd end up leaving that big technology company and creating his own app or something."

My throat tightens. I wish I could tell her that I've seen him. I wish I could tell her that what she wanted for him *did* come true.

"I had a dream about Jonathon," I say finally. "He said he misses you."

Mom sniffles on the other side of the line. "You'll come home for the anniversary?" she says, her voice breaking fully now. "Please."

"Yeah, Mom," I say, eyes stinging. "Yeah, I'll come home."

After we say goodbye and hang up, I sit on my bed feeling like a weight has been lifted. But as it gets later, and I'm incessantly checking my phone for any word from Jonathon, the dread starts to seep back in. I'm worried about my brother. Tomorrow, the Serpent will most likely get her powers back, *and* I'll have to face Crow again. Plus, it hits me that I might not be able to keep my promise of coming back for Jonathon's memorial. The world might end before I get the chance.

When it gets to around three in the morning and Jonathon still hasn't shown, I decide I should at least try to get some sleep. My head is starting to hurt, and I'll need my wits about me tomorrow.

It's hard though. For a long time, it seems, I lie in the dark staring up at the ceiling.

How the hell are we going to stop this Apocalypse?

Chapter Forty-One

I'm woken from restless dreams at around seven. It takes me a minute to realize the pounding sound isn't the stress headache creeping into my temples, but someone knocking at my door.

I shuffle to the door to find Jonathon in the hallway. He wears the same crimson football hoodie and jeans as before, but the black eye is new.

We stare at each other for a moment. Then I throw my arms around him, and he sweeps me into a hug. He smells like sweat and airplane food.

"You need a shower," I tell him.

He chuckles into my shoulder. "Thanks, sis. Good to see you too."

When we head inside, he sits on the edge of my bed, rubbing his face in his hands.

"You're hurt," I say, gently touching his eye.

"I'm fine. I actually got to Adam first, but the Omen I hired turned on me once he realized Adam had the apple." He shakes his head. "Omens, man. I should have gone alone."

I sigh. "I'm just glad you're okay."

"Yeah, but today's going to be interesting. I heard the trial's at twelve. I guess you'll have gotten the invite—" For the first time, he really looks at me. He narrows his eyes. "You look like you've been crying."

"I'm fine."

His jaw tenses. "It's that Omen, isn't it? Crow? What has he done?"

I exhale. "Long story. And I think we have bigger things to worry about."

"Want me to kick his ass?"

I roll my eyes but feel a swell of warmth despite myself. My brother is here, after all this time, threatening to get into a fight he won't win out of brotherly duty.

"No," I say. "It's okay."

"Thank God. I'm not much of a fighter. You were always the one with the talent in that department. I remember babysitting you when you were five and sending you to bed when you wanted to watch something on the Disney Channel. You came at me like a child possessed. Thought you were going to kill me."

"Oh, shut up. I wasn't that bad."

He grins. "Well, still, I don't envy this Crow guy." He gets to his feet. "Mind if I take a shower before the trial?"

"Please do. You're stinking up my room."

He laughs, messing up my hair as he walks past me to the door. But when he opens the door, he stops and says hello.

"Oh, my god!" I hear Josie say. "You're the brother, aren't you? I'm Josie. I've heard so much about you."

Despite it being 7:00 a.m., Josie is dressed as if she's ready for the club, complete with skinny jeans and a floaty green top that matches her earrings. She—unlike me, Gabriel, or my brother—*is* a hugger and pulls Jonathon close, giving him a kiss on both cheeks.

"Hey, yeah, nice to meet you too," he says awkwardly before escaping to the showers.

Josie watches him over her shoulder, then she takes a seat on my bed, folding one of her legs beneath her.

"He has the same eyes as you," she observes. "And he's kinda—"

"Do *not* say he's hot," I say.

She laughs, giving me a mischievous half-shrug. Then her brow furrows.

"You look like you've been crying." Her expression sours. "It's that Crow guy, isn't it? What's he done!"

"I'll tell you later," I say. "Got to get through today first. Did you hear—?"

"The trial? Yeah, babe. Darius told me. And if you're going, I'm coming too."

***

The Ethereal Courthouse is underground and, like the Purgatory Vaults, at an equal distance between Devils Inc. and Halo Corp. We take Jonathon's white Honda Civic to a public lot not far away and walk down the office-lined street together.

We considered not coming at all, but, apparently, trial attendance is compulsory for any employee of either company, and Jonathon and Josie didn't think I should come alone. Plus, we need to know what we're up against if she actually wins.

When I lead Josie and Jonathon into the Devils Inc. atrium, it's just as chaotic as a day ago. I'm wearing my black blazer, so no one looks twice as we follow the crowd and line up at the elevators. I imagine Gabriel doing the same over at Halo Corp. And Crow . . . I harden myself. Well, who cares how Crow gets anywhere?

When our elevator doors open, they reveal a black marble hallway lined with lush Hellscapes in ornate golden frames. We follow the stream of Demons parading across the black-and-white tile to a grand archway up ahead. Soon, we find ourselves in a circular underground courtyard fed by three other hallways.

My heart stills when I spot Crow walking with Kat. A half a head higher than the rest of the crowd, I can tell he hasn't dressed up for the occasion—unless you count the leather jacket. The fact he's on jovial terms with Kat must mean he's managed to get Adam into protection. Which is good. I suppose.

He must feel me looking because he stops and searches the room until our eyes lock.

We stare at each other, the bubble of noise around us suddenly faraway. There are smudges beneath his eyes, and he hasn't shaved since his visit to explain himself. Then he gives me a half-smile and raises his hand in a semblance of a wave.

I swallow.

"You okay, babe?" Josie touches my arm.

"Yeah, fine." I force a smile and drag my gaze away.

When I look back again, he's gone.

We spill into the actual courtroom, which has a high-domed ceiling painted with Michelangelo-style cherubs and Bosch-style Demons and the same checkered tile on the ground. Above us, two mezzanine levels curl around the space. The jurors, twelve people randomly chosen from Halo Corp. and Devils Inc., are already seated along a bench near the front.

The air smells sweet and musty like flowers and churches, but it's quickly overwhelmed by the scent of hundreds of bodies.

"This way," says Jonathon.

He leads us to a space at the back as the rest of the organizations' employees trickle in. I lean against the wall as I search for Gabriel. Finally, I spot a flash of red hair to my left.

When he sees my nod, he turns away so quickly I'm surprised he doesn't give himself whiplash. While I doubt anyone would care much about an Angel smiling at a Demon at this point, it seems he wants to be on the safe side.

He barges through the crowd to Crow, who leans against a column.

They appear to argue for a moment—Crow refusing to meet his gaze; Gabriel grabbing his wrist. I know Gabriel and I had a heart-to-heart last night, but I can't imagine him showing emotion in front of his colleagues on my behalf. Something else is going on.

"As soon as we find out the outcome, we need to head out," says Jonathon under his breath. "If Adalind gets her powers back . . ."

"Agreed," I mutter. "Gabriel wants us to reconvene at Evie's after the trial. Evie's given him the keys so we can use it as a base."

"What about Crow? Is he coming too?" says Josie.

I tense, trying not to think about the fact I might have to have a civil conversation with him. I can get over this, but not without space. I don't want to be in close proximity to the hard body that held me, or the stubbled jaw that brushed against my skin, or the mouth that moved against mine.

And I don't want to look into the eyes that filled with tears as he told me about his past.

Not now. I'm not ready yet.

"I guess so," I say with a casual shrug that doesn't fool Josie.

She narrows her eyes and shoots daggers at him across the room—which he doesn't see because he's still trying to bat Gabriel away as if he's an irritating fly.

What's going on?

A couple of minutes later, a hush ripples through the crowd. A stern-looking woman with a blonde bun and black-and-white robe takes her seat at the judge's bench. There's a murmur of interest at her appearance.

"Her name's Eleanor. Human once, but she's pretty senior now," Jonathon whispers in my ear. "She reports directly to Saint Peter. Only takes high-profile cases. She's very fair, which could be a bad thing—we could have done with a bit of bias against Adalind."

Eleanor nods at two guards standing on either side of a black door, and they open it to reveal Adalind. Silence descends as she saunters over to the witness stand. Her hands are stuffed in her suit trousers, and her white shirt is unbuttoned enough to reveal the snake tattoo coiling around her neck.

"Shall we begin?" Eleanor says, sitting down as she surveys the room. "We're here today to witness Adalind's appeal against the disciplinary action taken against her back in the Genesis period. Oaths, please."

Adalind scowls at the proffered Bible before placing her hand on top. "I swear by Almighty God to tell the truth, the whole truth, and nothing but the truth," she says in a low drawl.

Eleanor nods. "You have some evidence you wish to present to the court?"

"Yeah," says Adalind. "I'd like to present—"

Suddenly, a glint of silver slices through the court. One of the guards twists her fingers, and a shadow snatches the weapon out of the air when it's just inches away from Adalind's face.

It's an ornate dagger. Blood already on the blade. My heart sinks.

There's an eruption of noise as it clatters to the floor. Everyone turns toward the wannabe assassin. Crow stands at the edge of the room wearing a smirk that doesn't meet his eyes.

"Thought you might want it back," says Crow, his gruff tone carrying across the chaos.

Adalind smiles back coolly. "Nice try, Omen."

"Order!" yells Eleanor. "Guards, take him into custody. Order, please!"

Through the chaos, I see Gabriel grab Crow's thick arm and shove him toward the door, face pink with fury. As the guards make their way toward them, Kat laughs, twisting her hands together. A cloud of darkness conceals them both.

When it's gone, they've both disappeared.

I guess Crow's pointless assassination attempt is what they were arguing against.

"Order!" yells the judge again. "Order!"

The courtroom goes quiet, and the trial begins.

***

Given that the fate of the world rests on the outcome, the trial itself is surprisingly boring. And Adalind is surprisingly eloquent.

When she tells the jurors about the nondisclosure agreements, it causes ripple of intrigue. But when she presents the apple, disclosing the fact she recovered it from Adam—who initially stole it from the Vaults—it causes so much chaos that there has to be a recess while Eleanor decides whether to permit it as evidence.

For about twenty minutes, I wonder if this is all going to be resolved in our favor due to a legal technicality.

But when we reconvene, Eleanor allows the apple as evidence, having since reviewed a security tape depicting Adam's theft. Jonathon curses.

"We presumed she'd spike the jury with the apple," he whispers. "But she's done everything by the book. It's hard to argue against."

Finally, each of the jurors is presented with a very small segment of the apple of knowledge. The room goes completely silent as they eat them. There's another recess in which the jury disappear to determine Adalind's fate.

When they retake their places behind the bench, all eyes are on them.

"Verdict?" asks Eleanor.

The lead juror—a Devils Inc. employee with a blond man bun—stands. Adalind tries to look casual, eyes focused on her fingernails, but I can see the tension in her sharp shoulders.

"In the light of the new evidence presented to us today, it is of our belief that Eve would have taken the apple with or without interference from the Serpent. And therefore, Adalind is not accountable for the Sin committed in Eden."

Eleanor inclines her head. She raises her mallet and bangs it against the desk.

"Sentence overturned," she says. "Adalind, I grant you back your power."

Chapter Forty-Two

The noise of hundreds of Demons, Angels, and Omens echoes around the high-domed ceiling. Some cry, some speculate, and others celebrate.

Behind it all, Adalind remains a quiet force. She looks over the pews of people until her snakelike eyes find us. She smiles, and my heart goes cold.

Her mouth opens.

Then it keeps on opening, jaw dropping, until it's impossibly wide.

"Holy shit," I mutter.

Fangs erupt from within. Then her skin turns inside out, peeling off her to reveal something dark green and scaly. As she grows, a serpentine head erupts, brushing the domed ceiling as a tail coils out to whip at the far wall of the courtroom. Rubble begins to fall.

Eleanor bangs her mallet against the table. "Order! Order!"

Adalind laughs—a low, raspy hissing sound.

"Time to go, sis!" says Jonathon.

"Agreed!" I say.

He grabs my wrist, and I grab Josie's.

"Where are we going?" she yells as the hissing behind us deepens.

"We need to meet with the others!" I yell back.

Evie's Garden Bar is where all this started. Maybe we can come up with a plan there to stop it. Preferably before the end of the world.

***

After parking on a side street, we make it to the dark shopfront of Evie's, where a *"Closed"* sign is still taped to the glass. I try the door, hoping Gabriel made it.

As it swings open and we pile inside, though, it isn't Gabriel sitting at the bar beneath the unlit fairy lights and white apple blossoms.

It's Crow.

He sits at the bar, one big arm resting on the counter. His leather jacket rests on a stool beside him.

There's an awkward pause.

"Hey," he says.

"Where's Gabriel?" I ask.

"Not here yet."

"How did you get in?"

"I'm an Omen, little De—"

He stops and clears his throat. There's another awkward pause—one in which Jonathon folds his arms across his chest and Josie looks ready to say something. Then Crow's gaze fixes on something over my shoulder.

"Speak of the devil," he mutters.

Gabriel marches in briskly, key in hand, buttons of his stiff gray shirt not quite done up right.

"This is not good. This is not good," he repeats under his breath. Then he barges past us to yell at Crow. "Of all the stupid things you could have done, Ewan!" he says. "Throwing a dagger at an Ethereal while she was in human form? In front of everyone? What the hell were you thinking?"

Crow cocks an eyebrow. "Oh, was I just supposed to do nothing? Like you, mate? How did that work out? Because news is, she got her powers back."

Gabriel grabs Crow's chin. "And what if you didn't miss? What if you killed her? Then what!"

Crow jerks to his feet, shaking Gabriel off. "Then Adalind would be dead, there'd be no trial, and this whole mess would be over."

"And what about you?" Gabriel prods him in the chest.

"I don't give a shit about me."

"That's quite clear," snaps Gabriel. "Do you realize what would have happened if you'd killed an Ethereal unprovoked? Hell. For eternity."

Crow lets out a bitter laugh. "I'm pretty sure I'm already there, mate."

They stare at each other, Crow's jaw clenched, and Gabriel's cheeks pink with fury. Then Gabriel grabs his chin again.

"Pull yourself together," he says before releasing Crow roughly and stepping away.

"So . . . what are we going to do?" I ask, bringing the conversation back on track. "I don't know if you noticed, but Adalind turned into a humongous Serpent monster."

Gabriel rubs his face. "I don't know," he says.

"Shall I make us some drinks?" chirps Josie, breaking the awkward silence. "I think we could all use one."

Gabriel's gaze moves to Josie, seemingly noticing her for the first time.

"You're Rachel's friend, the bartender from Apocalypse."

"Yeah. Josie. You must be Gabriel."

She moves forward, arms widening to hug him, and his eyebrows lift with alarm. I touch her arm and shake my head.

"Oh. Not a hugger, huh?" says Josie. "Well, nice to meet you. Drink?"

Gabriel sighs. "Why the hell not?"

Josie slips behind the bar, surveying the numerous types of apple juice in the fridge, the basket of apples by the mirror, and the bottles of green liquor stacked on the shelves lining the redbrick wall.

"Wow, this girl is really into her apples, huh?" she says, trying to sound upbeat. "Everyone okay with appletinis?"

I head to the bathroom while Josie mixes drinks, more to get away from the tension than anything else. When I come out, though, Crow is leaning against the hallway wall, arms folded over his big chest. I stop.

"Hey," he says, his eyes wary.

"Hi."

"You okay?" he asks.

I incline my head. "Yeah. You?"

"Aye. I'm okay." He pushes away from the wall to step directly in my path. I catch that familiar Omen scent of woodsmoke. "Listen, Rach—"

"Crow," I say, meeting his stormy gaze, "I can't do this right now. It's all so messed up. And Adalind . . ."

"I know. I'm sorry." He exhales and pulls something out from within his leather jacket before looking at me sheepishly. "I, uh, got you something."

I don't take it. I don't even look at it. Instead, I take a step back.

"Why are you doing this?" I ask. "Are you trying to win back favor with my brother?"

His eyes widen. "No. I've screwed it up with you and your brother. I know that. I just . . . I saw it at the shop, and I thought you might like it."

There's something almost childlike to his demeanor as he shifts his weight from one foot to the other. I sigh and look at what's in his hand. It's a DVD. The *Godzilla* remake.

"You can throw it out if you like," he says when I just stare at it. "I just . . . well, you liked the old version, so—"

I snatch the DVD out of his hands.

"Er," Crow starts, but I'm already running back into the main room, not bothering to hold the swinging door open for him.

Gabriel and Jonathon are sitting at the bar—Gabriel plopping an umbrella into Jonathon's bright green drink and explaining that the decoration makes it taste better—while Josie cleans behind it. They all turn as I drop the DVD on the nearest high table.

"I think I have an idea," I say. "About how to get rid of Adalind."

"Really?" says Gabriel, absently stirring his cocktail.

I cross my arms. "There's no need to sound so surprised."

"Well—"

"Shush," I say. He falls silent. "Have you ever seen *Godzilla?*"

"The old version, or the remake?" asks Gabriel.

"Doesn't matter," I say impatiently. "Either."

"No," he says.

I look at him, perplexed. "They why did you—?" I shake my head. "Never mind. It's about these two monsters that fight each other."

I look around, my eyes catching Crow's. He's slumped back down on a stool, his expression dark.

"What on earth are you talking about?" says Gabriel.

"Beats me too, babe," says Josie, leaning against the bar.

I take a deep breath. "In Godzilla, there's this monster—"

"Godzilla?" says Gabriel.

"No. I mean, yes. But there's another monster. It's causing all this havoc, and the humans can't kill it. But Godzilla is this *worse* monster. They fight, and Godzilla wins."

Gabriel looks confused. "We're here to stop the Serpent before she kills Adam and Eve and thus puts an end to all humanity, not discuss movies. What are you saying?"

"She's saying that if we want to win this, we need a monster that's worse than Adalind, mate," says Crow, and I can tell from the way he's straightened that he's getting into the idea.

"And where exactly are we going to find a monster worse than Adalind? She's a giant, unkillable serpent with the intelligence of an immortal human," says Gabriel.

"I know where," I say, then I turn to Jonathon. "You said so yourself, she wouldn't want him here because he'd be *pissed* she did all this without his consent."

Gabriel gets it now. His face drains of color.

"You can't possibly be suggesting what I think you're suggesting," he says.

"It could work," says Crow.

Gabriel snaps his head toward Crow. "Do you really think that? Or are you just trying to get in Rachel's good books?"

Crow gives a half-shrug, eyes glinting, and takes a sip of his bright green drink.

"I mean, seriously," says Gabriel. "How would this not be making everything a hundred times worse?"

"Yet you're not saying no," says Crow. "Which means you know it has legs."

Gabriel's cheeks pinken as he looks down at the bar. "We can't . . ." His voice is quiet. "I'm an Angel. It goes against everything—"

"Think about it, mate," says Crow. "He doesn't want to be on Earth. Not yet. He knows he can't stay because he knows he can't win. That's why he was recruiting all those years ago. That's why *I* was murdered in the first place. But there's been no activity since, right?"

"No. But—"

"Don't get me wrong, he'll be *pissed* to be here. And he's a monster. *Much* worse than Adalind. We'll all be putting our lives and our souls in danger." Crow shrugs. "But we're in danger anyway if Adalind succeeds. As is the rest of humanity. And he's the only monster she fears; the only one with the power to drag her back to Hell." He raises his glass to me. "I'm with Rachel on this one."

I appreciate the support even if I'm not sure Crow, with his many schemes of self-destruction, is the person I want on my side.

Jonathon blows out hot air. "We're putting a lot of faith in the idea he won't want to continue with the Apocalypse once here," he says.

"Aye. But you're a man of science, mate," says Crow. "What would you say the evidence is suggesting?"

Jonathon stares at Crow, then at me. Then he sighs in the way that I know means I've won.

"Just so we're all clear, what exactly are you suggesting, babe?" Josie says, but when I turn to her, I can tell from the worry in her eyes that she already knows.

I pick up my drink and stick an umbrella in it, noting Gabriel was right—it *does* taste better with a bit of decoration.

"I'm saying we deliver the final Revelation Scroll," I say. "I'm saying we trigger the actual Apocalypse. I'm saying we summon Lucifer."

Chapter Forty-Three

An hour and a half later, Crow and I stand outside a tall, tired-looking apartment block in downtown Los Angeles.

"This the one?" he says.

I glance at the Afterlife app. Jonathon gave us the privileges we need to see where Adalind lives. Crow's black spot and my red one are right over it on the map.

"Yeah."

It's taken too long already to get here. The traffic was bad, thanks to what the radio reported was a sinkhole on the street leading to Devils Inc.

Adalind must be trying to get into Halo Corp.

We need to get the final scroll and deliver it to Apocalypse before it's too late.

Crow turns his head to look at me. The sky is overcast—a stark contrast to the bright sun and blue skies this morning—almost as if it knows what's coming. It darkens his already stormy eyes.

"Well, shall we?" he says.

I pull my gaze away. "Yeah. Let's get this over with."

He walks to the building's peeling white door and puts his hand flat against the buzzer. The shadows from the hanging basket of dead flowers and the traffic lights slide over to collect at his feet. Slowly, they travel up the doorframe.

As he does his Omen thing, I quickly check Afterlife. Gabriel's white spot is at Halo Corp, where he headed to draw up some forces should we need to fight. Jonathon isn't on the map, but I know he went with him to make sure Adam and Eve were safe. I quickly swipe over to find Josie's purple pinpoint at Apocalypse. She went as soon as we left Evie's to find out as much as she could about what happens once the end is triggered.

The click of the door draws my attention back to our breaking and entering. Crow steps in casually, as though he's entering his own home rather than the residence of a gargantuan serpent.

"You coming, little Demon?" says Crow.

Truthfully, I'd have rather brought one of the others, but Crow was the best for this Ethereal burglary job.

"Yeah. Don't call me that." I follow him into the mouth of the building.

"Sorry. Rachel," he says as we head for the stairs. "Which floor?"

"Third floor. Apartment fourteen," I murmur.

He takes the stairs two at a time, and I follow, the lights in the walls flickering as he passes. When we come out on the third-floor landing, the shadows are already sliding down the floor ahead of us to curl up Adalind's door and break the lock.

When Crow puts a hand on the handle and pulls, however, it doesn't open. He frowns, then bends down to peer through the keyhole. I wrench him back.

"Have you never seen a horror movie?" I hiss. "Because this is the point where some idiot looking through a keyhole gets their eye poked out."

"Nice to know you still care, little De—"

"Are you *trying* to piss me off?"

His gaze flicks pointedly down to my hand. "Aye."

Weak blue flames dance at my fingertips. I curse. I've tried my whole life to hide my feelings, and now I literally burst into flames when I get pissed off? I hate that Crow knows he can still get under my skin.

I hurl the small ball of flames at the lock. It shatters, creating a small hole in the wood.

"You're a dick," I say.

"She had an anti-Omen device built around the lock," he explains. "See the light around it? That prevents the shadows from—"

"You could have just said that."

"Aye. But where's the fun in that, little Demon?"

I have to swallow down another wave of irritation as Crow kicks in the door.

"Fun? This is fun for you, Ewan?" I ask as we step inside, and then I feel a burst of satisfaction at the way he tenses at the sound of his real name.

But I don't enjoy it for long because now we're in, and I have a scroll to find amid what turns out to be a lot of clutter. I guess when you've been alive since Genesis, you end up collecting a lot of crap.

The prominent features are a scuffed black sofa, a black leather recliner, an old boxy TV, a pile of leather books on an antique-looking coffee table, and a small writing desk littered with maps and law textbooks. There are used mugs everywhere and a black marble fruit bowl full of rotting apples on the chipped windowsill. Weirdly, the shelves on one wall are almost entirely filled with those Troll dolls with the brightly-colored hair.

Crow exhales next to me. "Not fun, no. Maybe I just want you to be angry."

"Why?"

"Maybe because anger is better than nothing at all."

I look at him hard. "Seriously, Crow. What the hell do you want?" But then I hold up a hand. "No. You know what? We don't have time for this. Let's just get the scroll and get out of—"

I stop talking, my eyes drawn across the room. Above the desk, there's a collection of photographs, including that awful "slutty Demon" photo of me from Instagram.

"Oh, god," I say.

"I know," says Crow, though he's staring at the wall of Trolls.

"Not that," I huff. I tug his arm. *"That."*

"Can't have a villain's lair without a photo collage of your diabolical plan," says Crow darkly.

"That's seriously creepy," I say, my irritation momentarily forgotten.

"Aye," says Crow, crossing the room to rip it down. Then he looks down at the desk and picks something up. "Oh, hey, scroll's here." He turns to face me, brandishing a yellowing piece of parchment sealed with crimson wax. He throws it in the air and catches it. "That was easy."

I fold my arms across my chest. "You just don't give a shit, do you?"

"Eh?"

"Who says shit like that right before an Apocalypse? Are you trying to tempt fate?"

A smile spreads across his face, and he shrugs, but then he runs a hand over his mouth.

"Just . . . talk to me, Rachel," he says. "Tell me I'm a dick. Throw a fireball at me. Whatever. Let's just get on with it."

"So you can feel better?"

"Aye. So I can feel better." He crosses the room, stopping close enough that I can smell his shower gel. "It may have escaped your notice, but I'm a selfish dick. Just hit me or something." His breathing is heavy, like he's bracing himself for what's next. "Go on," he says. "Just do it."

"I don't want to," I say through gritted teeth.

"Liar. Come on, little Demon. Hit me."

As I glare up at him, a lick of angry heat flares in my stomach. A part of me does want to lash out; to inflict some of my pain on him.

Instead, I take a step back. "You should have told me. It wasn't fair. Not what you did to me. Not what you did to Gabriel either. I'm not going to hit you to ease your conscience. It doesn't work that way."

"Fine. Don't do it to ease my conscience. Do it to make you feel better."

"I need time."

"We don't have time." His cheeks are flushed, and for the first time since I've known him, he seems genuinely agitated. "We're about to trigger the Apocalypse."

"Let's just go," I say, starting to turn away.

He grabs my arm. "I'm sorry. I truly am, Rachel. I didn't do it on purpose."

"Like hell you didn't," I say, spinning back around and wrenching my arm out of his grasp. Although I can see his satisfaction at provoking a reaction, I don't care. He's right. It does feel good to be angry. "You hid something from me. Something I deserved to know."

He opens his mouth to reply, but now that I've started, I can't stop.

"And I know, we had a casual thing. It didn't have to mean anything. But you did exactly what Gabriel said you would. You *worked* to hook me. You tried to make it seem like more than that. You tried to make me open up to you, to trust you."

"Rachel, listen—"

"No. You listen. I see what you do now. You flit around fabricating real connections until you get what you want because you've figured out that's what works best for you. It's messed up. For a moment, you made me feel like we actually had something, and I don't connect easily." I stop then, feeling flushed.

His eyes flash. "Has it ever occurred to you that you felt that way because we did have something?"

"No. You're married, Crow. You hid it. Who does that!"

"I know. And I know it's messed up. I love her, and ever since I lost her, I've had to focus on trying to make things right or I'll go fucking insane. I can't give anyone else what they want or deserve from me, so most of the time, I don't even try. But that doesn't mean I don't feel anything. It doesn't mean everything is fake. It just . . . I don't know how to do this."

I shake my head. "I might almost believe you. But you did the exact same thing to Gabriel."

"Aye. And I cared about Gabriel too!"

Even in the cramped apartment, the words echo.

With a sigh, he rubs his face. "I don't know how to do this," he says. "I love my wife. I always have. I always will. But it's over. I know it's over. I just . . . I just can't let it go. Ever since I died, it's been my only fucking purpose. Making things right. And if I do let it go, I'm scared I'll fall apart."

He looks at me then.

"I care about you, Rachel. Yes, I started out protecting you because I wanted something from your brother. I never lied about that. And at first, I slept with you because I'm a dick and I thought you were hot. I admit it. But the rest of it . . . I wasn't trying to mess with you, or fake something, or get a hook into you. It was just . . . me." He shakes his head. "You deserve better. I should have exercised caution. I—"

"You should have been honest with me," I say quietly.

"Aye. I should have been honest with you. I'm sorry. I truly am. And if this all goes to shit"—he glances at the scroll, then back to me—"I just want you to know that. Because if I get trapped in some depth of Hell and I can't get to you, I want you to know that you didn't mean nothing. I'll never be able to tell Maddie that. But I had to tell you. Before the end. I had to. Maybe that's selfish. But I had to. I just . . . I'm sorry."

We stare at each other. Then we both exhale at the same time.

"I know you're sorry," I say finally. "And I'm sorry about your wife. This situation. It's just—"

"Messed up. I know."

I sigh again. "Yeah."

He averts his eyes, nervousness making its first appearance. "Do you think—?"

Before he can finish, something shatters. Crow lunges forward, knocking the air out of my lungs as he brings us to the ground, sheltering my body. Just past his head, I see the light of blue flame. White plaster rains down all around us. The Revelation Scroll rolls just out of reach.

He raises himself on his forearms, my body caged within his.

"Let's put a pin in that," he says. "Looks like we have company."

I scramble for my cell in my pocket, then glance at Afterlife. The map shows a cluster of about fifty black and red dots outside Adalind's apartment.

I turn it to Crow. "You think Adalind sent them?"

"Aye." His face darkens. "She has admin level on Afterlife— she'll have seen we were here. Bit of an oversight, really."

"Shit," I say under my breath.

There's another crashing sound as a new fireball hurtles into the wall. Crow stays on top of me, the falling plaster turning his black hair white.

"Shouldn't we get going then?" I ask.

"Aye. Let's."

I shove him off me and grab the scroll. After he helps to pull me to my feet, we run out of Adalind's door. Footsteps echo up from the stairwell.

My eyes lock on Crow's, and he pulls me toward a wide window at the other end of the hallway. The lights flicker, and he uses the new shadows to pop the glass from its frame.

We're not high enough to die if we jump out, but we'll probably break our legs.

"Do you trust me, little Demon?" he says.

"No," I say. I don't slow down though.

"Probably wise."

With his hand still curled around my arm, he turns just as we hit the window, pulling me into him and locking my body against his chest.

Revelation Scroll clenched in my fist and a horde of Demons racing toward us, we hurtle toward the earth.

Chapter Forty-Four

We're falling.

A ball of blue fire sparks out of the window above us, cutting through a sky filled with ominous clouds. The breeze whips my hair, and my stomach is in my throat. Even with Crow wrapped around me, the ground will be brutal.

Then Crow twists the fingers of his free hand, and darkness rises around us—thick, and malleable, and suffocating.

Our fall slows.

But not completely.

We thud hard onto the concrete. Crow grunts, a raw sound scraping his throat, as he takes most of the impact. We're shrouded in shadow still, and all I hear within the cocoon of darkness is his low, hot breath against my ear. I gulp in smoky darkness.

Then the shadows fade.

Demons and Omens close in on both sides, a mass of black blazers and leather jackets.

Crow's black Mini Cooper is parked just down the road. We need to get to it. Fast.

I wriggle away from him to take a better look. Shit. There's a dribble of blood leaking from the corner of his mouth, and his face is contorted in pain.

"You okay?" I ask him.

He groans again, eyelids flickering. Then he rolls onto his forearms and spits out blood.

"Crow?" I say.

He makes another raw sound. I move closer, grabbing his shoulder.

"Crow? Are you okay?"

"Aye. Bid my tongue. Hurts like a motherfuc—"

I slap his arm. "I thought you were dying or something! Jesus Christ. Can we save the dramatics and get going, please?" I jerk my head toward the pack of Demons headed our way.

He looks over my shoulder. "Ah, shit," he says.

I see the reflection of blue flames in his eyes and throw him to the concrete just as the fireball smashes into the window of a first-floor apartment. Soon after, the door of the building crashes open, the Omens and Demons that were in the stairwell spilling out.

"This isn't good, little Demon."

"I noticed."

Another fireball crashes from our right, but Crow manages to fizzle it using the shadow from the traffic lights. When he cocoons us in another wall of darkness, I can't see anything. Cold adrenaline drowns any heat in my veins. I'm breathing hard. There are so many of them. How can we beat them all?

"Crow!" I yell.

"I'm thinking!" he yells back.

A screech of tires cuts through our panic. Crow drops the shield as a Honda Civic brakes on the sidewalk just in front of us.

The door flies open, and Jonathon leans over from the driver's seat.

"Get in!" he yells.

We don't need to be told twice. Under the cover of Crow's darkness, I throw myself into the passenger seat while Crow piles into the back.

"Good timing," I say, my voice breathless as we slam the doors shut.

"Been keeping an eye on Afterlife," says Jonathon, putting his foot down on the accelerator. "Noticed a load of Demons making their way here."

Under cover of shadow, the car lurches forward, knocking through a bunch of Demons who don't see us coming. They yell and hit the car, creating a cacophony of fists against metal, before Jonathon breaks us free and we hurtle down the road.

"Get off me, Omen," a sharp female voice says as we swerve around the corner.

"Evie. Pleasure as always," Crow replies. "And with the hubby as well."

Eve, the bartender I met just before I signed away my soul, sits in the backseat, her black hair swept into a long ponytail that hangs over one shoulder of her green blouse. She's perched stiffly between Crow and a man wearing a linen top. Adam. His skin is the same creamy brown as Eve's, and he has beautiful dark brown eyes.

Crow smirks. "How . . . awkward."

That's when I notice their bodies are angled away from one another.

The back window cracks, and we all flinch as a ball of blue fire bounces off it. When I peer back again, I see we have a new tail.

"You got the scroll, sis?" says Jonathon.

"Yep," I say, holding it up.

He nods, eyes wide, as he looks through the rearview mirror. "We need to get to Trinity Falls as soon as possible. Before Adalind realizes I've got Adam and Eve."

"Where's Gabe?" Crow says, leaning between the seats.

The question is casual enough, but I notice the knuckles of the hand on my seat are white.

"Still at Halo Corp." Jonathon overtakes another car. As the driver honks, Jonathon swerves onto the sidewalk to overtake a line forming behind a red light. "It's pretty bad over there. But Gabriel tipped them off that the end of the world is happening. He's pulling together a team to come over to Apocalypse and fight with us."

We dodge a fireball on our way onto the freeway. The traffic is bad enough that Jonathon has to slow down, dodging cars as we swerve across the nine lanes. Demons and Omens swerve with us. This isn't good.

Crow slumps back and looks through the rear window. "Come on, Gabe," he mutters, then he yells for everyone to duck.

This time, the back glass shatters, revealing a hatchback Porsche close behind. A blonde drives, while a girl with a brown pixie cut hurls blue flames from the passenger seat. The air is filled with the angry honking of a thousand innocent passengers' road rage.

The road beneath us trembles.

"What was that?" I whirl in my seat.

"She's coming," says Adam coolly. "She knows we're not at Halo Corp."

"Thanks for stating the obvious," snaps Eve.

The momentary distraction stops us from seeing the red Ford Fiesta until it barges into us from the right side and manages to run us into a metal barrier. We jerk forward against our seat belts as sparks fly, and a number of cars have to swerve out of our path. As soon as we screech to a halt, a fireball hits the back of the car.

"EVERYONE OUT!" yells Jonathon.

Sweat rolling down my face, I stumble into the road still gripping the Revelation Scroll. Crow, Adam, and Eve fall out of the back as Jonathon hurries to my side. Flames roar behind us as cars full of Demons screech to a halt on all sides.

"Shit!" I say.

Adam pulls a dagger from his belt and twirls it with a performative air. Eve scowls, then she strides to the trunk of the car, making a low sound as she touches the scalding metal. Once it's open, she pulls out a great-sword, flames dancing along the blade.

The corner of Crow's lip lifts. "Looks like your wife has the bigger—"

"Oh, shut up," says Adam. "I've only known you five minutes, and I already despise you."

The Demons have gotten out of their cars to form a circle around us. The floor trembles.

The girl with the pixie cut steps forward, and I see she's wearing a Devils Inc. blazer.

"You're one of us now, intern," she says. "Give us the scroll, and you won't die horrible, painful deaths. We don't care about the Serpent's gripe with humanity, but we can't have you summoning the boss. He'll be pissed."

"Any ideas?" I mutter, sliding my gaze to Crow, only to find he has his eyes closed and is muttering something under his breath, big hands clasped together. I nudge him.

"Shh," he says without opening his eyes.

The Demon gives a twisted smile. "Oh well. Worth a try. I wanted to do it the murderous way anyway."

Heat hits us from all directions as the Demons draw their blue flames.

The floor trembles again.

That's when Crow puts his finger and thumb in his mouth and whistles. A crow caws somewhere in the distance. Another answers it. And then the sky darkens as the sound of flapping wings fills the air. Big black birds nosedive from the clouds, tearing at our attackers. Adam and Eve join the fray, slicing down any Demon who comes close.

"We need to get to Apocalypse!" I yell.

"Don't worry," says Crow. "I called you a cab."

"Huh?"

As if on cue, something hurtles through the black, cawing mass. A topless Gabriel skids to a halt in front of us, white wings shuddering behind him.

"I got your prayer," he tells Crow. "I'm surprised you remember how to do that."

Crow shrugs. "Never forgot, mate."

Gabriel spins on his heel to face me. Despite the fact he's just been hurtling through a sky full of birds, his red hair is perfectly neat.

"Rachel. You have the scroll. Excellent work." He shifts from one foot to the other. "We should probably get going."

I stare at his chest. "Uh, so you mean, I should . . .?"

He runs a hand through his hair. "Yes. Well . . ."

I step closer to him, not really sure what to do.

"Just put your arms around my neck," he says.

I do as he says, gripping my wrist to make a solid lock while also keeping hold of the scroll. As my knuckles brush against his wings, he tenses. I tense too.

"Sorry," I mutter.

"This is uncomfortable to watch," observes Crow over the murder of crows.

"Yeah," agrees Jonathon.

"Oh, shut up," I say.

The corner of their lips continue to twitch until Jonathon's eyes meet Gabriel's over my head, suddenly fierce.

"Look after her."

"Of course," says Gabriel.

Carnage rages around us, fireballs flying and swords flashing as birds swarm through the air.

I look at Crow. "Look after my brother."

He inclines his head, his face unusually serious. "Aye. I won't let anything happen to him," he says, then he looks to Gabriel. "Good luck, mate."

"And you," says Gabriel.

"See you at the end of the world."

Gabriel nods back. Then he brings his gaze to mine, face close. "Ready, Rachel?"

I suck in a breath. "Yeah."

Gabriel locks his hands around my waist as Crow whistles for the black, swirling mass of birds above to part. Gabriel bends his knees, and then his huge white wings make a strong, violent movement.

And the road drops from beneath my feet as we start to fly.

Chapter Forty-Five

We leave the fighting behind in mere seconds. The cars look like toys from up here, and as my hair whips my face, I can taste the clouds.

We're so close together that I feel the toned muscles of his stomach against mine, but thanks to the elation—and terror—surging through my body, I'm feeling more at peace with the strange physical contact than expected. My eyes are entranced by his wings as they move behind him—slowly, powerfully, the hard feathers brushing my knuckles every so often.

After five minutes, I ease my hold just a little. His embrace is surprisingly strong despite his slender frame, and I know I won't fall.

Soon, I catch the familiar white church surrounded by palm trees at the end of the Trinity Falls main street, and Gabriel starts to drop height. I feel a mixture of relief, dismay, and dread. The muscles in my arms might ache, and the Angel carrying me might not be enjoying the experience, but it feels good to be flying.

Gabriel's body suddenly tenses against mine, his arms tightening around my waist.

"Gabriel? What is—?"

My voice is drowned out as the churchyard below erupts in a volcanic burst of mud, stone, and bone.

Gabriel swerves roughly, turning me away from the blast as dirt rains down on his red hair. My eyes widen when the Serpent's head rears into the sky behind him with a thunderous rumble, fangs like knives, eyes like fire.

"GABRIEL!" I yell.

He changes course, narrowly avoiding impact with her wide mouth. But her black tail lashes out and clips his wing. He cries out, and we plunge toward the ground.

He manages to gain control just in time, and we drop clumsily into the churchyard. Wind knocked out of us, we rest our weight on our forearms as we catch our breath.

We're trapped within a prison of green and black scales as her body coils around the perimeter of the church. Her large head has thrown the yard into shadow, and her sharp tail has broken the window by the arched door. I catch a scattering of old gravestones and the ripped wood of coffins, splintered like kindling.

I shift, feeling something hard piercing my palm. When I realize it's a fragment of bone, I fight a wave of nausea.

Adalind lazily turns her head to look down, her amber snake eyes catching mine. Then her laugh fills the air, raspy and terrifying.

"Nice try, intern," she hisses.

I swallow hard, holding the scroll. Even though adrenaline surges through my body, it doesn't bring the heat I need to fight. I turn to Gabriel. He's red-faced and muttering in pain. His eyes are squeezed closed. His wings are still shuddering behind him, and the hard feathers on his left one look ruffled and out of place.

He's hurt. Out of action.

We're well and truly doomed.

Or—no, I can't think like that. The nearest part of Adalind's scaly body is thirty feet away, pressed up against an iron fence. If I could distract her, then climb it. . . God, I can *smell* the fried onions from Diablos' hot dog stand.

Apocalypse is so close. And yet so far.

"It's a shame," continues Adalind, slowly dropping her head to our height. Her fangs are covered in blood. I can smell it on her breath, coppery and sour. "I actually kind of liked you, intern," she says, forked tongue slipping out. "But you are becoming a pesssst."

"Says the big lizard," I retort, not managing to hide the quiver in my voice.

She laughs. "Any lassst words? No, never mind. I can't be asssed with that."

She rears back to her full height, ready to lunge.

Figures drop down from the sky around us, ten in total. Angels. They wear white suits that must have some kind of slits to accommodate the great white wings that fold into their backs as they land.

Gabriel lets out a relieved sigh. "The military department," he says under his breath.

Adalind's eyes make a strange movement. If she wasn't a giant serpent Demon, I'd think she was rolling them.

"Oh. Some Halo Corp stiffsss. How sssscary."

She lunges at one of them, a muscular guy with dark skin, and he dives behind an upturned tombstone before throwing a ball of white light at her. There's shouting and chaos and blurs of light as the Angels' attacks bounce off Adalind's scales.

"You summoned them?" I ask Gabriel. "The Angels?"

"Yes. By prayer," he says. "But they're no match for her."

Adalind's tail whips out, hurling broken pieces of white wood from the church across the lawn and wobbling the cross on its roof. Gabriel and I roll and duck as a big gray boulder shatters inches from where we lay. Another Angel, a guy with blond hair, is hit in the head and rendered unconscious.

Adalind laughs and begins to slither in a circle, drawing us all closer to its center.

"We need to get out of here!" I tell Gabriel, pulling him to his feet. The barrier between us and Apocalypse is only getting higher.

"If I heal my wing, I can fly us over her body," he says.

"Great!" I say.

He stares at me. Nothing happens.

"Go ahead and do it!" I say.

"I can't." He thrusts a hand through his neat red hair. "I'm panicking."

I rub my face, aware of Adalind's hissing laughter and the cries of more fallen Angels.

"Okay, well . . . calm down, Gabriel. There, there." I use my best soothing voice as screams and shouts fill the air. "It'll be all right. We're absolutely not going to be squeezed to death by a giant serpent monster."

"Not. Helping."

I'm about to try again when we're interrupted by a loud whinnying sound. Something flies through the air over Adalind's body. We both stagger back as a large, pale white horse skids to a halt in front of us, its eyes black as death. Its black saddle is adorned with silver markings depicting scythes.

Josie sits atop it like a conquering queen, hair wild, eyes bright.

My mouth drops open.

"Don't even ask, babe. Need a ride?"

I glance at Gabriel, and he nods. "Go," he says.

"Your wing?"

"Getting rid of you drastically alleviates the stress."

"Thanks," I say.

He gives me a half-smile. "I didn't mean it like that. Go!"

He nudges me to the beast, and Josie helps me clamber onto its back. I grab her waist, the scroll still in my hand. Her sandalwood perfume mingles with the earthy scent of horse.

"You're coming too, right?" I ask him.

"I'll be right behind you," he says.

Gabriel closes his eyes. He shudders, and soon, his wing snaps back into place. Then he hurtles up into the air in front of Adalind, distracting her just long enough for Josie to cry out and dig her heels into the sides of our mount.

It leaps. And for the third time today, I'm hurtling through the air. When we clear the Serpent's body and come back down on the street, Apocalypse is just a short gallop away.

"So the horsemen *literally* have horses then?" I yell as we pass Diablos'.

"Yeah. Darius isn't allowed to interfere in this, but he let me borrow his horse," she yells. "He's waiting for us in the basement of Apocalypse. We just need to get there before—"

There's a rumbling behind us. Adalind's seen through the distraction, and her serpent eyes are fixed on us.

Shit.

She lurches toward us, sending the iron fence and one of the palm trees crashing down the road. Ahead of us, cars screech to a halt, and Demons pile out. My stomach lurches. Where are Jonathon and Crow?

Josie pulls the reins and swerves the horse into Apocalypse. We both duck down beneath the blue sign, and then we're tucking our legs in as we gallop down the dimly lit hallway. My hair flies behind me, and my pulse mimics the loud thunder of hooves on linoleum. Seconds later, we're bursting into the blue-lit main club and catching the scent of old alcohol and lime wedges.

The dance floor trembles beneath us. Then a hissing sound follows.

Adalind.

Josie pulls back the reins, and we leap over the central bar, both crying out as we hit the ground with a skid. Then the horse bursts through the black double doors at the far end of the room. *Employees and horses only,* I think wildly as we take another flight of stairs down.

The horse slows to a stop, and I raise my head to study our new surroundings.

The four Horsemen are lined up by one wall in front of a closed elevator, all wearing off-white linen shirts over brown pants. From their faces, it looks like they're about to head into battle. Chris stands at the end with a huge bow, blond hair tousled. Beside him is Will, with his neat dark hair and sly mouth. He holds a giant sword. Felix stands next to him, sleeves rolled up over his muscular forearms to reveal a scales tattoo similar to the large brass pendent around his neck.

And Darius stands at the end, tall and menacing, with dark, penetrating eyes. His hand is clasped around his scythe.

They emanate power. Static, and cold, and heavy. My arms turn to gooseflesh. My breath mists in front of my face.

"Josie and Rachel, we've been expecting you," says Darius, his voice a silky shroud.

Josie's breathing quickens. So does mine. The magnitude of what we're about to do crashes down on me.

"Darius," she starts.

"Death." His dark eyes catch hers. "You must call me Death in here, my darling."

There are a series of frantic thuds behind us. We jerk around as a tangle of limbs tumbles and skids into the room. It's Gabriel, wings out, with Crow. One of the Omen's muscular arms is hooked around Gabriel's neck, the other clamped around his waist.

When Crow untangles himself, he looks a little sick. Gabriel's wings shudder into his shoulder blades, his expression haughty. Without looking at him, Crow shrugs off his leather jacket and throws it to Gabriel, who slips it on, zipping it up to cover up his bare chest.

"Where's my brother?" I ask.

Crow was supposed to look after him.

On cue, Jonathon stumbles into the room, a motorcycle helmet tucked under his arm. "Here now," he says. "Helped Adam and Eve steal a car, then got one of my old contacts to lend me a bike."

"His idea, little Demon," says Crow, raising his hands in surrender.

"Are they safe?" asks Gabriel.

"The Demons weren't interested in them," says Jonathon. "Only the scroll. With Adalind distracted, they should be fine. For now."

Before anyone can say anything else, Darius coughs pointedly behind me.

"I'm so sorry to interrupt your conversation, but I believe you have something you wish to deliver?"

His three brothers smirk. My heart beats fast. Is this really a good idea? Summoning the Devil? But Crow gives me an encouraging nod. So does Gabriel.

As soon as I slide off the horse, Josie jumps down beside me.

"How does it work?" she says. Her Afro is wild from the horse ride, and her shoulders are tense beneath her floaty green top. The silver cross she wears around her neck glints in the eerie blue light.

The brothers step to the side to reveal the elevator with an *"Out of Order"* sign behind them. Instead of call buttons, there are four holes in the wall.

Three of them have scrolls sticking out of them.

"When the final scroll is turned in the lock, the wax seal breaks, and the Elevator is called," says Darius. He deliberately peels the sign off the doors and lets it float to the black linoleum.

"Where from?" I ask, a cold ball of dread growing in my stomach.

He smiles. "Hell, of course."

Josie makes a soft noise in her throat, touching her cross. I hold her gaze, heartbeat quickening. She doesn't want me to do this. I'm not sure I want to do this.

But . . .

We both flinch as the ground shakes. I hear footsteps above as dust falls from the ceiling. Someone screams. Then a hissing sound vibrates through the wall.

What choice do we have?

"Well?" Darius says, holding out his hand.

Before I can second-guess myself, I hand him the scroll. His strong, tattooed hand curls slowly around it. Then he strides to the elevator, slips it in the lock, and slowly turns.

There's a click. Then a whirring sound.

He smiles at his brothers. "The end is nigh, boys."

Cool adrenaline surges through my body as Josie and I take a step back to rejoin the others. My arm brushes against Crow's. I instinctively start to pull it away but then decide to leave it, given this might be the end of the world anyway.

Lucifer is coming.

My heart beats fast against my chest. I can't believe we're doing this. I can't believe we're summoning the Devil.

This moment seems to last forever.

Then the elevator pings.

The doors slide open.

Chapter Forty-Six

The man who emerges is tall, with broad, muscular shoulders and dirty blond hair shaved close to his scalp. He's shirtless, and there are glistening patches of frost on his exposed skin that seem to burn and crackle as he moves. In one hand, he holds a bronze trident. A sharp, pointed tail curls out the back of his black pants.

Lucifer.

The scent of brimstone is suffocating.

Cold air follows him as he steps further into the room. He's taller even than Crow, and his whole being emanates menace. His tail hovers in the air behind him—obsidian-black, with a sharp point at the end.

Horror unfurls in my gut when his gaze hits me. He looks like a man, but I see no humanity inside his neon-blue gaze, only coldness. And in this moment, I understand Gabriel's initial reluctance to raise him.

He is a monster.

What have we done?

The faint sound of screaming can be heard upstairs, but none of us flinch. There's a greater threat in here, with us.

Lucifer narrows his eyes as he looks at the door beyond.

"Dante," says Lucifer.

"Yes, my lord?"

That's when I see that Lucifer didn't come alone. A tall, thin man stands in the corner of the elevator, his black cloak making him one with the shadows.

"Hold the elevator," he says. "You won't be taking the journey back down alone."

"Yes, my lord."

I glance sideways at Crow, the cold, hard ball of dread growing. It sounds like he plans to fight Adalind, but that doesn't mean he's going back after.

Crow's cheeks are flushed, and his hands are held in fists. He looks angry. I wish I knew what he was thinking.

Lucifer slides his hand up his trident, fingers curling around the bronze. I'm steeling myself for a fight when the back wall behind us caves in with an explosion of rubble.

I grab Josie, and we crash to the floor to the side as bits of concrete and plaster spray the room. Something hits the side of my head, and I grunt. When I touch my hair, my fingers come away red with blood. Dizzy, I look to see if I can spot the others.

For a moment, all I see is darkness and two unblinking neon-blue eyes. All I hear is the whinnying of Darius's horse and the thunder of its hooves as it clears the room. I can smell dust, and brimstone, and the metal of blood.

And then a low, soft hissing enters the space. Something is slithering in.

The hairs on my arm stand on end. My eyes, stinging from the dust, adjust just enough to see the head of the Serpent rearing up between us.

Shit.

I roll to the side as she lunges at me, bare arms scraping roughly across sharp bits of brick and concrete. She gnashes her head, and I roll back, narrowly avoiding her fangs—each one as sharp as a blade and the length of my arm.

Somewhere, my friends call my name. Suddenly, Adalind's head is pulled back, and I see Crow attacking. She thrashes him away, and there's a loud crash of a body hitting the wall before she lunges at me once more.

"The ssscroll," she hisses.

"Get away from my sister!" I hear Jonathon running toward her.

She flicks her tail and sends him skidding across the floor.

I feel my power then, hot, in my stomach. No one touches my brother. I send a fireball at her face before scrambling to the side. It misses, but it lights the room enough that I see a glimmer of Lucifer as it hurtles past.

He's just standing there. Unmoved.

Adalind laughs, then she drops her head toward mine. Her eyes are bright in the darkness, and I can make out the inky blood dripping from her fangs.

"It'ssss over, intern. Give me the sssscroll."

When I don't respond, she raises her head, preparing to strike.

"I can't. I already gave it to *him*," I say, jerking my head to the right.

She pauses. Then she looks to her left, and her snake eyes catch Lucifer's. She hisses, then rears back so sharply her head bangs into the ceiling.

A new dusting of plaster falls, coating his muscles and dirty blond hair, yet he remains stoic. There's a predatory look in his too-blue eyes; the look of a wolf who knows he's about to devour his prey.

"You dare to defy me, Adalind?" he says in a voice laced with sweet poison.

She attempts to slither back through the hole in the wall she's created, but enough has fallen that she's trapped. She stops, and her yellow eyes narrow.

"You left me," she hisses. "I sssserved you. And you left me."

"Yes," he says. "And I had you where I needed you."

"You let them take my power. You abandoned—"

"Silence," he says in a tone that doesn't allow for disobedience. He takes a step forward, muscles rippling, patches of burning frost crackling on his skin. "I had you in a position where you could be my eyes and ears on earth, where you'd know everything that happened within my corporation so that when I returned, you could serve at my side. You were the first Greater Demon I managed to station on earth, ready. You were mine. You were one of my greatest weapons for the Final War to come."

Her head jerks back. "My lord. You never told me."

"I did not realize, Adalind, that I had to run my plans past you."

His voice is light, but there is a coldness behind it. He begins to pace as though lecturing a recalcitrant child.

"So now, what are we to do with you? You have come into your powers prematurely. The Ethereal laws will not allow you to stay on earth for long. And thus, you force my hand. Do we go ahead with Revelation and begin a War for which we're unprepared?"

"Yesss, my lord. We can win. The Angelsssss are weak."

"It is certainly tempting."

I glance at Josie, who's taken refuge behind a large slab of concrete. Her eyes are wide with horror. I can't see Crow and the others, but I think I hear Jonathon's groan.

This is *not* how *Godzilla* plays out.

"No doubt, this cowering assortment of misfits thought they could summon me, Lucifer, King of Hell, to do their bidding as if I were some common Devils Inc. intern," he continues, sliding a finger along one of the points of his bronze trident. "Insolence cannot go unpunished."

"Yessss, my lord." Adalind's venomous voice vibrates around the dark room, and I suppress a shudder, edging back to take a seat near Josie, who shifts to make room for me near the wall. She gives me a dark look.

"This is bad, babe," she mouths.

I nod. "I know."

I wish I could see the others to determine if they have any ideas, but Adalind's scaly body blocks everything, including the hole in the wall.

And even if we got out, then what? We let Lucifer end the world?

I squeeze my eyes shut, clasping my hands together in prayer. It worked for Crow and Gabriel earlier. *Dear Gabriel,* I think. *Can you hear me? Is this a prayer? Any ideas? Please keep my brother safe. Um, yours sincerely, Rachel. Amen?*

Nothing happens.

"Come to me, Adalind," Lucifer says. "Bow down to your King, and let us put this business behind us so we can work toward a greater future. Together."

I open my eyes just in time to see Adalind bring her big face level with his. When he touches her scaled cheek with a huge hand, she nudges into it like a cat.

"My sweet Adalind," he says.

She bows in deference.

Then, in a sudden movement, he thrusts his trident up into her throat.

She screams as it pierces through her dark scales, and black blood spills like ink over Lucifer's shoulders. I throw my hands over my ears as Adalind's pain and fury vibrates through me, then I cover my head as her body convulses, bringing more of the ceiling of the small room down.

"You basssssstard!" she screeches. "You bassss—"

"Enough," he commands.

He wrenches his weapon out, and Adalind crumples to the ground, her head thudding against the ground so hard the whole room shakes. As we look on in horror, her skin shrivels, then begins to shed, decomposing until there's nothing left but the body of a girl covered in dust and gore.

Now she is small, I can see the others. Jonathon has pushed himself against the far wall, breathing fast, while Crow is beside him, crouched as though ready to spring into action. Gabriel stands in the shadows, his eyes fixed on Lucifer, his face rigid yet oddly devoid of fear.

"Dante," says Lucifer. "Give me your cloak."

The Demon in the elevator slips off his dark cloak and throws it to his master. Lucifer swipes it from the air with one hand, then throws it on Adalind before scooping her up in his arms.

"My dear Adalind," he whispers to her dead body. "You may hate me now, but do not think me cruel. You will one day have your revenge. As will I."

He carries her past the Four Horsemen, each watching impassively, and passes her fragile human body to Dante. Turned away, I see two jagged scars mark his shoulder blades where his wings were once ripped from his shoulders.

"Now," he says without turning, "as for this other matter of insolence . . ."

My eyes fly to the hole in the wall as I debate whether we can make a run for it. But no—even if we did, we can't let him stay on earth.

"Lucifer, I must interject," says Darius.

Lucifer turns his head, and the two lock gazes. Despite the menace in the Dark Lord's eyes, Darius doesn't so much as flinch.

"You forget yourself," says Lucifer. "You are in no place to question my decision to punish."

"In Hell, perhaps. But we are in my club, and I do not work for you," says Darius, his voice smooth and calm. "I have a higher calling. Still, for reasons of diplomacy, should you make the call for the Revelations War, we will ride out and bring about this Apocalypse, as is our duty. Should you wish to punish those who summoned you, we will not stand against it." He raises an eyebrow. "We do not like to be used as pawns in Ethereal games either."

My pulse quickens, and Josie tenses beside me.

"But the girl, Josie," he continues. "She is one of us. And you will not touch her."

There's a pause, long and silent. Sounds of fighting still filter down from the main club upstairs. Adalind is gone, but they don't know that yet. Or perhaps they do. Perhaps this is the start of the Final War.

"Very well," says Lucifer, still facing away from us. "Take your girl. Await my instruction. I will have a moment alone to deal with the others."

"Very well," says Darius, then he strides toward us. "Josie, my darling . . ."

"No. You can't do this," Josie says, shaking her dust-covered head. "You're not leaving them. I'm not leaving them." When Darius offers her his hand, she bats it away.

I grab her wrist. "Josie. It's fine. Go."

She snaps her head toward me. "*No.*"

Darius pauses for a moment before turning to his brother, Felix, who swoops in to throw Josie over his shoulder.

She yelps, struggling against him, but he holds her tight. When she angles her head enough to scream my name, I hold her bright eyes for a moment before tearing my gaze away. She's safer with them than us.

The rest of the Horsemen follow him through the room's new opening, riding boots crunching on the rubble.

Then there's only us left—Jonathon by the wall, Gabriel standing in the corner, Crow on his knees, and me sitting in the rubble.

And Lucifer.

"So," he says, slowly turning to face us. His inhumanly blue eyes glint with menace. "What shall I do with you four?"

Chapter Forty-Seven

The elevator to Hell gapes behind him.

"Rise," Lucifer says, imperious despite the black serpent gore still dripping from his chest.

We do. His tone doesn't allow disobedience. Not that I want to be sitting on my ass when faced with the literal King of Hell anyway.

"Which one of you delivered the scroll?" says Lucifer. The question is simple, but there's something poisonous in his tone.

Cold dread rolls in my stomach as his eyes slide over me. Crow and Jonathon start to offer up themselves, but I cut them off.

"Me," I say, ignoring their angry looks.

Lucifer's too-blue eyes lock on mine.

"So tell me, did I do my little errand to your satisfaction?" Lucifer asks as his fingers caress his trident. "I mean, that's why you summoned me, isn't it? To do a little job for you."

"Aye. You did it well enough," says Crow.

Out of the corner of my eye, I see Gabriel stiffen. Lucifer turns his head to look at Crow, but when his tail lashes out, it's my neck it wraps around.

I give a choked scream as he yanks me toward him, and although I grapple at the obsidian cord, it remains tight. *It burns*, I think, and then I realize that's not true. No. It's freezing. Frantically, I try to free myself, shortened breaths misting in front of my face.

Jonathon lurches forward, but Gabriel grabs him and throws him back toward the wall.

"Your power, Rachel," he says.

My vision blurs as I search for something hot in my veins to fight the cold burn of Lucifer's pointed tail.

I think about how I was tricked into signing away my soul. I think about how I've been damned to Hell when I didn't do anything to deserve it. I think of stupid coffee runs and filing and defending bad people at Devils Inc., and how I'll probably be stuck doing that for all eternity. I think of my brother forced into hiding, and how everything Adalind did was because Lucifer didn't intervene when she was punished. I think of Crow being murdered so he could be part of Lucifer's army, and how something inside of him has been broken ever since. I think about how that broken part of him hurt me.

It's all Lucifer's fault. He's going to end the world if we don't stop him.

I'm not going down without a fight.

The burn lessens, but my vision is blurred, the room swimming in and out of focus from the pain of it.

Crow twists a finger and sends a shadow surging toward us.

Lucifer reaches out and grabs it, wrapping it around his wrist as if it were a real thing. He pulls, and Crow stumbles toward us until he's close enough for Lucifer to wrap a hand around his neck. Crow punches him in the side of the face. Lucifer doesn't even flinch.

"Do you think I don't know what you desire, boy?" says Lucifer as Crow struggles for breath on his tiptoes. "I'm the Devil. And what a soul desires—well, it's the only thing about a soul worth knowing. It's how I recruit. It's how I keep souls in my employment. It's how I torment. It's how I punish."

He forces Crow down on his knees, then releases him. Crow coughs and wheezes for breath, hand moving to his throat, where red fingerprints mark his skin.

"What I desire is for you to piss off back down to Hell, mate," he rasps.

"No." Lucifer stares at him coolly. "That's not what you want. You want redemption. You'd like nothing more than for me to snap your neck so you can sacrifice yourself to save the others and absolve yourself of your sins. To make your pitiful existence mean something. But I'm not going to give you that, boy."

When he reaches down and raises Crow's chin with a finger, Crow grabs his wrist.

"Get the Hell off me, you piece of—"

"But I could give you something better. I could give you her."

Crow stills, his stormy gray eyes suddenly unreadable. The two stare at each other. My heart clenches.

Her. His wife.

Oh, no.

As Crow uncurls his fingers from Lucifer's arm, a thin smile curls across the Devil's face.

"I wouldn't be the Devil if I didn't know what each of you desired," he continues, dropping Crow's chin. "And I wouldn't be the Devil if I didn't know how to give it to you."

"What about what you want, Lucifer?" asks Gabriel, taking a step out of the shadows.

Lucifer's cool gaze shifts to Gabriel. "Like you, for example. Michael's boy. Do you think I don't know what you desire? It radiates off you. You reek of it." He breathes in sharply. "I can smell it in the air. Hot and raw and laced with Sin. Do you think I don't know you'd do anything to be in my position right now? To have this reprobate on his knees before you, ready to submit to your every whim?"

Gabriel flushes, but his expression remains impassive.

"Let them go," he says, "and let's talk about what you want."

"I could give him to you, if you wanted," says Lucifer. Then he sniffs the air again. "But no, that's not your biggest desire, is it? What you really want is Daddy's approval." He inhales deeply. "Or, wait—it goes deeper even than that." He laughs—a harsh, cold sound devoid of joy. "How precious. The Angel desires to be loved."

"Let my sister go," says Jonathon. He moves to stand by Gabriel.

Lucifer flicks a hand in dismissal. "Quiet, boy. You are irrelevant. Pointless. Nothing."

Gabriel pushes my brother behind him again as Lucifer turns to me, bringing me closer with his tail.

"Not you, though, Rachel. No. You're special." He touches my cheek, and I try to jerk away. "That's what you want, isn't it? To be special. The girl who lived in her brother's shadow for so very long wants to have the light shine on her face." His tail uncoils from my neck, but his hand remains. "Well, you are special, my girl, because your soul belongs to me. But if you wanted, I could make you more special. So very special."

"I don't want anything from you," I say, holding my ground even though there is no humanity behind his eyes.

"That's not true. You wanted me to defeat the Serpent for you. You triggered the Apocalypse to bring me here." I can smell him, brimstone and fire and dry ice. "Would you like me to end the world for you, Rachel? Wouldn't that make you so very special?"

"You'll lose," I say as his cold breath mists my face. "You can't win the Revelation War."

"Yes. The game is rigged against me." He smiles. "But in summoning me, you have presented me with moves that were hitherto unavailable. New pieces on the board that I can use."

"Lucifer. Stop this," says Gabriel, his tone sharp. "There's nothing for you here."

"Isn't there?"

Lucifer drops his hand from my cheek and makes as if to turn. But when I try to dart away, his tail whips out and curls around my neck once more. I gasp at the renewed burn.

"Crow. Rise, my boy," Lucifer says.

Crow gets to his feet, his expression blank.

"I can give you your heart's desire," Lucifer continues, "but first, I need you to show me you're mine."

"Crow," I wheeze.

He doesn't look at me. "What do you want?"

Lucifer smirks and drags his gaze over to Gabriel. "Michael's boy."

Jonathon tries to step in front of the Angel, but Gabriel pushes him aside yet again, eyes unmoving from Crow's.

"Crow. Don't," I say. I try to sink my nails into the tail wrapped around my neck, but it's hard; impenetrable.

Crow runs a hand across his stubble, then exhales.

"Don't make me hurt you, Ewan," says Gabriel.

Crow sighs again. "You won't hurt me." He sounds almost sad.

I struggle against Lucifer, but he holds me tight. I can't breathe. I can't move. I can only watch as Crow strides across the rubble and gore to stop a few feet away from Gabriel.

"I trust you, Ewan," says Gabriel.

They both stare at each other. Silence hangs heavily, mingling with the sulfur in the air. Then, in a sudden movement, Crow lunges forward.

"No!" I gasp.

Gabriel doesn't even fight as Crow slips behind him. He jerks him into his body, one big arm locked around his stomach. The other is around Gabriel's throat.

Panic floods me. Panic and anger. What is Gabriel doing? *Fight.*

Flames lick at my fingers, and I try to burn the tail. Lucifer doesn't even look at me.

"Good," Lucifer says with that same cold smile.

Crow tightens his fingers around Gabriel's neck.

"Easy, boy," says Lucifer, putting a hand up. "I didn't command you to kill him. Bring him to the elevator."

Crow doesn't move, only continues to squeeze. Gabriel finally puts a hand on his wrist, but he doesn't try to pull it away.

"What are you doing?" says Lucifer, tone hard. "Put him in the elevator, and I'll give you what you desire."

Crow is breathing hard now. "I'm going to kill him," he says.

Lucifer releases a harsh chuckle. "No, you're not."

"Aye." The word scrapes from his throat. "I am."

Lucifer frowns. "Stop. I command you to stop."

"No use to you dead, is he?" says Crow.

Gabriel's eyes water, unfocused. His fingernails dig into Crow's skin as he wheezes for breath.

"Crow, don't," I splutter, but my voice is so hoarse it barely travels.

Jonathon lunges at the two to try to intervene, but he's stopped by one of Crow's shadows. As he flies toward the wall, I scream, lurching forward.

Lucifer pulls me back as my brother slides down the wall, unconscious.

"You think I don't know what you desire, mate?" spits Crow. "Gabe would be a good bargaining chip for Michael, but his soul doesn't belong to you. If I kill him, he'll end up in a place neither you nor I can enter."

Lucifer and Crow stare at each other—Lucifer's eyes cold; Crow's filled with some raw, primal intent that scares me just as much. I can't tell if he's bluffing. As it is, Gabriel looks ready to pass out.

Then Lucifer laughs.

"Kill him," he says. "Let me show you how little I care." With that, he hurls his trident across the room.

Crow's eyes widen, his hand instantly releasing Gabriel's throat as he spins, his back acting as a shield against the three bronze spikes headed straight for them.

I scream, but just as it's about to make impact, Gabriel's wings rip through his shoulder blades, cocooning Crow and emitting a blinding white light.

Lucifer's trident bounces off them, landing with a loud clatter on the gore-coated linoleum.

For a moment, all I see is light. I feel it too. Warm. It eases the burn around my neck as Lucifer's hold on me wavers.

Then I see Gabriel. He looks as hard and impenetrable as any statue in a churchyard. Magnificent. Not of this world.

"Enough," says Gabriel, his voice low. "You've had your fun. Now, go back to where you belong before *I* call my father here."

Lucifer's too-blue eyes glitter with intrigue and malice. "Perhaps I don't need to take you to Hell to distract your father, Gabriel," he says with a laugh. "Perhaps your fondness for this good-for-nothing Omen will prove disturbing enough."

He clucks his tongue, moving his gaze to Crow.

"And you . . . well, it's too bad, my boy. I could have given you what you wanted. I could have granted you your heart's desire. Still. Corrupt his soul, and perhaps we can renegotiate. And as for you, Rachel Mortimer . . ." He pulls me forward and grabs my face. The rough thumb he runs along my cheek leaves a cold trail in its wake.

"Get off me," I snarl, grappling at his wrist, but I may as well be fighting a piece of metal.

"I did you a favor when I rid your world of The Serpent," says Lucifer. "So it seems to me that you are in my debt."

"Enough," says Gabriel.

Lucifer releases me roughly, his tail uncurling from around my neck to snap up his trident from the ground. As I gasp for breath, he takes his weapon and strides back to the elevator, where he stands in the open doorway, his back muscles rippling in the blue light.

"I always collect my debts," he says, his voice hard with icy promise.

Dante emerges from the shadows to push a button. The doors slide shut, and a whirring sound competes with the pounding blood in my ears.

And with that, Lucifer goes back to Hell.

There's a moment of heavy silence.

Then Crow releases an inhuman roar that rips at my soul and falls to the ground.

Gabriel's wings snap back into his shoulder blades, and he drops down on his knees in front of him. He pulls back Crow's arms to reveal the tears rolling uncontrollably down the Omen's cheeks.

"It was a trick, Ewan. It was a trick," says Gabriel, holding Crow's face with both hands. "He's the Devil. He would never have given her back to you. There would have been a loophole. It was a trick."

Crow shakes his head, jerking away, but Gabriel holds him there.

"You did the right thing, Ewan. You did the right thing."

Something changes then. One of Crow's arms curls around Gabriel as he sobs, clinging to him for support. That's when I realize Crow never would have harmed Gabriel. He never would have harmed any of us. And it cost him the only thing he ever wanted.

I glance at Jonathon to make sure he's okay. His brown hair is ruffled and dusted with rubble, and there's a cut on his forehead, but his eyes blink open. When they find me, I see his slender shoulders relax.

Then I go to Crow, kneeling down to tentatively touch his shoulder. His T-shirt is damp with sweat, and his muscles tremble beneath my fingertips as he cries into Gabriel's neck.

Gabriel meets my eye. I see the silent question in them: *Are you okay?*

I nod even though I'm not sure that I am.

With a sob, Crow curls his other strong arm around my back. He holds me like he's afraid he's going to fall away. His skin burns; his big body shakes.

"Shh," I say. "It's okay. We're here. It's going to be okay."

"I let her down. Again," he says through shuddering breaths.

"You didn't, Ewan," says Gabriel softly. "It was a trick. It was just a trick."

A hand squeezes my shoulder.

"I'm going to go tell the Horsemen and Josie that it's over," Jonathon says softly. "Stop the fighting upstairs."

I give him a half-smile, squeezing his hand with my free one, before he steps over the rubble and through the hole in the wall.

And we're left alone. The room is dark, the blue lights in the floor distorted by the mess of fallen rock. The elevator doors are shut. And Lucifer has returned to Hell, where he belongs.

We're Team Apocalypse. And we won.

Yet the victory feels hollow as Crow's sobs echo through the room.

Chapter Forty-Eight

The more things change, the more things stay the same. That's the thought in my head when I walk through the doors of Evie's Garden Bar a week later and see the blackboard behind the bar is back to advertising half-price appletinis.

Eve's behind the bar again, looking like she always does, in a black waistcoat over a white blouse, with her dark hair tied back in a ponytail. But the way she looks at the slender guy on the stool in front of her is different. Adam. She arches an eyebrow, then deliberately bites into an apple.

Then she looks at me and inclines her head toward one of the high tables by the window.

I slide onto the chair opposite Gabriel, taking off my black leather jacket and dumping it beside me. I leave the silk polka dot neck scarf I borrowed from Josie in place, however. I still need it to hide the burn marks from Lucifer.

Looking pristine in his white company blazer, Gabriel fidgets with a white folder. Two teacups and an ornate teapot decorated with apple blossoms grace the table.

"Tea?" he says.

"Sure," I say, then I decide to jump right in. "So. Any news? Did you manage to get me out of my contract with Devils Inc.?"

He picks up the teapot and pours a cup, forehead creased as though it's taking all of his concentration. It's only after he slides my cup toward me that he exhales.

"I'm sorry, Rachel. I've looked at the contract every way that I can, but there are no loopholes we can exploit as of now. Adalind recruiting you was out of the ordinary, but given she worked for Devils Inc., it was all aboveboard."

"Okay," I say, then I take a sip of tea, swallowing down the disappointment with the rich flavors of Earl Grey. Since meeting Lucifer and hearing his promise to collect on the debt he's decided I owe him, I have even less desire for my soul to belong to him. I absently touch the scarf. Even Gabriel couldn't fully heal the burns left by his tail.

Gabriel watches the movement, concern in his eyes.

"There is one potential avenue we can explore, however. Given that I was right about the Apocalypse, I've been promoted to a more senior position."

"That's great, Gabriel. Well deserved," I say.

He pretends to not be pleased with the praise. "That's not why I mention it. You see, I hoped I could get you transferred to our organization, but our legal department didn't want to get involved. But, as a one-time offer, as a token of their thanks, they're willing to offer you a small Miracle."

My eyebrows raise. "Really?"

"A fairly low-level one, let me clarify," he says hurriedly. "I mean, you can't use it to raise the dead, or destroy the world, or turn back time. But, well, you *can* use it to destroy your contract with Devils Inc."

I set my tea down with a thunk. "Why didn't you lead with that?"

317

Gabriel frowns and takes a sip of tea. "I thought it was human custom to lead with the bad news then end with the good."

I laugh. "You're such a dork." Then the smile dies on my lips. "What about Crow? Does he get one too?"

Gabriel sets his cup down and folds his hands together. Something clenches at my heart.

"Are you serious?" I say.

"I tried, Rachel. I did. But given his pattern of untrustworthy behavior, they wouldn't see reason."

I think of Crow in Apocalypse, howling with grief after he gave up everything.

"That's not fair." A crackle of blue flame bursts from my fingertips and engulfs my teacup. *"Shit."*

Gabriel points a finger, and the resulting white light encases my hand like a glove. Then he sighs.

"I know."

We both slump a little and stare out the window. A construction worker passes by on his way to the churchyard in scuffed orange overalls—part of the team working on fixing the destruction caused by Adalind. Across the road, there's scaffolding around the entrance to Apocalypse too.

A vision of Crow on his knees on the floor in there, crying, floods my mind. Lucifer offered him the only thing he ever wanted, and he turned it down to save the world. Yet Halo Corp. won't even give him a small Miracle to say goodbye to his wife.

Biting my lip, I turn back to Gabriel. "So this Miracle? What do I do?"

Gabriel opens the folder and slides a piece of paper and a pen across the table.

"Just write out the Miracle that you want, then sign at the bottom," he says. "And then it's yours to do with as you wish."

I hold his gaze a moment, heart thrumming hard in my chest. Then I scribble what I want and sign it.

Gabriel watches. For a moment, I think I catch the corner of his lip quirk up. Then it's gone.

After he slips it back into his folder, we fall into heavy silence.

"How's Josie?" he asks after a while.

"She's good," I say. "She was pretty pissed with Darius and the others for forcing her to leave, but since we're all okay, she's agreed to keep her job there." I take a sip of tea and smirk. "He asked her to go to dinner with him to make it up to her—which she told me she refused out of principle. But I think if he asks her again, she'll probably accept."

"It was unusual for Death to stand up for a human like that," says Gabriel. "She must have made quite an impression."

"Yeah, Josie tends to have that effect on people." I pull a face. "And supernatural harbingers of doom, apparently."

Gabriel laughs. "How about your brother?"

"He's fine too," I say, warmth spreading through my body. "He's looking for an apartment here in LA. Said he's going to stick around now the whole Adam and Eve thing has blown over. *And* I've persuaded him to come back to New York with me next week. I'm visiting our parents. I know he's not allowed to speak to them, but he's promised me some moral support."

"That's great news," says Gabriel, taking a sip of tea.

"Thanks for making sure he didn't try and fight Lucifer or anything," I say. "Did you get my prayer?"

The corner of Gabriel's lip quirks up. "Yes. It was very . . . unusual."

"Hmph. Why didn't you reply?"

"Doesn't work that way."

"But I can get into your head? Like, if I wanted, I could just pray to you all the time? About menial stuff. Constantly?" I take a sip of tea. "Interesting."

Gabriel rolls his eyes. "There has to be desperation, love, or good intent there for the message to come through," he says.

"Otherwise, I'm sure Ewan would have enjoyed using that to torment me over the years."

"Have you seen Crow?" I ask.

Gabriel shakes his head stiffly. "I've tried to get in touch, but he's not answering his calls, and he's set himself to offline on Afterlife." Gabriel exhales again. "I think he just needs some time to process."

"When we were in Apocalypse, I thought he was really going to drag you into that elevator," I say. "And then I thought he was really going to kill you. But you never fought him. And when you stopped that trident from hitting him, and when you stood up to Lucifer . . ." I shrug. "Well, you're more powerful than you look."

"Thanks," says Gabriel.

I roll my eyes. "I didn't mean it like that. I just mean . . . it seemed like you could probably beat Crow if it came down to it."

Gabriel inclines his head. It's not an arrogant notion, just an assertion of fact.

"You knew he wouldn't do it though," I say.

Gabriel sips his tea and places his cup down carefully before him. "He thought about it. But I have faith in him. I always have. Deep down."

"If he *had* done what Lucifer asked? What then?"

"Then I'd have been dragged to Hell. I doubt my father would have been too bothered."

I stir my tea absently with the small silver spoon. "The fact Lucifer wanted your soul proves otherwise. I mean, he knew us. He knew exactly how to push our buttons; to get under our skin. How to break us."

"Yes," says Gabriel. "That's true."

We both fall quiet, and I wonder if the same image of Crow's soul-wrenching roar has been haunting his thoughts too.

"I think maybe your father cares more than you think," I blurt after a bit. "Otherwise, why would Lucifer want to kidnap you?"

DEVILS INC.

Gabriel's coppery eyebrows rise almost imperceptibly, his expression pensive. "Perhaps."

We finish our tea, avoiding the serious topics and talking about lighter things—such as how Gabriel hopes to use his more respectable position to get a sabbatical to do some research for the Purgatory Vaults. Finally, Gabriel tucks my Miracle under his arm, and we make to leave. As we do, I give Eve and Adam, now bickering, an awkward wave.

On the street, Gabriel tells me how to use the Miracle. I wait until he's gone, then I pull out my phone and check Afterlife.

Once I have the address I need, I order a cab.

***

An hour later, I'm sitting in front of a prestigious redbrick manor house. The place reminds me of one of the stately homes you see on period dramas. Sitting on acres of green land, with a giant fountain, it's hidden from the rest of LA by thick trees and wild hedges.

I sit on the steps to finish replying to Josie's message that we should go watch Lucas's *Faustus* dress rehearsal tonight.

Sure. There's just something I need to do first.

A shadow looming over me causes me to jerk my head up. Crow stands before me wearing a pale blue shirt, sleeves rolled up. His jaw is covered with a layer of stubble, and there are smudges beneath his eyes. One of his hands is in his jeans pocket; the other holds a bunch of white lilies.

"What you doing here, little Demon?" he asks, his voice gruff.

I push myself to my feet. "I wanted to give you something." When he seems confused, I add, "Can I come in with you?"

He rubs the back of his neck. "Little Demon. . ."

"It's weird, I know. I just want to try something. Please?"

He exhales. "Aye. Okay."

321

After he checks in at reception, he leads me through a maze of disinfectant-scented hallways. When we pass a TV room full of elderly people in worn armchairs, a number of nurses smile and say hi. He seems to be well-liked here.

Finally, he pauses outside a wooden door. Taking a deep breath, he pushes it open. Hesitantly, I follow him inside, into a small bedroom.

The first thing I see are vases full of lilies everywhere—on the chest of drawers, on the windowsill, on the table next to the bed—their floral note mingling with a heavier, mustier smell. That's when I spot the old woman sitting in a rose-print armchair by the bed. She's petite, with white hair brushed back in a bun, and a long green skirt covering her knees. She has a scar down one side of her face—probably from the car accident that left her unable to care for herself. And left Crow unable to care for her too.

She doesn't react when we step closer. Her blue eyes are vacant; unseeing.

"Maddie, love?" says Crow.

Her head moves slowly to the pair of us. "Who are you?" she asks sharply. "If you've come to bring me some lemon cake, I've been waiting for hours."

"No, Maddie, love," says Crow before he replaces a bunch of dying lilies by the bed with the fresh ones in his hand.

As he does, I crouch down in front of his wife. Crow stiffens but doesn't stop me. I take her hands in mine, gnarled and old.

"What are you doing?" he asks.

I turn to meet his gaze. "If this works, Gabriel says the department can't make the effects permanent. So it won't last long. But I hoped it would be enough."

Something vulnerable crosses his expression when he understands what I'm saying.

"If you don't want me to—if it will make things harder—I don't have to do it," I say.

DEVILS INC.

He opens his mouth, cheeks flushing. But then he nods.

I do what Gabriel told me. Closing my eyes, I send my prayer to the Halo Corp. Miracle Processing department. As I'm muttering under my breath, a warmth begins to buzz beneath my skin—not hot and harsh and needing release like Devils Inc. power. More subtle than that. It's like the feeling of Gabriel's light when he fought Lucifer. Or the feeling of hugging Jonathon after all that time. It's like soft sunlight and gentle bathwater. It feels like love.

I hear Crow breathe in sharply behind me. I open my eyes to see white light radiating from my hands and engulfing Maddie. Then it disappears.

I let go of Maddie's hands. When I look up, the glaze is gone from her eyes, making them a brighter, intelligent blue.

"Ewan?" she says, eyes fixed on a spot over my shoulder.

Crow crashes down to the floor beside me, taking her small, frail hands in his big ones. "Maddie, sweetheart, I'm here."

"Ewan, you haven't aged a day." She smiles, touching his cheek. "You'll have to share your skincare routine."

He lets out a half-laugh, half-sob.

"Maddie, I'm so sorry." Tears stream down his cheeks. "I'm so sorry, love."

She laughs. "Whatever for?"

"I'll give you two some privacy," I say.

Quietly, I slip out of room, only pausing in the doorway long enough to see the two of them start to talk. Then I head out of the building and explore the grounds, enjoying the late-afternoon sun on my skin.

After a while, I stumble upon a small man-made lake with a white iron bench to the side. Sitting, I reflect on everything that's brought me here.

I could have used the Miracle to save myself, but I don't feel bad that I didn't. I'll find another way to get out of my contract with the Devil. Crow saved the world—given what he gave up for

323

that, it only felt right that he should get a chance to tell his wife he's sorry. Maybe he can finally move on. He deserves to.

A couple of hours pass before Crow silently takes a seat beside me. The sky is starting to pinken as evening approaches, and it colors the water.

"Thank you," he says, his voice thick with emotion.

I turn my head to look at him. His eyes are red and swollen, but the tension has left his shoulders.

"You okay?" I ask him.

He runs a hand over his mouth. "Aye. It was hard. But I told her everything," he says. "She said it wasn't my fault, that there was nothing to for her to forgive." He taps his chest. "I feel like a weight has been lifted. Or something. I feel better. That I got the chance to tell her."

"I'm glad."

We fall into silence for a while, watching the water.

"How did you get hold of a Miracle anyway, little Demon?" asks Crow.

I shrug. "I'm diabolical."

He chuckles, putting an arm around my shoulders. "Aye, that you are," he says before releasing me to rest his hand on the bench behind me. "Seriously, how did you get it?"

I tell him what happened, leaving out the part about what else I could have used the Miracle on. I think he's carried around enough guilt over the years.

Still, he frowns. "You should have used that for yourself. Gotten yourself something good. Or sold it."

I shrug. "Nah. Nothing I wanted."

His frown deepens. "Maybe you could have used it to get out of your contract," he says.

"I need the internship, don't I?" I say, raising my eyebrows. "College credit. Plus, we're friends. And that's what friends do. They help each other out."

He stares at me a moment longer. Then he follows my gaze across the water.

"So Gabe offered you a Miracle and let you sacrifice your soul to give it to me?" The corner of his lip quirks up. "Perhaps our mate Gabe is the true diabolical one."

"It wasn't like that," I say. "And why is that diabolical?"

"You'll see."

"What will I see?"

He mimes zipping up his lips. I give him a playful slap on the arm.

"You're *still* going to be this annoying?"

"I think Gabe will want to tell you himself."

We fall quiet for a bit.

"So . . . friends?" he says after a little while.

"I think so. If you want?"

He smiles. "I'd like that."

We watch the sky turn a burnt orange over the lake. All I can hear are Crow's deep breaths, and the sound of the breeze rustling the nearby trees. After about half an hour of sitting with our thoughts, Crow nods to the water.

"You've probably got some aftereffects of that Miracle in your body, you know?" he says.

"What do you mean?"

He gestures to the lake again and makes a stomping movement with his feet.

"You're trying to tell me I can walk on water?"

He raises his eyebrows and nods.

"Screw you," I say. "You're just trying to get me to drench myself."

He chuckles. "Am not!"

"Yeah, you are."

"I bet my life you can walk on that lake!"

I hold his gaze. Then, with an eye roll, I get up and go to tentatively touch the lake with my Converse. When I look back, he gives me an encouraging nod.

I sigh. "Fine."

I take a step, bracing myself for the plunge into dirty, ice-cold water. But it doesn't come.

"Holy shit," he says, approaching the water's edge. "It actually worked."

"Are you serious? You didn't know for sure!" When he simply shrugs, eyes glinting with mischief, I laugh. "You're such a dick."

"I know."

I hold out my hand to him. "Come on."

"I bet you'd love that, wouldn't you?" he says.

Leaning forward, I pull him onto the lake with me. Both of us remain standing atop the surface. His eyes widen.

I laugh again. "Oh, my god, I didn't think that would work!"

Dipping his sneaker into the water, he kicks some up, drenching me. I yelp, splashing him back. Then he throws me over his shoulder, and we mess around on the surface of the lake as the sun sets behind us. It feels good to blow off some steam, as friends, after everything that happened.

An attempt to tackle Crow goes horribly wrong, and he has me in a headlock when he freezes.

I twist out of his grasp to see Gabriel striding across the water toward us, a disapproving look on his face, and a white folder tucked under his arm.

"Glad to see you two are keeping our Ethereal secrets safe, dancing out here in the middle of a lake," he says. "Not at all unusual for anyone watching."

Crow grins, and I look at my feet.

"Sorry, Gabriel," I say.

"Yes, well . . ." He looks at Crow, eyes softening. "Did everything go all right, Ewan?"

A smile spreads across Crow's face. "Aye." He puts his arm around Gabriel and pulls him close, brushing his lips against his forehead. "Thanks, mate."

Gabriel lets himself be held for a couple of seconds before awkwardly shrugging him off. Crow watches him, amused.

"So what's up?" I ask Gabriel, trying to bring the conversation back on track.

"I have some news," he says brightly. "You see, as it turns out, there's a get-out clause in all Ethereal Contracts. Including your Devils Inc. one." He puffs with pride. "It's called the Redemption Clause."

"That's how Jonathon got out of his contract with Halo Corp.," I say. "He sacrificed his soul to save me."

"Yes," says Gabriel. "He gave you his Miracle. As for you, I could never have actually used the Miracle to save your soul," he says. "Halo Corp. wouldn't have meddled with a contract with Lucifer. But *you* thought that was the case, and you gave it to Crow anyway. You sacrificed your soul for someone else. It was enough to exercise the Redemption Clause in *your* contract."

When I look to Crow, flabbergasted, the Omen grins. "Told you he was diabolical."

My eyes widen, something warm swelling inside me. "So I'm out of the Devils Inc. contract?"

"Yes. You're out," says Gabriel. "It doesn't mean Lucifer won't still collect on his debt, though, so be careful."

"No more signing up to free Wi-Fi without reading the terms and conditions then?" I say with a half-smile.

"Well, that would be a start," agrees Gabriel. "But I also thought . . . well, you'll still be needing an internship. And it would be good for both Ewan and I to keep an eye on you. So I pulled some strings, and . . ."

He passes me the white folder. My pulse quickens as I take it, a thrill of excitement buzzing through my veins.

"Your new contract, should you choose to sign it," says Gabriel, and then he smiles.

"Welcome to Halo Corp."

Acknowledgements

Thank you to everyone who read Devils Inc. in its early draft stages online. Your comments and reactions kept me smiling and helped to shape the story.

Thank you to Andrea Robinson for your invaluable insight when it came to the developmental edits. This is the second book we've worked on together, and as with the first, I felt like you understood exactly what I was trying to do and really helped to take Devils Inc. to the next level. Thank you to Bryony Leah for all your hard work on the copy edits. It was a joy working with you.

Thank you to Robynne at Damonza for your work on the Devils Inc. cover. I love it!

Lastly, thank you to my friends and family for your support. In particular, thank you to Jamie for listening to my constant chatter about Angels, Demons, and Omens over the past year!

About the Author

Lauren Palphreyman is an author based in London. She likes to write books full of magical organizations, modern myths, silly jokes, and lots of kissing. She writes serially on Wattpad and Radish Fiction where her stories have garnered over 60 million views. Her first book, Cupid's Match, was published in 2019. Devils Inc. is her second published novel.

Connect with Lauren by following her on Instagram (@LaurenPalphreyman), Twitter (@LEPalphreyman), or Facebook (@LEPalphreyman). Or visit her website: www.LaurenPalphreyman.com.

Also by Lauren Palphreyman

Devils Inc. Series:

Devils Inc.

Halo Corp. (Coming Soon)

Cupid's Match Series:

Cupid's Match

**Follow Lauren Palphreyman on social media to find
out more:**

Instagram: @LaurenPalphreyman
Twitter | Facebook: @LEPalphreyman

Website: www.LaurenPalphreyman.com

Cupid's Match

He's mythologically hot, a little bit wicked, almost 100% immortal. And he'll hit you right in the heart.

Seventeen-year-old Lila Black is sick of the Cupids Matchmaking Service spamming her. But her world is turned inside out when she learns not only that cupids exist, but that she's been matched with the infamous god of love, Cupid.

The only catch? She can't actually fall for Cupid; if she does, all of mythical hell will break loose, and it won't be pretty . . .

As arrows fly and feelings become stronger, can Cupid and Lila resist each other's magnetic pull? And will Lila find herself part of a deadly supernatural war that could cost her life, and her heart?

Find out more:
www.LaurenPalphreyman.com

Made in the USA
Columbia, SC
23 June 2025

59749086R00202